# the **tree** of seasons

foreword by Sir Elton John
& David Furnish

# Stephen Gately

HODDER &
STOUGHTON

First published in Great Britain in 2010 by Hodder & Stoughton
An Hachette UK company

1

Copyright © Stephen Gately 2009
Written in collaboration with June Considine and Jules Williams

Pictures © Keith Wilson

A CIP catalogue record for this title is available from the British Library.

ISBN 978 1 444 70652 9

Typeset in Minion by Hewer Text UK Ltd, Edinburgh
Printed and bound in the UK by Clays Ltd, St Ives plc

Hodder & Stoughton policy is to use papers that are natural, renew-
able and recyclable products and made from wood grown in sustain-
able forests. The logging and manufacturing processes are expected to
conform to the environmental regulations of the country of origin.

Hodder & Stoughton Ltd
338 Euston Road
London NW1 3BH

www.hodder.co.uk

# acknowledgements
## by Andrew Cowles

The following few paragraphs are the most difficult that I've ever had to write. Although the purpose of this page is traditionally to thank all the people who've helped make this book become a reality – a fairly simple and perhaps even enjoyable task – writing it on Stephen's behalf is not easy.

Stephen grew-up in 1980s Sherriff Street, one of the poorest parts of Dublin city. It was a time of civil unrest and terrorist activity. Whilst his parents, Martin and Margaret, struggled to provide for their family of five children, Stephen dreamed of a better life, a life like the ones he'd seen in his favourite Disney movies.

A combination of hard-work, talent, and wishing on the occasional star paid off and Stephen's dream became reality when he joined Boyzone – soon becoming one of the world's most successful boy bands. However, at no point did he lose touch with his roots, he was proud of where he had come from and of all that he had achieved.

Achieving his dreams made Stephen an incredibly grateful person. His former manager and dear friend, Louis

Walsh, once told me that Stephen was the only person he'd worked with who always said 'thank you' after every television appearance, gig and record release – every time they'd worked together in fact. Stephen really meant it too, and he felt privileged to have been given those opportunities. And so, the first acknowledgement should go to Louis Walsh. 'Thank You Louis.'

After seven years at the top, Boyzone parted ways and Stephen enjoyed success as a solo artist and West End musical theatre performer, but without his former bandmates, there was always something missing. In 2008 Boyzone reformed, and being on tour with his old buddies was the final piece of the jigsaw that filled the void for Stephen. His band-of-brothers was complete once more, and these lads, who had been his best friends for so many years were there again to offer him hugs and support. Performing to crowded arenas filled with screaming fans, he fizzed with positive energy and a new found confidence. So to his 'brothers': Ronan, Keith, Shane and Mikey, goes of course a huge 'T'anks Lads.'

Along with his Boyzone brothers, Stephen's real family were incredibly important to him, and although he'd chosen to make London his home, he maintained regular contact with his parents, brothers, and sister Michelle – with whom he spoke on an almost daily basis. So to them all, he'd certainly want say a huge 'Thank you for supporting and loving me.'

For coming to his rescue at his darkest moment, for match-making the two of us, and not least for writing the foreword to this wonderful book, Stephen would be ever so grateful to Sir Elton John and David Furnish. Two incredibly busy men, but men who found time to offer him support and direction when he badly needed it. To them he'd say 'EJ, David, thanks for looking out for me.'

During the last few years, and whilst writing this book, Stephen's closest friends included Phyllis the Butcher (of Highgate Butchers) and her friend, Pat the Baker. I should point out that Pat isn't really a baker but the nick name stuck – she is however a very good cook. Many pages of this book were written on summer days spent in Phyllis' garden or with her at The Red Lion & Sun. To these girls he'd say 'Thank you both for being my good friends and for brightening my days. Thanks Phyll for the sausages that brought us together, for the champagne that kept us together, and for always losing at cards!'

Stephen loved his fans, and through his website www. stephengately.co.uk was able to stay in touch and keep them informed of events. He'd want to send special thanks to April Nelson for building and maintaining the website. To her, and his loyal fans he'd say 'You guys made me so happy. You were always there for me, and without you I would've been nothing. Thanks for the support. I love you all so much.'

Special thanks should also go to David Byrne and Keith Wilson. David is Stephen's oldest friend, and supported him through so much. It is his partner Keith's art which adorns the pages of this book. To them he'd say 'T'anks Daíthi, knowing you and Keith made my life so much better. I loved our times in Windsor, and Keith's beautiful images make this story extra special.'

There are a great many people Stephen would want to thank, for various reasons, and here I'll list a few of their names that come to mind, but to those I miss, please forgive me.

Carla, Hannah, Caroline, Rachel, Chris, John, Claire, Bernie, Cocky, Fadi, Jason, David, Kelly, Lee, Paula, Gavin, Lol, Laura, Jean, Lew, Mark, Sue, Alan, Pieter, Bernie, Rob, Seb, Sam, Shelina and Eloy – to you all he'd want to say at the very least 'Thank you for being in my life. God bless you all.'

I suppose lastly, he would want to say a few words about me, and to thank me for reading excerpts of his first draft, for helping with his spelling and punctuation and for the sleepless nights when he'd sit up in bed tapping away at the laptop. But mostly for my love and support over the years... and not least for being there when he was scared of the dark.

So his final acknowledgement goes to Andrew Cowles, his husband. To me he says, 'Thank you, woofy!'

To which I reply, 'No Steo, **Thank You!**'

# foreword
## by Sir Elton John and David Furnish

The first thing I noticed about Stephen was his smile.

Stephen was one of those completely transparent people. When he smiled, his sweetness, gentleness and kindness shone out of him. He also had a huge love of life and whenever he appeared in the doorway with his dimples and infectious laugh, we all new we were going to have fun, fun, fun. From the moment we met, Stephen and I were great friends.

Friends are people who are on your side, even when you are in the wrong. Both Stephen and I have had times when we've been down, and I was very glad to help him in the period after Boyzone split up. He said he missed the guys, and I think he may have worried he was losing their friendship. Of course, he wasn't, and by the time of his tragic death, Stephen, Ronan, Mikey, Shane and Keith, were reunited.

As well as being highly sensitive, Stephen was also incredibly brave. He was described in the Times as 'A hero of gay rights', being the first ever boy band member to come out. David and I are very proud that we introduced

Stephen to Andy, who was to become his life's partner, at a party in 2002. We are also very proud of Andy because, despite his terrible loss and grief, he has seen this book's publication through to the end, knowing that this is what Stephen would have wanted.

_Stephen often talked about his childhood. He was proud of the backstreets of Dublin, where he was raised by loving parents. The family was very poor, but Stephen would always laugh about the times he had to sell firewood door to door at 10p per bag, or walk to school in shoes stuffed with cardboard to keep the rain out. Stephen never forgot what it was like to be a child, and it was perhaps this quality that made his star shine so brightly. He and I shared a love of the films of Disney and The Wizard of Oz, and both of these are big influences on the magical story that is *The Tree of Seasons*.

I miss Stephen. I miss him so much. But his book reminds me of many of his best qualities, and just thinking about it makes me smile too.

# 1

# strange happenings in grimsville woods

The first time Josh saw the lights flaring like a beacon above Grimsville Woods, he decided he was suffering from one of three things. He was hallucinating. He was dreaming a particularly vivid dream in green and purple colours. He needed to have his eyes tested . . . and fast. There was a fourth option, of course. The lights casting those eerie, grotesque shadows across the dark sky were real. But that was so unbelievable he'd had to wait until last night to check it out.

The checkers-out were Michael and Beth. Needless to say, they'd not believed their older brother when he described what he'd seen. Why should they? Lights over Grimsville Woods in the middle of the night! Get real, Josh. Or get glasses. Oh, they scoffed and laughed but last night they were standing by his bedroom window when the time came, waiting just as eagerly to see for themselves if he was suffering from delusions – or if a mystery really was unfolding right in front of their eyes.

Josh had used his binoculars to see exactly what was going on. But everything was a blur, colours swirling at such speed that he'd staggered back from the window, suddenly dizzy and nauseous. It was the same sensation he used to get when he spun for too long on the spinners in the playground. It was a long time since Josh had been on a spinner but he remembered the sensation only too well, and Michael had had to hold him steady until the bedroom furniture stopped swaying.

Beth had been the timekeeper. She announced that the colours flashed for thirty minutes. Then, just like the previous night, they abruptly stopped. The sky and the woods merged back into darkness and the children were staring into an inky-black landscape. It still seemed like a dream but Josh had heard Michael's gasps of wonder, and Beth's whimpers of fear (understandable as she was only eight years old and the lights had been awesome to watch).

This morning, with the sunshine spilling into his bedroom, Josh had no difficulty using his binoculars. He leaned out the open window and adjusted the lens. Apart from a few bobtail clouds, the sky was blue, the sun was up, and birds were singing their hearts out in the garden. Suddenly Grimsville Woods rushed towards him. The trees waved their branches and he could make out each distinct fluttering green leaf.

Merryville Woods was the proper name for the woods but Josh had nicknamed them Grimsville because there was nothing merry about the *Trespassers Will be Prosecuted* notices that had appeared over the past year, nor the thorny hedges growing around the perimeter.

Apart from the waving branches, nothing was stirring this morning in Grimsville Woods. There were no birds flitting from bough to bough, no small creatures scurrying between the trunks. The narrow path that led from the back of their house to the woodlands glinted with flecks of mica but the trees looked as they always did, grim, mysterious, unwelcoming and, now, definitely worth exploring. Big problem. The woods were out of bounds since Great Aunt Graves had had the threatening trespassing notices erected. Josh figured she must have poured gallons of plant food over the hedgerows because they looked even more thorny and vicious that usual. Like rolls of barbed wire, he thought, lowering his binoculars and glancing across the room at his sleeping brother.

This was the first day of their school summer holidays and Michael wouldn't rise before noon. Beth's bedroom door slammed. Her light footsteps sounded as she ran across the landing and down the stairs. Josh wondered if she was also thinking about last night. Probably. She was the one who had suggested they break the number-one rule and investigate. Below in the kitchen, he heard the clinking, clunking morning sounds as his mother set the table for breakfast. But the sounds were leisurely instead of the usual hurried footsteps and loud voices as everyone rushed to beat the clock. Josh sighed with absolute contentment. Freedom. Such a wonderful word. Freedom from lessons, homework, school rules and, most importantly of all, freedom from Johnny Welts.

Unable any longer to stand the sight of his sleeping brother, he shook Michael's shoulder. "Wake up!" he said. "You can't lie in bed all morning."

Michael opened one eye then closed it again just as quickly. "Why not," he growled. "I'm on holidays. I can do what I like."

"But what about the woods?" Josh said. "We decided last night that we'd investigate."

"Nothing to investigate." Michael pulled the duvet over his head and snuggled deeper into his bed. "It was probably just kids setting off fireworks in the village." His voice was muffled but determined. "Leave me alone. I'm not getting up for hours and *hours*."

Josh sighed as he put on his jeans and laced his train-ers. He rummaged in his drawer for a tee-shirt and pulled on his favourite black one with the Superman symbol on the front. Last night had nothing to do with fireworks. Fireworks mean celebrations and illuminations scattering like stars across the sky. This was different, more like laser beams, and, anyway, the village of Merryville was nowhere near the woods. As for the noises . . . that was really scary. The first time Josh hadn't heard anything but last night mysterious clashes and thuds had carried clearly on the wind.

Unable any longer to watch his brother sleeping when they had so much to discuss, he grabbed a pillow and jumped on Michael's bed.

"Get up," he yelled. "Get up! Get up!" He swatted the duvet with the pillow until Michael emerged from under-neath it and grabbed his own pillow. The light of battle banished the sleep from his eyes and the fight was on in earnest.

"Cut out the racket, you two!" their mother yelled from the bottom of the stairs. "You'll bring the ceiling down on top of us."

"What about the woods?" Josh collapsed on Michael's bed. "Do you really believe it was fireworks?"

"What else could it be?" Michael threw his pillow to one side and placed his hands behind his head. "Fairies?"

5

The two boys guffawed at the thought of fairies playing with lasers in the middle of Grimsville Woods.

"Not fairies," said Josh. "Elves, maybe?"

This made them laugh even louder.

"Goblins?" said Michael, not to be outdone. "Pixies, leprechauns, brownies?"

"Demons?" retorted Josh. "Ghouls? Sea witches?"

"Vampires?" Michael hissed in mock-terror.

"Werewolves?" Josh arched his hands into claws and dived on his brother. They wrestled for a few minutes until the breakfast smells drew them down-stairs, shouting, as they always did, "Last one down is a rotten egg!"

"Ah! The samurai wrestlers have decided to join us at last." Mr Lotts lowered his morning newspaper and stared over the top of his glasses at his sons.

"Sorry, Dad," said Josh, pulling his chair to the table. "We were just messing."

"Well, mess a bit quieter in future." Their father returned his attention to his newspaper and Mrs Lotts – still in her dressing gown – placed a platter of pancakes in front of the boys. Easy knowing the summer holidays had started. Their mother, who was a school teacher, never had time to make pancakes in the morning. She had also made Josh's favourite breakfast – a soft-boiled egg with toast soldiers – and as she bustled about the kitchen she looked as happy and carefree as her children whereas Mr Lotts, gloomily reading the property pages, was dressed in his suit and tie.

"Mum, did you see anything strange last night?" Josh finished his egg and reached for a pancake.

"Strange?" Mrs Lotts paused, teapot in hand. "What do you mean by strange?"

"Flashes of light from Grimsville Woods."

"You mean *Merryville* Woods?" she replied.

"Yeah . . . whatever." Josh shrugged. "Did you see anything?"

"Why on earth would there be flashes of light coming from the woods?" said Mr Lotts. "No one ever goes there."

"You must have been dreaming, Josh," said Beth, spreading her third pancake with a thick layer of maple syrup. She shot him a warning look. "You *always* have such weird dreams."

"I guess so." Josh squeezed lemon over his pancake and took the first delicious bite.

"Flashes?" said Mr Lotts, folding his newspaper and placing it in his briefcase. "Maybe your great-aunt was inspecting her property."

At the mention of Great Aunt Graves, the three children pulled faces at each other across the table.

"You're spoiling my appetite," said Michael.

"Mine too," said Beth, reaching for another pancake. "I don't want to visit her horrible house *ever* again."

"You can't refuse an invitation when you haven't been invited." Mr Lotts sighed heavily and picked up his briefcase. "Unlike me. I've to go there tonight for another meeting."

"I'm not going with you," said Josh.

7

"Me neither," chorused Michael and Beth.

Mr Lotts raised his eyebrows and stared at the three mutinous faces. "As it happens, I'm going there as her estate agent, not as her nephew. So it's not a family visit."

"Whew!" Josh dramatically wiped his forehead.

"Double whew!" Beth's long hair swung forward as she tried to grab the maple syrup from Michael. She and Josh were blonde like their mother while Michael, with his brown curly hair, was the image of their father.

"Is she still determined to start felling the woods as soon as planning permission comes through?" asked Mrs Lotts.

"She's ready to roll," replied Mr Lotts. "Before we know it, there'll be new houses stretching as far as the village."

"Cut down the woods?" Josh gasped. "When she bought them, she told me she wanted to turn the woods into a conservation area."

Mr Lotts nodded. "That was last year, Josh. But things have changed since the trees became diseased."

"The trees are not the only things that are diseased," muttered Michael.

"Enough of that kind of talk, Michael." Mrs Lotts, knowing exactly what he meant, frowned. "Your great-aunt was very ill. Let's be thankful she's recovered her health."

"Recovered?" Beth swallowed loudly and pushed her plate to one side. "She's turned into a horrible old witch. I don't like her any more."

"Me neither," said Michael and looked across at Josh for support.

"She's a weirdo." Josh always felt disloyal when they said nasty things about their great-aunt. He had loved her once but Michael and Beth were right. She was horrible, rude and crotchety, and always made them feel so unwelcome when they called to visit.

After Mr Lotts drove away, the children stacked the breakfast dishes in the dishwasher and tidied their rooms. From the window Josh watched his mother, now dressed in her gardening trousers and a straw hat, enter the garden shed. She'd spend the summer working in the garden, preparing her fruit and vegetables for the annual Merryville Horticultural Festival. Until Great Aunt Graves had turned into the most unpleasant person Josh knew, she and his mother used to compete in the gardening section. Sometimes Great Aunt Graves won first prize for her tomatoes and courgettes, sometimes his mother was the winner. But it never mattered who won or lost. The two women had been the best of friends until last summer when the accident happened and everything changed.

Suddenly, thinking about Great Aunt Graves, the idea of exploring the woods became less attractive. Those noises last night . . . the more Josh thought about them the more he became convinced there had been a fight going on. Sticks and knives and spears and maybe even guns, because now he could remember a popping sound, and blasts, as if bolts of electricity were being released.

When the chores were done, Beth, her hair tied in a ponytail and dressed like her brother in jeans and a tee-shirt, rushed into their bedroom to discuss the woods.

"We have to find the way in first," Michael reminded them. "That hedge is like a fortress."

"We could crawl underneath it," said Beth. "We've never *really* tried, not seriously, I mean."

"If Great Aunt Graves finds out we're on her property, we could end up in jail," warned Josh. "And I'll be blamed . . . as *usual*."

Being the eldest was tough going at times. If his parents found out, he'd be grounded and have his pocket money cut while Michael and Beth would probably get off with just a warning. "There's some really weird stuff going on there," he continued. "I think we should go to the lake for a swim instead."

"What!" Beth looked disgusted. "Last night we said—"

"I know what we said. But there could be gangsters in the woods."

"They're not gangsters," said Beth. "I think it's magic."

"Magic!" Josh snorted. "Don't be daft. There's no such thing."

"Please, Josh. You promised." Beth folded her arms and gazed challengingly at him. "I bet you're scared."

"I am not. But I'm responsible for you—"

"You're not in charge of me," Michael interrupted him, indignantly.

"Or me," said Beth. "I *really* want to do something different and exciting today. I vote we go to the woods right now."

"I'm the eldest." Josh was determined to keep his cool. He knew what Beth was like when she wanted her own way.

She would say, "please . . . please . . . pretty *please* . . . " until he felt like gagging her, and Michael would sulk for the rest of the day. But Josh was twelve and a half years of age (the extra six months was important as they added to his authority) and he was expected to be fearless. Like Superman. He touched the 'S' symbol on his tee-shirt. Superman wouldn't have hesitated for an instant. But then Superman had the ability to fly and watch danger from a safe distance whereas he, Josh Lotts, would have to crawl through a spiky hedge and probably be caught by Great Aunt Graves, who was far worse than any enemy Superman ever had to confront. But, despite Josh's uneasiness, the woods beckoned and he was just as anxious as the others to find out what lay behind those extraordinary lights.

"OK, this is the plan," he said in his best Superman voice. "We don't let on we're going near Grimsville. If either of you tell Mum and Dad, I'll never speak to you again. *Ever.* Understood?"

They nodded and Beth solemnly crossed her heart.

"We'll go to the woods the long way. That means walking to the village and entering from the far side," he said. "Maybe the hedges won't be so thick there. We stick together. No splitting up and going off on our own. And at the first sign of trouble, we run like hell. Agreed?"

Again, Michael and Beth nodded, their eyes shining with excitement.

When they emerged from the house, their mother stopped digging and leaned on the handle of her spade. "Where are you going?" she asked.

"To the village," said Josh. Strictly speaking, this was not a lie. They'd have to walk through West Merryville Street but, as usual, Beth could not help embroidering the truth.

"We're going to the playground and then to the lake and then to the park," she said. "So we'll be gone for ages and ages."

"Sounds like a busy morning," replied Mrs Lotts. "Just make sure you're back by lunchtime."

"We will . . . we will," said Beth, who just knew the day was made for adventure. And how right she was.

The sun was high in the sky and the day promised to be a scorcher. Their house was set in a Wicklow valley, surrounded by wild meadows and lush green fields. After a fifteen-minute walk, they reached Merryville. This small, busy village had shops lining the main street and a play-ground on the outskirts. They hurried through the village and passed Merryville Lake, which was in the centre of Merryville Park, so, to be fair, Beth had not been lying either.

When they left the village behind, Grimsville Woods appeared like a thin black line on the horizon. They climbed through the bars of a gate into a field. The sheep stopped grazing and gazed after the children as they ran across the grass. When they reached the end of the field they climbed over a stile. The narrow road they entered twisted and turned along the lie of the woods. But they were unable to find an opening in the dense hedgerow. Usually, at this time of year, the whitethorn was heavy with white blossom but all they could see were thick branches of thorns trailing the ground and spiking the air.

"Look!" After they'd been walking for some time, Michael pointed into the distance where the outline of a roof had become visible. "That's Great Aunt Graves's house," he said. "We'd better not go any further."

In the same instant, Josh noticed a small arched opening in the hedge. From where they stood it looked like it could form a tunnel into the woods. Their footsteps slowed. They'd been warned about the woods so often. The trees were diseased, the ground was full of hollows and slippery dead tree trunks, and it was easy to get lost in the labyrinth of dark, narrow trails.

"We don't *actually* have to go into the woods." Doubt entered Beth's voice for the first time. "We could just get close enough to see what's *actually* going on."

But Josh was in full Superman mode. "You two can stay outside. I'll do the exploring and report back to you if I find anything."

"Oh no you won't," said Michael. "If you go, we all go. Right, Beth?"

"I guess . . . " She gripped Josh's hand and walked a little closer to him as they approached the hedgerow. Thorns tugged at their clothes, dragged at their hair. Josh was stung by nettles but he was too excited to notice the pain. They emerged into a dusty trail, just wide enough for them to walk in single file. But the trees remained impassable. Even Beth, who was slight and wiry, was unable to force her way between the gnarled trunks. The sun shone through the rustling, leafy canopies and cast dappled shadows before them as they continued along the trail.

"Well, looks like there's nothing here." Josh didn't know whether to be relieved or disappointed. "Come on, let's go back and find the opening."

"Wait!" Michael stopped, abruptly. "Someone's coming."

Josh listened intently but was unable to hear a sound. "It's your imagination," he said. "Now come on, let's go." He turned back, hoping the others would follow. One part of him wanted to continue exploring. Somewhere, there had to be an opening between the grim, silent trees. But the more sensible part of him – the part that belonged to being twelve and a half years old and responsible for their safety – wanted to leave this mysterious green space where brilliant lights shone at dead of night and eerie noises suggested that Beth could be right and magic was afoot. He'd only taken a few steps along the path when he heard a voice behind him. And, before he turned, he knew it didn't belong to either Michael or Beth.

# 2

# the arrival of forester

Josh blinked. Unable to believe his eyes, he blinked again. Earlier, he'd laughed uproariously with Michael at the idea of supernatural creatures. He'd scoffed when Beth mentioned magic yet here he was, only a few hours later, staring down at a little man who most definitely belonged to the enchanted underworld. Josh was unsure if he was an elf, pixie, brownie or leprechaun. Not that it mattered. No such creatures existed . . . apart from fairy stories. The obvious answer was that the sun, now at its height in the noonday sky, had got to him. He was suffering from severe sunstroke. But one look at Michael's stupefied expression, and Beth's delighted smile, forced him to face reality. Somehow, he, Michael and Beth had stumbled into the realm of magic.

The air was still and hushed as the children and this strange little man stared curiously at each other. The little man stroked a bushy, russet-brown beard. His hair was the same rich shade – and a green hat with a pointy tip sat jauntily on the side of his head. He was dressed in tight black trousers and a moss-green jacket. Two brown patches on either side of his hat were so carelessly stitched on that they waggled every time he moved his head.

"Hi, there," said Beth, as if it was perfectly normal to meet such an unusual creature in the course of her day. She hunkered down until she was almost eye level with him. "Who are you?"

"Never mind who I am," he replied as he removed a satchel from his shoulders. It was made from hemp and had a thick rope strap. It looked heavy but that did not bother the little same. Despite his size, he looked tough and brawny, and his skin was ruddy from the outdoors. His eyes were most extraordinary. They glowed with a purple sheen and, right now, they were busily scrutinising each of the children.

"Are you allowed in the woods?" he asked. "Haven't your parents warned you that it is a dangerous place?"

"We were . . . eh . . . we were looking for our dog," said Beth.

"He ran off into the woods," added Michael.

"You won't find any dog in these woods," the little man replied. "Canines sense danger and no sensible dog would venture any further than the spot we're standing on now."

"What kind of danger could be in there?" asked Beth, pointing at the trees. "It's only Grimsville Woods."

"So, that's what you call it?" said the man. "Grimsville Woods?"

"That's the name Josh gave it," said Michael, sitting cross-legged on the ground. "But it's really called Merryville Woods."

"Once upon a time Merryville was an apt name," the man replied. He looked directly at Josh, who felt so awkward standing before such a small person that he also hunkered down. "But you named is wisely, Josh," continued the little man. "There is nothing but grimness and decay here now." Then he turned to Beth and asked, "Do you really have a lost dog?"

Beth hated being caught out in a lie but there was something so compelling about the man's gaze that she lowered her eyes and said, "Actually, no. We don't even *own* a dog."

"I thought so much. Why did you lie?"

"Because we're not allowed in the woods," she replied. "I'm sorry for lying. I said the first thing that popped into my head." She paused and moved a little closer to him. "Can I ask you a personal question?"

"By all means," the little man politely replied.

"Are you a leprechaun or a pixie?"

"My name is Forester." He made a slight bow to each of the children and continued in a matter-of-fact tone. "I'm the gatekeeper and protector of these ancient woods. What is your name?"

"I'm Beth and this is my brother, Michael."

Forester shook hands with each of them in turn. His hand was tiny yet it fitted comfortably into their own hands, which made no sense, as far as Josh was concerned. Or it made as much sense as anything else that was happening.

The little man continued talking. "Keeping humans from entering the woods is one of my tasks so I command the trees to shelter us. I also protect them with my spells so that they grow strong and tall."

"You haven't protected them very well," said Michael. "They're all diseased."

"Is that a fact?" Forester sounded indignant. "Are you suggesting that I don't know how to care for my trees?"

"It's what we've heard," said Josh. "A man from the county council did an inspection and said they were suffering from some kind of weird mildew. And you said yourself that the woods are decaying."

"I said there is decay within the woods, not within my trees." He glanced around, checking that no one could overhear. "Appearances can be deceptive. And enemies come in many guises. I would lay down my life rather than let anyone harm my trees. No humans can penetrate these woods—"

"But the man from the council—"

"Hush!" Forester put his finger to his lips. "Sound carries in the wind and our enemies have sharp ears."

"Who are the enemies?" Josh whispered.

"You'll be in danger if I tell you," the little man whispered back. "Be sensible and do not venture any further along this trail."

"But we want to know about the lights," said Michael. "We saw them last night and Josh saw them the night before."

Forester tilted his cap to one side and scratched his head in astonishment. "How could you see the lights?" he asked. "No one in the mortal world has the vision to see such sights." He stepped back from the children and closed his eyes. He seemed to be concentrating, his forehead furrowed. He uttered an occasional word, then nodded, as if someone had replied.

"What's he doing?" muttered Michael, shifting uneasily on the dusty ground.

"I think he's communicating the way we do on the phone, only he's doing it through his mind," Josh whispered back.

Forester gave a final nod and opened his eyes to stare directly at Josh. "Did you also hear noises?" he asked.

"We did," Josh replied. "Like spears clashing. And we heard blasts as well."

"You heard correctly." Forester settled his hat back on his head again. "There have been skirmishes taking place in the woods these past few nights. Oh, nothing too serious . . . as yet . . . but the time will come . . . " he stopped at the sound of dead wood snapping. This was followed by a rustling noise, as if someone or something had brushed against leaves.

"Go now," he whispered. "Go quickly back to the safety of your home. You can't be seen here."

The children scrambled to their feet and stepped backwards, uncertain what to make of the little man's strange behaviour. "Will we see you again?" Josh asked.

"Perhaps . . . " Forester waved them away with his hand. "But you must leave immediately. I say this to protect you. You have entered a dangerous space."

His urgent tone added to their nervousness. Without another word the children turned back towards the opening. They had only taken a few steps when Beth spun round. "I want to ask him about the lights," she whispered but Forester had disappeared.

They stared at the spot where he'd been standing just seconds ago.

"How strange is that?" asked Michael. He bent forward, half expecting the little man to be still standing between the burgeoning roots.

"Really weird," agreed Beth.

"You heard him," said Josh. "Danger! Let's get out of here."

They hurried along the trail. Sunshine no longer filtered through the branches and the shadows grew mottled and dark. The trees groaned and tossed their green, heavy crowns.

To his relief, they found the opening and climbed back to the road.

"Did we imagine that?" asked Michael.

"Of course we didn't," said Beth. "He's the gatekeeper and protector of the woods. I told you it was magic."

"But magic doesn't exist," said Josh. "At least, it didn't until today."

"You looked *really* scared," said Michael.

"You were shaking in your shoes," retorted Josh.

"I wasn't scared at all," said Beth, smugly. "That's because I believe in magic. And I liked Forester. He's got a cute little face."

"There's no accounting for taste, especially if you're into little green men," said Michael.

Beth punched his arm and ran ahead. He chased after her, shouting, "Beth's got a boyfriend."

By the time they arrived home, they were out of breath and still amazed by their encounter.

"Mum, who said the trees in Grim . . . I mean Merryville Woods are diseased?" Josh asked.

"A tree specialist," replied Mrs Lotts. "Apparently, he's a very famous expert on tree diseases."

"Mmm." Josh cut his pizza into triangles and wondered if he was treading on thin ice by even mentioning the woods. His mother had an uncanny knack of picking up on her children's thoughts. Between that and the eyes in the back of her head, very little escaped her attention. But magic was too serious, or too crazy, for adult discussion.

"Why do you ask?" she said. "I hope you children weren't hanging around the woods?"

"Of course we were," said Beth in her merriest voice. "We had a *really* interesting conversation with a tiny little man in a green jacket and a high pointy hat."

Mrs Lotts laughed and shook her head, despairingly. "Beth Lotts! Some day your tongue will tie you up in knots. Eat your pizza and stop telling whoppers."

When lunch was over, they escaped to the garden and sat on the wall.

"*Very* funny, Beth." Josh stared sternly at his sister.

"I told Mum the truth." Beth giggled so much she almost fell off the wall.

The morning's sunshine had disappeared. Dark rain clouds swept across the sky. "I want to go back to the woods tonight," said Michael. "We know the way in now."

"But Forester said it was extremely dangerous." Josh tried not to sound too alarmed. "And that was during the day. Night-time must be even more dangerous."

"But he said there were skirmishes going on," said Michael. "I want to see one up close."

"What's a skirmish?" asked Beth.

"It's what happens when Josh and Johnny Welts get together." Michael grinned and ducked when Josh pretended to cuff his ear.

The last person Josh wanted to think about was Johnny Welts. He tried to avoid doing so whenever possible but Johnny Welts was the bane of his life, his torture, his torment, his nightmare. Josh had once enjoyed school, now he dreaded it. He'd liked his teachers and was a reasonably bright student so school should not have been a place where trouble lurked. But it did – and it lurked in the shape of Johnny Welts who never missed an opportunity to pick a fight and usually chose the schoolyard as the boxing ring. Josh had lost count of the number of detentions the two of them had received, not to mention his ballooning eyes, grazed fists, aching ribs, duck egg bumps on his head. He sighed and forced Johnny Welts from his thoughts. There'd be time enough to think about him when school started again and that, thankfully, was not for two whole months.

"But Josh and Johnny Welts fight with their fists." Beth was unconvinced by Michael's definition of a skirmish. "The little people sounded as if they were fighting with spears."

"That's why we can't go back to the woods tonight," argued Josh. "What would happen if you got a spear plunged straight into your heart?"

"I'd pull it out," said Beth. "It'd be so tiny it'd be just like getting an injection."

"That's where you're wrong," said Josh. "Did you notice how Forester's hand seemed to fit into ours yet it was much, *much* smaller. It would be the same with the spears."

Beth looked thoughtful but Michael was determined to get his own way. "If it's anything bad then we could call the police and report it."

"Oh, yeah," said Josh, putting on a mock-official voice. "Please, Mr Policeman, I want to report a skirmish in the woods. The elves, or maybe it's the leprechauns, are to blame. Arrest them immediately."

But Michael refused to be amused. "Nothing ever happens around here, *ever*. I think this would be a really exciting adventure. We can't back off now."

"Oh please, Josh, we have to go," pleaded Beth. "Please, please, pretty *please*."

"Shut up," yelled Josh. "I have to think this through. What if there are sea witches in the woods? What then? Do you want your heart torn out and eaten?"

This stopped Beth in her tracks but Michael tossed his head, defiantly.

"Don't be stupid. A sea witch can't live in woods. She's a *sea* witch."

Once again, Josh was losing control of the situation. Being twelve and a half and in charge meant nothing to Michael, who never respected their two-year age gap. As for Beth, she was a law unto herself. Josh wouldn't put it past her to creep out her window and head off on her own to investigate. He'd have to go with them, even if it was only for their own protection. But, despite his misgivings, he was also intrigued by his meeting with Forester and just as anxious to know what was going on behind the sinister ring of trees.

"OK then." He nodded in agreement. "Listen carefully, this is my plan." The children bent their heads close together. "When we go to bed tonight, we'll watch for the lights. If nothing happens we stay put. Understood?"

They nodded in agreement.

"But if we see them?" prompted Michael.

"Then we climb down the ivy ladder under Beth's window. We don't make a sound. If Mum and Dad wake up we're in major trouble."

"What happens if we're missing when they come in to say goodnight?" asked Beth.

"The lights happen when they're asleep. Wear your pyjamas then change into warm clothes. It's getting colder already. We won't have to go through the village 'cause no one will see us in the dark, so we'll take the shortcut from the back garden. I'll bring my torch. At the first sign of danger you follow me and get out of there as fast as possible. Understand?"

"Agreed," said Michael.

At that moment, the weather broke. Lightning forked across the sky, followed by a distant clap of thunder. Rain began to fall. Sheets of rain that soaked through their clothes as they ran from the garden to the house.

It rained for the rest of the afternoon. They passed the time watching television and playing board games. The rain had stopped by the evening. Aware that they were about to disobey their parents in the most serious way possible, they set the table for dinner and asked their mother if she needed help in the kitchen. Needless to say, she became suspicious of such well-behaved children but she spotted nothing to alarm her when everyone sat down to eat.

Mrs Lotts was a splendid cook and the roast chicken, crispy on the outside, juicy on the inside, was exactly the way they liked it. She served it with roast potatoes and fresh vegetables from her garden. Their father talked about his day at the estate agency. This was the most boring conversation ever but Mrs Lotts seemed to enjoy hearing about the new houses for sale and the ones that had been sold. When he mentioned Great Aunt Graves, the children exchanged their usual agonised glances.

Memories, that's all they had left of the woman they used to love. Only last week Josh had been looking through a photo album and had seen her in so many of their holiday snaps. Other photographs had been taken in Merryville Manor. Her house had been warm and welcoming then. Climbing roses grew along the walls and her garden was full of flowers, hollyhocks, sweet william, foxgloves, poppies, lupins and a sweet-smelling lilac tree that always bloomed in May. There was an apple tree that bore the sweetest apples Josh had ever tasted. The horse chestnut at the very end of the garden had a stout branch that was perfect for making a swing. Great Aunt Graves was . . . had been . . . terrific fun. Josh had looked at the holiday photographs taken on the roller coaster at Alton Towers two summers ago. Great Aunt Graves's mouth was wide open in a scream as she hurtled along, clinging to Josh, laughing wildly when she was not screaming, enjoying the thrill every bit as much as he was. Impossible to imagine. He'd closed the album with a snap. Could he once have called her Lily-May until she ordered them to call her by her proper title and her surname? Great Aunt Graves. How formal it sounded, how unfriendly. Nowadays, she scared him. Her once smooth silvery hair had grown long and frizzy. It smelled greasy, as if she never bothered shampooing it. She'd grown a wart with stubbly hair on her chin. Her hands had become thin and as bony as claws, and were dotted with liver spots.

"It's the accident," said Mrs Lotts when her children made insulting remarks about their great-aunt. But there were other equally puzzling changes. Her garden had disappeared under weeds, brambles and thistles. The trees had been chopped down. Her house had become damp and chilly, even in sunny weather, and the high-ceilinged rooms had such a scary echo they were almost afraid to raise their voices. Perhaps they could have tolerated all the unpleasant changes if Great Aunt Graves had pretended to like them. But she made no secret of her feelings and they could never wait to escape her cold, echoing rooms.

"She's having a bad day," Mrs Lotts would say on the drive home. But she never sounded convincing and Josh suspected she dreaded visiting Great Aunt Graves as much as they did.

Tonight Mr Lotts sounded relieved when he announced that the meeting with his aunt had been postponed until tomorrow night.

"No warning," he grumbled, just to prove he was a busy man. "She just rang my office at the last minute and said she had something more important to do. She wants me at her beck and call, and never a word of thanks for all I do for her."

"What do you do?" asked Josh.

"I'm trying to organise planning permission for the felling of the trees," his father replied. "As they are so seriously diseased, they need to be removed as soon as possible."

"What will happen then?" asked Michael.

"A motorway," said Mr Lotts. "It's going to take at least twenty minutes off my journey home."

"But we won't have the woods," cried Beth.

"The diseased woods," Mr Lotts reminded her. "Woods that no one ever enters because they're too dark and dangerous. A motorway with trees and shrubs growing along either side sounds like the perfect solution. Don't you agree?"

Josh felt his anger rising as he remembered the shiny green leaves he had seen in the woods, and the respectful way Forester had spoken about his trees. "I know the land belongs to Great Aunt Graves but she should never have sold the woods for a motorway," he said.

But Mr Lotts was rubbing his hands together at the sight of Mrs Lotts carrying a delicious chocolate cake and a bowl of vanilla ice cream to the table. Beth, the sweet tooth of the family, helped herself to seconds and would have gone for thirds if Mrs Lotts had not removed the remains of the cake to the kitchen.

"She used to make brilliant muffins," said Josh.

"Who did?" asked Mrs Lotts.

"Great Aunt Graves."

"In your dreams," said Michael.

"She did . . . " Josh stopped. Had there ever been a time when Great Aunt Graves baked muffins and brownies and cookies? Now, when they visited her, she served weak tea and bread with mouldy blue spots round the edges. It seemed that the only thing Great Aunt Graves loved was money . . . but only if she did not have to spend it, especially on children. No more pocket money or surprise presents. No new clothes, which they'd always worn because, unlike most adults, their great-aunt had known exactly what they liked to wear.

Michael sidled from the table. "I'm off to bed to read my book," he announced.

"Michael reading a book?" exclaimed Mrs Lotts. "Is the sky about to fall?"

"Me too." Beth gave such an exaggerated yawn that Josh could see her tonsils.

He cleared the table and watched television. The evening news came on, followed by the weather forecast. Normally, he never watched the weather reports. It was either sunny or wet. That was the way the summer went. If it was sunny they played outdoors. Rainy days meant Scrabble, Twister, Connect Four, comics and jigsaws. But, tonight, if their plan was to work he needed to know the forecast and so he watched a woman pointing at charts filled with strange, voluminous clouds. Usually, at this time of year, they were either grey or white, with a little sun like a fried egg attached to some of them. But to his amazement, the weather forecaster announced that there would be strong winds, even snow and hailstones in some parts of the country. These would be followed by clear spells and showers.

Somehow, although Josh had no idea why, the forecast added to his sense of apprehension. What would happen if they disappeared in Grimsville and were never seen again? Or if Michael and Beth were captured and he was left to explain their disappearance to his parents? Sweat broke out on his forehead at the thought of their reaction. He would lie on the ground and let Johnny Welts jump on his bones for a week rather than face that. Sighing, Josh left the television with its ominous weather charts and climbed the stairs to his bedroom where his sister and brother waited for him to take charge.

They took turns keeping watch by the window but nothing extraordinary happened. When their parents came in to say goodnight, they were surprised to see that Beth was still in the boys' room.

"We're playing Monopoly," said Josh, which was perfectly true as they had to find something to keep them awake.

"You can buy the rest of Ireland tomorrow," said Mrs Lotts and ordered Beth to bed.

The boys continued watching and waiting. Downstairs, the television was switched off and the usual night sounds faded. As soon as their parents went to bed, Beth tiptoed back to their room.

"Anything yet?" she whispered.

"No," said Michael and flopped down on his bed. "Now it's your turn to watch."

After another hour passed and there was still no sign of the mysterious lights, Beth's shoulders began to slump. "I'm *really* tired now." She sighed with disappointment. "It doesn't look like anything's going to happen tonight."

"She's right." Michael crawled under his duvet and pulled it up to his chin. "I'm going to sleep now."

"You're the ones who wanted to investigate." Josh stretched his arms in the air and yawned, unsure whether to be relieved or frustrated. "I guess we'd better call it a night and try again tomorrow."

Just then they heard it. The blast was so loud and clear it could have come from underneath their window. This was followed by the same popping noise they had heard the previous night. All signs of tiredness disappeared. They ran to the window and stared towards Grimsville Woods where the sparkling, luminous colours rose about the trees and lit the night with streaming ribbons of green and purple. Now they could make out another colour. It was a cold, clear blue – and it made them shiver as it arched upwards and illuminated the trees in an icy glaze.

"Wow, just look at that!" gasped Michael as the colours whizzed through the air at incredible speed. He unbuttoned his pyjama top. "Let's get dressed and go."

31

Josh pulled his tee-shirt on last and touched the 'S' for courage. The flashing lights looked even brighter. Could the aurora borealis possibly be as splendid? he wondered. He had learned about the Northern Lights in school but they shone above the icecaps of the Arctic, above snow mountains and igloos and polar bears. If anything, the lights flaring across the sky were even more splendid. Forester had said humans could not see them yet something – and he had no idea what it was – had made it possible for them to witness this extraordinary sight. This 'something' was drawing him onwards, forcing him to overcome his fear and lead his brother and sister on this extraordinary adventure.

# 3

# an encounter with shift

Last year their father had erected a strong, wooden trellis under Beth's window to encourage ivy to grow along the back wall. The ivy was still sparse enough for them to see the criss-crossing slats as, one by one, they eased themselves onto the window ledge. Their hands searched for secure grips as they carefully climbed to the ground. Michael went last and almost fell off as the masonry nails securing the ladder to the wall began to loosen. But it remained upright and he jumped from about the halfway mark, landing like a cat on the grass.

"Did you bring your torch?" Beth whispered.

"Yes." Josh pulled it from his pocket. "But the batteries are low. I hope it holds out."

The children had lived all their lives in the country. They were unafraid of the dark and walked confidently behind the beam of the torch. The night air was cool and crisp. No clouds in the sky but the lights from the woods made it difficult to see the stars. They climbed over the back garden gate, as it was inclined to creak, then took the shortcut to the woods. This was usually a busy road during the day but now it was empty of traffic. They passed a thatched cottage and three bungalows. The Welts family lived in the middle one. All were in darkness. Soon the grim outlines of Merryville Manor loomed before them. Thankfully, it too was in darkness.

"Can you feel it?" Beth whispered.

"Feel what?" asked Michael, who was beginning to sound a little shaky.

"Magic, I can feel magic." Suddenly, she flapped her hair and looked upwards. "Bats!" she shrieked as a colony of bats swirled through the flashing lights.

"They won't harm you," said Josh but he hurried a little faster along the road. A full moon sailed above them. It dipped behind the trees then reappeared when they turned another corner. As the wondrous lights continued to flare across the sky, they noticed occasional shadows flitting above the branches.

"It's *really* scary being so close." Beth's voice trembled.

"Do you want to go back?" Josh whispered.

"No." She gripped his hand. "You'll keep me safe."

"You bet I will." Josh wished he felt as confident as he sounded.

"Do you think the sea witch—?"

"There's no such thing," he reassured her. "And even if there was, I'd tear her heart out first."

The noises sounded much louder and the flashes were so vivid that Josh turned off his torch to save the batteries. At last they reached the hedgerow surrounding the woods and found the arched opening. Quickly, they crawled underneath.

"Ouch! Mind those thorns," Michael warned them as they huddled together and peered out at the tight rows of trees guarding the woods. "Do you think we should *actually* enter the woods?" he asked.

No doubt about it, Michael was as scared as Beth. Their fear added to Josh's courage. He touched his Superman symbol and said, "We've come so far. No sense turning back at this stage." Then he made the mistake of looking through the thorny branches at the tree on the other side of the dusty trail. The bark was so gnarled he imagined a pair of eyes, sunk deep into the hollowed wood. They were staring directly at them, and the mouth . . . he was sure there was a mouth with thick, wrinkled lips grinning at them. He blinked and the image disappeared. It's only the moon playing tricks, he decided, but he wasn't taking any chances.

"We're not moving from here," he decided and, for once, the others did not argue back.

By now the lights were so dazzling they had to shield their eyes. The clamour had also increased, thuds like wood clattering against wood, and a whizzing noise, as if arrows were flying at great speed through the air. They could hear the clash of steel and something else, something so horrifying that they tensed, unable to move. Screams. The full-throated screams of people in pain.

"What is it?" Beth whispered.

"Could be an animal caught in a trap," said Josh, wishing with every fibre of his being that he was safely back in bed.

"It's a skirmish," hissed Michael. "And someone's hurt."

Beth whimpered and pressed her fingers over her mouth.

Thorns pricked through their jeans, caught against their jackets, dragged at their skin, but they remained in their hiding place until the lights and screams grew fainter, and darkness once again surrounded them.

"We'd better go," said Michael.

"Wait," said Josh, grabbing both their arms and peering out from the hedge. "Someone's coming."

The moon cast a silvery shadow across the trail and by its light he saw a dark, smoky shape weaving towards their hiding place. At first he thought it was a shadow but it was more substantial, like a coil of heavy smoke emerging from a chimney.

Michael peered between the leaves then drew back, his shoulders hunched. "What is it?" he whispered.

Beth took one look and buried her face in Josh's shoulder. His mouth was so dry he was afraid he'd never again be able to swallow. The smoke shape was followed by a tall figure wearing a dark-green velvet cloak. The cloak was so long that Josh was unable to tell if it was worn by a man or a woman. The material shimmered in the moonlight and appeared to have been woven from iridescent threads. The smoky shape flitted to and fro in front of the cloaked figure. Both of them looked eerie and insubstantial enough to be ghosts, thought Josh, who held tight to Beth and also to Michael, whose hand was hot and sweating.

"We're safe here," said Josh. "They can't see us."

They remained frozen in their crouching positions, unaware of thorns or any other discomfort, hardly able to breathe as the smoky shape drew nearer to the hedgerow. It began to glide upwards and over to the far side, then returned to the trail, sniffing loudly all the time. Josh knew with a sudden sickening certainty that the shape could smell their presence, no matter how deeply they huddled among the leaves and thorns. The cloaked figure lifted what looked like a cane. A pulsating green light emerged from the tip, glowing brighter and wider with each second that passed. The figure reached their hiding place. The green glow from the cane was so bright it lit up their terrified faces.

Through their terror, they heard the hooded figure speak. "Shift, we are not alone here. There are mortal children spying on us."

Josh lifted his head. Although his heart was beating frantically, something about the sinister voice was familiar. He watched as Shift, the smoky figure, hissed like a snake and began to change shape. It swirled around the hedge one last time then slowly began to thicken into a monstrous-looking creature with huge red eyes, scales along its back and a horn on top of its head.

It's a gargoyle, Josh thought, remembering a book about monsters he had borrowed from Merryville library. The gargoyle's teeth were long and razor sharp. As Josh watched, Shift sprouted a pair of ugly, scaly wings.

Beth's face was streaked with tears and Michael looked as if he was about to faint. The gargoyle flapped its wings and flew next to the hooded figure.

"I can smell them." The voice hissed, the sound so sibilant and threatening that shivers raced up and down Josh's spine. A nightmare, even the worst possible nightmare, would be easier to endure. With dreams he could always force himself awake but this was as real as the thorns catching in his hair. As real as the damp smell of earth and mouldering leaves. He had only one thought in his mind. Somehow, he had to save his brother and sister. But he had absolutely no idea how he was going to do so. Being twelve and a half, and the eldest, had never seemed so difficult to Josh Lotts as at that moment.

He decided they should make a run for it then changed his mind in the same instant. He'd seen how fast Shift moved. They would never make it back to their house in time. But it was their only option. The thought of being touched by either creature was too terrifying to even consider. His knees were cramped from crouching but just as he was about to give the command to run, the children heard a popping noise and there, right beside the hedge, Forester appeared.

# 4

## a journey through the wood

The watchman and protector of the woods showed no sign of fear as he approached the hooded figure and the gargoyle.

"Can I help you, Gridelda?" he addressed the hooded figure. "And you too, Shift? I see you've been up to your usual foul deeds tonight."

"How dare you spy on me?" The voice that came from beneath the hood was shrill and definitely female. Josh strained forward, struggling to recognise the voice. He had never heard of anyone called Gridelda – but the name that came to his mind was so horrendous he refused to even consider it.

"You know I don't spy," replied Forester. "My responsibility is to protect the woods."

"There are children hiding nearby." Gridelda pointed a bony finger towards the hedge. "Shift can smell them. He does not make mistakes. Move aside, you pathetic watchman."

"Shift's sense of smell is ill-timed," said Forester. "There were children here earlier today looking for a lost dog. I can assure you, no child could pass my watch and enter the woods. Now if you don't mind, I must be on my way."

Gridelda raised her hand and drew the hood from her face. The light from her cane continued to pulse as she stared angrily down at him. "If I thought you were up to anything suspicious, I would crush you like a grape. Do you hear me? Like a grape between my fingers. Do we understand each other?"

"You can't harm me," Forester calmly replied. "I do no harm to living things and no living thing can harm me."

"You may be safe for the moment but not for much longer. And you will pay dearly for all the trouble you have caused me." Gridelda pulled her hood up again and snapped, "Shift, take me home. You and I will celebrate tonight's victory in my mansion. We will sip from the Chalice of Elentra and allow the trees to sleep for the short time that is left to them." She laughed loudly as the branches, as if understanding her threat, cast forlorn shadows over the illuminated trail. She swept her cane through the air one last time and the bats swerved above the trees, as if they too were terrified by the luminous green shadows.

Shift waggled forward on four sturdy legs. By now it had grown to the size of a winged horse. It bowed to Gridelda who leaped effortlessly upon its broad back. Up they rose into the air, flying about the trees, rising even higher into the starry firmaments. The mysterious green light faded then plunged one last time like a shooting star disappearing from view.

"Come children, it's safe to emerge now." Forester opened his satchel and removed a twig. It flamed as soon as he pressed it and lit the way as the children crawled through the hedge that had provided them with shelter, as well as so much discomfort. Forester shone the flaming twig upwards on their horrified faces.

Michael was the first to speak. "Tha ... tha ... *that* ... wo ... woman ..." Terrified, he could only stutter a few words. ""What's she ... she do ... do ... doing, she's our ... our ..."

Forester stared sternly at them. "What did I tell you?" he demanded. "I warned you that this is a dangerous place. It's bad enough in daylight but for you to come out at night . . . you could have been killed. Go home and for your own safety, forget about me and Shift, and, particularly, Gridelda. And don't let me catch you around these parts again. Next time you might not be so lucky."

"We're sorry we didn't listen to you," gasped Josh, "but that woman, that dreadful woman, we know her."

"She's our Great Aunt Graves," Beth blurted out.

"Your Great *Aunt* Graves?" Forester looked astonished. "Are you telling me you're related to Gridelda? Impossible."

"It's not impossible," said Josh. "It's true. She's our father's aunt and she lives in Merryville Manor. We've been there loads of times."

The little man tugged at his beard and stood for an instant deep in thought.

"If she is your great-aunt, then it's no coincidence that you are here tonight. I've cast my spells throughout the woods to prevent humans finding out what we are protecting. Yet you've proved once again to be immune to my magic. You must be gifted with special powers that allow you entry to the woods. I must go now and seek permission to bring you to its heart."

"To go where?" Josh felt his brother and sister shivering beside him.

"Don't be frightened," said Forester. "You will be safe with me."

44

"But what if Great Aunt Graves comes back?" he said. "Or that thing . . . that gargoyle? What if they find us here?"

Forester faced the hedgerow with its barbed branches and recited a short rhyme.

*"Hedgerow! Please draw back your thorns.*
*We need to vanquish she who scorns*
*These woods that shelter us from harm.*
*Obey my wish – and with this charm*
*Keep these children in your arms.*
*Cause them no fuss or false alarms*
*And save them from the gargoyle's wrath*
*Until I return along this path."*

As he spoke, he stretched his hand towards the hedge. The children watched in disbelief as the thorns pulled back into the branches and the leaves began to increase. The little arch grew wider and when they crawled through they found a roomy dome with a floor of soft pine needles. The entrance was covered by a dense leafy screen.

"That's amazing," said Michael. "How do you do that?"

Forester waved his hand dismissively towards the hedge and said, "We all have our gifts. Mine is to commune with nature and like all precious gifts I never take it for granted."

Before the children could ask any more questions, they heard a loud pop and he disappeared as quickly as he had done that morning. But, by now, they were beyond amazement.

"Where do you think he goes?" asked Michael.

"We'll soon find out." Josh was beginning to recover his nerve. "What do you think Great Aunt Graves was doing with that creepy gargoyle?"

"I'm not a bit surprised," said Beth. "I always knew she was horrible and wicked. And now I know she's an evil witch as well."

"But she wasn't always like that." Josh had no intention of defending her but he kept thinking about the accident. Could there be any connection or had she always deceived them? Could he actually be related to a woman who kept a hideous gargoyle as a pet? He had to be dreaming . . . any minute now he would wake up and tell everyone over breakfast about his most amazing nightmare yet. Some wish. Josh sighed and sifted pine needles through his fingers. Great Aunt Graves had been fried alive. At least, that was what his father had said afterwards. Fried alive and lucky to be alive.

It had happened on a sunny day, rather like today, only there had been no sudden storms and rain. The weather had been balmy and he had been weeding his great-aunt's garden when he heard her scream. He rushed into the kitchen and slipped, landing with a ferocious bump on his bottom. A baking bowl lay in pieces on the floor and a golden batter mix had spread in a pool below the cooker. His great-aunt was sprawled on the floor, her head resting in the batter. The cooker, where she had been making pancakes, made a sparking sound and smoke was still rising from the rings. Josh did not hesitate. His aunt was unconscious. She had been electrocuted, maybe she was already dead. He rang an ambulance then ran back in and crouched beside her. A faint pulse was still beating in her neck. He called her name, "Lily-May . . . Lily May . . . " but she never moved. But when the ambulance men arrived and lifted her onto a stretcher, her eyelids flickered. Then her eyes opened and she stared at Josh as if he was a stranger, and one she did not like very much. One she loathed, in fact. At first he thought she was still dazed but she spoke quite clearly to one of the ambulance men.

"My name is Graves," she said. "Miss Graves. And that boy is trespassing in my house." She turned back to Josh and waved brusquely at him. "Out, boy, out! I don't want to see you near my house when I return."

"It's the shock," the second ambulance man whispered kindly to Josh. "She'll be as right as rain in no time at all."

But he was wrong. The accident marked the beginning of the change and now, sitting inside the domed hedge, Josh had a sudden desire to cry. Not that he would. No way. What would Johnny Welts do if he heard? But everything was so confusing. He was still struggling with his thoughts when Forester reappeared before them.

"I have been permitted to reveal certain secrets before I take you into the woods," he said. "Come closer and listen carefully."

He waited until the children formed a semi-circle around him then he spoke in a low voice. "The most magical great oak tree in the world grows inside these woods. Since time began, it has been protected from harm. I have made sure that no human took an axe or chainsaw to its precious bark. This great and wondrous tree is called the Tree of Seasons."

"The Tree of Seasons," whispered Josh. It sounded ancient and magnificent.

Forester nodded, as if he could read Josh's mind. "The Tree of Seasons contains four parts. Within its trunk there are four doorways leading into four magical lands, each one representing the seasons. It has been thus from its beginnings – spring, autumn, summer and winter. Each nation has its own independent ruler. The land of winter is called Icefroztica and is ruled by the king goblin, Darkfrost. As you can imagine, this is the coldest land and it is occupied by goblins. They are cold creatures, brave in battle, smart and wily. I used to believe they were loyal . . . " He paused for breath and frowned. "But I've discovered that their hearts are small and unloving."

The goblins, Josh figured, must have created a fair amount of trouble in the land of Icefroztica.

"Then there is the land of spring," continued Forester, his expression lightening. "This is called New Blossomdale, and is ruled by the noble elf, King Leafslear. This magical place is populated by elves, who are warm and caring, and have great powers of healing. They too fight with great skill and are courageous in battle. The land of summer is called Brightisclearen and is populated by fairies, who are gifted spell casters and always ready to help people in trouble. Their ruler, Queen Glendalock, is as wise as she is beautiful." He smiled briefly but when he spoke again, his voice was edgy, the words low and hurried. "Lastly and least, the place I've come to hate is Duskcanister. It represents the season of autumn but it has become a dark and dreary place, full of rot and mould. A land to be avoided, if possible."

"But autumn is wonderful," said Josh. "After summer, it's my favourite season."

"Sadly, since Queen Gridelda came to rule over Duskcanister, it has become a fearsome kingdom," said Forester. "Once it was ruled by wise queens who understood that it was a time to harvest the summer's bounty, to slowly fade in a splendid blaze and gently give way to winter. But now I'm afraid Duskcanister is ruled by the woman you call your Great Aunt Graves. She is the evil queen of autumn."

"That's unbelievable," gasped Josh. "Our aunt can't be the queen of autumn. She's evil, all right. But she's not a queen."

"I've never seen her with a crown," said Beth. "Not once. Queens are beautiful and wear long gowns with frills."

"You can't expect us to believe such a crazy story," scoffed Michael.

"You saw her with her gargoyle," retorted Forester. "Is that any crazier than what I'm telling you now?"

"I suppose . . . " Josh shuddered and closed his eyes against the image of Shift and the menacing hooded figure that had walked behind him.

"I've been given permission to tell you these truths," said Forester. "But it is important that you believe me."

"We do . . . sort of . . . ." said Beth. "Maybe she keeps the crown in her wardrobe."

"She wears no crown but she has achieved a mighty power," said Forester. "Now if you will follow me—"

"Follow you?" Beth's eyes widened with excitement. "Where are we going?"

"To the Tree of Seasons," replied Forester. "My instructions are to take you to meet Queen Glendalock immediately. So please, we must hurry."

The children emerged from their hiding place. Immediately, the thorns reappeared and the hedgerow looked as menacing as ever. Now that they were expected to venture into the woods, Josh's terror resurfaced.

"How are we going to get through the trees?" Josh looked nervously towards them. Hunched under the moonlight, their trunks seemed alive, twisted limbs and branches like muscular arms waiting to strangle those who stepped too close.

Forester stretched his hand towards two of the biggest trees and spoke in his rhyming voice.

> *"Oak and willow, birch and elm*
> *We seek to enter magic's realm.*
> *Alder, cedar, pine and beech*
> *We must make haste and swiftly reach*
> *Queen Glendalock, whom I obey.*

*So please assist us on our way*
*Along the path where branches sway*
*Towards the kingdom of the fey."*

The earth shook beneath the children's feet and rumbled deeply. They watched in disbelief as the roots of the trees began to emerge from the earth and quiver like the legs of a giant spider. It was almost like a domino effect, Josh thought, except that the trees didn't knock each other over. They just rippled like a gentle wave as each tree moved to create a path.

"That's *really* amazing," said Beth as the roots sank into new earth and the path widened before them. She looked at Forester in awe but the boys were beginning to take the little man's power for granted.

"I take care of the trees and they take care of me," Forester replied. "It's a tradition that has run in my family for thousands of years." Once again he put his hand out and said,

*"Grass grow soft as feather down*
*And lead us to the fairy crown."*

When grass appeared on the newly formed path, he smiled at the children. "Nature has made you welcome in our kingdom." He rummaged in his satchel and produced three twigs similar to the one he had used earlier to light his way. As soon as the children held them upwards, the twigs glowed brightly.

They had only walked a short distance when a voice began to ring inside Josh's head. Not sure if he was imagining it – and who would blame him? – he looked at Michael and Beth. Michael jabbed his finger at his head and Beth looked as if she might swoon with happiness so he had to assume that they too could hear the same soft, wispy voice.

"Do not be afraid, my dear ones." The voice was as calming as a gentle, melodic tune. "I shall let no harm come upon you on your journey here. But come quickly to my side. We have important matters to discuss."

"What a beautiful voice," sighed Beth.

"Mesmerising," said Josh. "Who is it?"

"Queen Glendalock, the queen of Brightisclearen," said Forester.

Holding up their twigs to light the way, they entered Grimsville Woods. They jumped nervously when they heard two loud popping noises.

"It's just my ears," explained Forester.

"Your ears?" Josh bent down to inspect the little man. By the light of his twig, he saw that the patches in Forester's hat had shifted to one side and two elf-like ears were jutting through the holes.

"My ears only come out in the woods," he explained. "In the outside world, I don't need to hear the grass growing. And, besides, what would people say if they saw my ears popping in and out?"

His ears did indeed look funny to human eyes and the children laughed with him as they stepped across the cushiony carpet of grass.

"How long before we get there?" Beth asked, after they had ventured deeper into the woods.

"Not long now," said Forester.

Shortly afterwards they saw a faint glow rising above the trees. "Almost there," he said. "Just another couple of turns."

"What's the glow coming from?" asked Michael.

"The Tree of Seasons always has a magical light around it," Forester paused to study the glow but the children walked a little faster, eager to see the magical tree.

When they reached the last corner, a wide clearing opened before them. Forester turned back the way they had travelled and stretched out his hand.

> *"We offer thanks to grass and trees*
> *Who carried us with greatest ease*
> *To where the Tree of Seasons dwells*
> *Midst chant and charms and magic spells."*

The trees began to uproot themselves and moved across the path until they found their original positions and rooted themselves back into the soil. The grass vanished and the woods became dark and dense once again.

But the children, surrounded by brightness, were drawn forward as if by invisible strings to stand in awe before the Tree of Seasons.

# 5

## entering the tree of seasons

A white glow flowed from the Tree of Seasons. It seemed as if the trunk and boughs, every twig and every broad green leaf were sending out waves of energy in all directions. Josh was amazed by its enormous height and girth. Michael and Beth seemed equally enthralled. They tilted back their heads and stared towards the topmost branches. They lived in a part of the country known as the Garden of Ireland. They were used to trees, could tell the names of any tree growing in the forests and along the roadsides. But they had never seen anything like this amazing tree with its streaming pearly light.

Josh was filled with a sense of calm and warmth as he imagined the tree's energy expanding beyond the woods, reaching out to the greater world and bringing with it the same soothing peace. A leaf brushed against his cheek. All his fear disappeared. All the anxiety, anger, humiliation, uncertainty, unhappiness, embarrassment, all these painful emotions he sometimes felt just disappeared. He would never be afraid of anything or anyone again. Everything was possible. He would conquer the world. No, not conquer, he decided . . . he would live in harmony with the world.

"It's so cool," gasped Michael. "But it's night-time. Where is the light coming from?"

"The sap released by the Tree of Seasons at night reacts with the air and glows like candles," Forester replied. "Candles without flames seems very wise to me."

"Amazing," agreed Josh. "I've never seen anything like it before in my life."

"Nor will you ever again." Forester sounded proud and pleased by their reaction. "The Tree of Seasons inspires pure emotion within those of us who stand beneath its branches. But we also have free will when we step outside its healing light and our queen of autumn has brought a blight upon this wondrous tree. But that talk is for later. For now, allow the Tree of Seasons to welcome you to its kingdoms."

"How come we can't see the tree from outside the woods?" Beth was puzzled. "It's so tall, surely other people must be able to see it."

Forester smiled at her. "The Tree of Seasons is protected by my spells," he explained. "It is invisible to the mortal eye but the seasons that it contains are visible throughout your world. Move closer to the trunk. The tree means you no harm."

Up close, the waves of energy felt even stronger. As they walked around its girth, the children saw that it did indeed have four parts, each one representing a season.

The first section was filled with the sweet aroma of cherry blossom. The smell of gorse was heavier. When spring came and the fiery gorse blazed across the hills, the scent always reminded Josh of coconut. Flowers peeked shyly between the budding leaves, buttery-shaded clumps of cowslips and primroses, daffodils and tulips. Nests had been built within the crooks of branches and the breeze blowing through the heavy boughs was frisky, warm then cold, warm again. The

unfurling leaves were a delicate shade of green and fluttered light as feathers.

They moved towards the strong, vibrant colours of
summer. The air was sweet with the scent of straw-
berries. Roses climbed upwards and wove around this
section of the trunk. Clusters of wild meadow flowers
bloomed between the sturdy roots that bulged above the
ground – poppies, daisies, buttercups, London pride,
violets, snapdragons, eyebright, forget-me-knots, hare-
bells, dandelions. Birds sang behind a shield of bright-
green leaves.

As they left the balmy breezes and moved to the next
section of the tree, the ground grew damp and mulching.
Leaves were scattered everywhere, red, bronze and yellow.
The smell deepened and became mouldy, reminding Josh
of rotting wood. The same smell that, nowadays, made him
recoil when he entered his great-aunt's manor. Sheaves of
wheat and corn hung from the branches but the grain was
mouldering and released a pungent stench. Apples, pears
and plums, mottled and wrinkled, rotted on the branches.
Worms crawled in and out of the slimy flesh, and there
were no sign of birds, not even a lone swallow waiting to
fly to sunnier climes.

Josh thought about the apples he used to pick in his
great-aunt's garden. They had smelled of roses and the
juice ran down his chin when he bit into them. Not any
more. Men had come in a truck with a chainsaw and cut
down the apple tree, than felled the lilac. The only one
left was the horse chestnut but that would probably also

disappear. One thing for sure, Josh would never again sling a rope over the toughest branch and swing on a tyre.

"Forester, is this where Great Aunt Graves comes?" he asked.

"Yes, this is her kingdom," replied Forester. "Now quickly, we must move on. It is dangerous on this side of the tree."

As the children walked to the last section, they shivered in the grip of freezing temperatures. Bright red holly berries glistened on the branches. Thorns jutted dangerously between the leaves. Icicles hung from twigs, a frozen mist chilled their fingers and snow silently drifted to the ground.

"How pretty," said Beth, catching snowflakes in her hands. A robin stared forlornly at her from the bleak, icy branches.

"Sadly, it's not that pretty inside this part of the tree," said Forester. "But we must not delay any longer. Queen Glendalock anxiously awaits us."

The children followed him round to the summertime side of the tree. They stopped at its centre and Forester once again held out his hand. "Brightisclearen, we are here to see Queen Glendalock. We await to enter."

The climbing roses parted and a circle began to glow. Slowly, it started to move. It was a door, Josh realised, and it creaked slowly open to reveal a large hole in the trunk.

Forester looked at the children and asked, "Are you ready to venture within the Tree of Seasons?"

Josh nodded reassuringly to each of them. He had no idea where they were going. Or what they would discover when they reached the end of their journey. But one thing was certain. They were embarking on the most exciting experience of their lives and nothing would stop him taking that next step forward.

They entered a tunnel. Although it looked tiny, it must have expanded because the children had no difficulty walking along it. The walls were decorated with summer flowers and they stepped on a path of purple clover. At the end of the tunnel they caught the faint hue of a blue sky. They emerged into another woodland. But this was different to Grimsville Woods. Here the trees bore many different varieties of fruit. As well as peaches, apricots and cherries, the children saw exotic foreign trees, wide-leafed banana trees, the slender trunks of swaying coconut trees, lemon, grapefruit and orange trees, and strange star-shaped fruits they could not name. Crystal streams flowed through the orchards. Valleys and hills rolled onwards towards a castle perched on the highest hill. It was a splendid sight, with many turrets and balconies, and surrounded by a great wall.

As they looked around them in wonder, they noticed two dark specks flying towards them.

"What are they?" Beth pointed upwards.

"Ah, they would be fairies," said Forester. "They are coming to escort us to their queen."

"Fairies!" Beth could hardly contain her excitement.

"I've only ever seen them in books and on television. I never thought for one moment that they *really* existed."

"Well, now you know." Forester grinned as the fairies drew closer. How effortlessly they flew, swifter than birds, lighter than butterflies.

"Oh, how I wish I could fly," Beth sighed enviously as they glided above the children before landing beside them.

The two fairies, who, like Forester, stood about a foot in height, were male. They wore glistening, silken loincloths, one in green, the other blue. The colours matched the crown of flowers sitting carelessly on their blond, tousled hair. They stared at the children with wide-set green eyes.

"Greetings," said the blue fairy. "I'm Bowrain. We have come to welcome you to Brightisclearen."

"I'm Partlant." The second fairy smiled warmly. "Be kind enough to follow us. Queen Glendalock awaits your arrival."

He gave a shrill whistle and immediately four huge butterflies emerged from the trees. Their yellow wings – speckled with luminous green spots – flapped gently through the warm air as they approached.

"Bet you've never flown on a butterfly before," said Forester.

Beth gasped in delight. "Are we *really* going to fly on them?"

"Yes. We need to make haste to the castle. Butterflies are the quickest way."

The butterflies landed next to the fairies, who patted their heads then gestured to the children to climb on board.

Forester mounted the first butterfly and settled himself in the slight bend between the head and thorax. "Hold on to their antennae so that you don't fall off," he advised the children.

As Beth was too small to manage on her own, Bowrain hoisted her upwards. He also flew to Josh's side and shifted him a little to one side so that his weight was more evenly balanced on the butterfly. Josh was surprised at Bowrain's strength. He smiled to himself and wondered what Johnny Welts would say if he heard that a fairy, dressed in a blue loincloth, had just assisted him onto a butterfly. The thought made him laugh out loud. He was filled with exuberance as the butterfly's wings began to flap and Partlant yelled, "Hold on tightly, children."

The fairy stepped back and waved his hands in a signal. "Butterflies, to the castle please."

Before they could utter a word, the children were airborne and on their way to meet Queen Glendalock. The two fairies flew alongside them. The sensation, thought Josh, as they flew over the hills, was even more wonderful and exciting than the great roller coaster he had once ridden with Great Aunt Graves. He put her out of his mind. Time enough to think about her later. With the wind blowing in his hair, he floated over a land of flowers and trees. He could see inside the castle walls.

Small houses ringed the castle. It looked like a miniature village with shops and pavement cafés and fairies
bustling through a village square. No cars. Why would
transport be necessary when all the inhabitants had to do
was flap their wings?

Fairy children stopped playing in their gardens to wave
up at them. Beth was so intent on waving back that she
leaned over too far and released one of her butterfly's
antennae. Before she realised what was happening, she
lost her balance. She tried to hold onto the butterfly with
her legs but it was too late. Suddenly she had a glimpse of
the butterfly's fat underbelly and long dangling legs. Then
she was tumbling through the air, the wind whipping her
screams and casting them over the hills.

"Forester! Beth's fallen off her butterfly." Josh, pale with
shock, yelled at the watchman, who seemed unperturbed
by the sight of Beth disappearing below them.

But her butterfly knew exactly what to do. It dived down
at great speed and flew beneath her, waiting for her to land
safely back in her seat.

"Are you OK, Beth?" screamed Josh.

"I'm fine," she replied and held on tightly to the antennae for the rest of the journey.

"Don't worry," said Partlant. "It happens a lot to anyone
riding a butterfly for the first time. But our butterflies
have great eyesight and will always catch you, no matter
what."

Onwards they flew towards the castle. They could see
activity around it. Fairies flew above the turrets, others

crowded the balconies or gathered in the courtyard to greet them when they landed.

"We must be going," said Bowrain as the butter-flies floated to a halt beside a marble bridge. "But we'll return to take you home. Bellatinks will escort you to the queen."

"Who's Bellatinks?" asked Beth, as the fairies flew out of sight.

"She . . . um . . . " Forester coughed into his beard. "She's the queen's handmaiden."

"Why are you blushing, Forester?" Beth tilted her head to one side and giggled. "Is she a pretty hand maiden?"

Forester cleared his throat once more as a petite fairy with a crown of daisies twined in her long, red hair stepped over the bridge. Unlike Partlant and Bowrain's untidy tresses, her hair was neatly combed and gleamed in the sunlight. She was barefoot and her dress, the same fiery shade as her hair, swayed around her dainty ankles.

"Gr . . . greetings, Bellatinks," said Forester, flustered for the first time since the children met him. "It's ah . . . it's nice to see you again."

Bellatinks's pale cheeks flushed. "You are welcome to Brightisclearen, Forester." They stared at each other for far longer than a polite stare should last. Then she lowered her eyes and turned her attention to the children.

"Dear children, we bid you welcome to Locksun Castle. Please follow me." She led them over the carved marble bridge and through the great doorway of the castle.

They entered the square courtyard where fairies were also eating and drinking at tables. The four sides of the courtyard were lined with long, stained-glass windows. Images of fairies had been painted on each window. Each fairy wore the same golden crown rimmed with glistening roses, and their expressions, although regal, were also compassionate.

"Who are they?" asked Michael.

"They are our beloved past queens of Brightisclearen," replied Bellatinks.

They stopped in front of a large door. It slowly opened and they entered a grand hall with a white marble floor, flecked with emerald. Marble statues of fairies, similar to the images in the stained-glass windows, were lined around the hall and the chandeliers, hanging from the high ceilings, threw out a faint rosy beam.

They passed through the hall and reached a wooden staircase with carvings on the banisters of fairies dancing. The carvings were intricate, each tiny movement and expression precisely cut into the wood. Everyone remained silent as they climbed the stairs, afraid that if they spoke aloud, the sound would echo all around them. They faced a smaller door at the top of the staircase. Bellatinks gently knocked and waited. After a few seconds the door was opened by a fairy and they stepped into Queen Glendalock's throne room. Six steps led upwards towards a dais where the fairy queen, wearing the same crown the children had seen in the courtyard windows, was seated on a throne.

Queen Glendalock's long dress was woven from fine silver threads. Her hair fell in curls to her shoulders and had the same silvery sheen. Her face was radiant with welcome as she arose from her throne and flew towards them.

She held out her hand to Forester. "My dearest Forester, it is such a joy to see you again. Thank you for your kindness, and for guiding the children safely here."

Forester bowed and kissed the ring on her finger. "As always, it is a pleasure to serve you, Queen Glendalock."

"Josh, Michael, Beth, you are most welcome to my kingdom." She smiled warmly at the children. Her voice had the same wispy softness they had heard in their minds. "You have journeyed far and must be hungry. Please, sit at the Meeting Table and eat, then we shall talk. We shall shortly be joined by King Leafslear and two of his greatest warriors."

A large table and chairs – much larger than the other furnishings in the throne room – had been arranged for their arrival. The table was laid with bowls of fruits from the orchards and the jugs filled with elderflower juice. Long-stemmed glasses, twined with flowers, were arranged beside crystal plates.

Forester filled his plate with fruit but could not resist glancing towards Bellatinks, who caught his glance and blushed. The children, their mouths filled with nuts and berries, grinned at each other. Josh made a swooning expression as he patted his heart, and the queen, seated on her throne, smiled. But Bellatinks and Forester noticed only each other.

When the children finished eating, the door opened and three male figures, dressed in jerkins and trousers, entered. King Leafslear moved with a lithe, willowy grace. His large green ears were as pointed as the first plants that thrust upwards from the spring earth. Like Queen Glendalock, he also wore a crown but he was armed with a bow on his back, and a quiver full of arrows tied to his side. The two elves who accompanied him were sturdier, more muscular. From the protective way they moved around him, Josh suspected they were his bodyguards. Their clothes were a deeper green than the pale leaf-green shade worn by the king.

"I came as quickly as I could, your Majesty." King Leafslear's voice resonated throughout the throne room as he bowed to Queen Glendalock. He turned his attention to the children, who had jumped to their feet when he entered, and bade them be seated again.

"It is a great pleasure to meet with mortals from the outside world," he said. "You have come to us in our time of need." He joined them at the table. "Let the meeting begin. We have little time to waste."

The queen flew to a gilded chair positioned at the head of the Meeting Table. It had a high back and velvet padded armrests.

"Forester informs me you are related to Queen Gridelda." The queen addressed the question to Josh.

"We're sorry ... but yes," he replied. "She is our

great-aunt. Until we saw her in the woods tonight, we had no idea she was so evil."

"We knew she was evil." Beth contradicted him. "We were always saying how horrible she was."

"But not like tonight," said Josh. "Not with a gargoyle and all."

"Shift," said Michael. "That's his name. He changes shape. We never saw anything like that in her stinking house."

"Tell us what you saw tonight." King Leafslear laid his bow on the table and leaned towards the children.

Quickly, Josh described the scene they had witnessed. The king and queen listened quietly, their expressions grave but not surprised.

"It is as I expected," said Queen Glendalock when Josh fell silent. "We are going through a very dangerous time within the Tree of Seasons. But let me tell you our story from the beginning. Many moons ago, just when life was starting, the Tree of Seasons was born. As Forester has already explained, it has four magical kingdoms, each representing a season. Each ruler was given a crown to signify their season. My crown is woven with roses. King Leafslear wears the crown of primrose. In Duskcanister, Gridelda has claimed maple as the crown of autumn and King Darkfrost once knelt to receive the crown of mistletoe. Each ruler also possesses an enchanted shard. This helps us to control the seasons in the mortal world. I hold the Shard of Light, and with the help of everyone in Brightisclearen, it brings summertime."

"I control spring with the magical Shard of Spirit," said King Leafslear. "This has the power to bring new life back into the world. It also has the power to heal the sick and wounded. My elves are great fighters and will do anything to protect our shard from evil and danger."

"Queen Gridelda holds the Shard of Decay," the queen continued. "But in her hands it has changed from the shard of gathering and celebration to the shard of decay. These days it brings rot, depression and sorrow to the mortal world, and those who are ill suffer greatly when she wields her power."

"But why was she elected Queen of Autumn?" asked Josh.

"Our rulers are not elected," the queen explained. "They are chosen by the king or queen when they are departing our enchanted kingdoms."

"Do you mean your rulers die like mortals?" asked Josh.

"When they have lived their span, they return to the earth," replied Queen Glendalock. "But before they depart, they name their chosen successor. The shard is taken from its repository where it is closely guarded and placed in the old ruler's hands so that it may be passed to the new. When the Queen of Autumn was dying, she chose Patina as her successor. But Patina disappeared and Gridelda stole the Shard of Decay. She now rules in Patina's stead, aided by Shift and her army of ghouls."

"Ghouls." Michael shuddered. "They're evil."

"Very evil," agreed Queen Glendalock. "Duskcanister

was once the land of sylphs. But those who follow Gridelda have been transformed into ghouls. They are meant to terrify and they succeed. Since then, the situation has worsened."

When she sank into her own dark thoughts, King Leafslear took up the story.

"The Shard of Frost was held by King Darkfrost, who ruled the kingdom of Icefroztica."

"Goblins?" said Michael.

"Yes, goblins." King Leafslear also sighed heavily.

"Did you say the shard *was* held by King Darkfrost?" asked Josh.

"Sadly, yes. The Shard of Frost was taken from the goblin king by Queen Gridelda. The king has been imprisoned in his castle, frozen into immobility. His power cannot be restored until the shard is returned to its cage of ice. But it is hidden within the mortal world and we have no idea where to search. We can only exist within your world during our seasons but Gridelda has found the power to survive outside for however long she wishes. She plots to steal the remaining two shards. If she succeeds, she will control our world. That also means the mortal world. But, as the Tree of Seasons has given you permission to shelter under its branches, I believe you have been sent to help us."

"How are we supposed to help?" asked Josh. "We're just kids. We've no weapons, no magic. We're not great fighters. Why doesn't the tree ask for assistance from stronger people? Adults maybe, or an army?"

"You have the most unique knowledge," replied the queen. "You can tell us everything you know about Queen Gridelda and how she exists in the mortal realm. Have you noticed anything curious happening in your world recently?"

"Curious?" Michael sounded puzzled. "What do you mean?"

"The weather," said King Leafslear. "Has the weather changed from its seasonal pattern?"

"Now that you mention it, yes," said Josh. "The weather forecast was really weird this evening. There's snow over some parts of Ireland . . . snow in *summer*. It's crazy." He paused, frowned. "There's something else. Great Aunt Graves owns the woods. She has hired lumberjacks to chop down the trees."

"That can only mean one thing," King Leafslear bellowed and smashed his fist repeatedly on the table. "Gridelda has failed to steal our shards but now she seeks the help of humans to destroy the Tree of Seasons."

"Humans wouldn't destroy the seasons," said Josh.

"Unwittingly, and often deliberately, they *are* destroying the seasons," said King Leafslear. "They will wreak devastation on the trees and bury the roots of our kingdom under cement. If that happens, our door into your world will be lost forever. Gridelda will have succeeded in her plan to rule the seasons. Imagine your world in the grip of decay? Imagine your world slowly dying with no hope of renewal?"

King Leafslear's bodyguards moved closer to him, as

if they too understood the horror that could soon unfold within their kingdom.

The queen shivered. Even her silvery wings trembled. "As you can see, the Tree of Seasons desperately needs your help." Her voice was even wispier than usual. "Can you find out when she plans to carry out this carnage?"

"Our father is going there tomorrow night," said Josh. "We can go with him."

"We've seen how evil she is." Michael was beginning to sound quite alarmed. "She could squash us like a grape . . . that's if Shift doesn't tear us apart first."

"I can't stop thinking about Shift." Beth's bottom lip trembled.

"Me too," said Michael. "And I won't be able to hide how much I hate her."

"You must not let her see you acting strangely or suspiciously," warned the queen. "She is powerful and shows no mercy. King Leafslear's warrior elves and my soldiers have battled bravely to keep her and her army at bay. But many of our brave fighters have been injured and some have perished where they fell. Thanks to the healers in New Blossomdale, our wounded soldiers are recovering but her war is only beginning." She shielded her face, as if she could not bear the sights that flashed before her eyes.

"If she steals the remaining shards, she will have the power to rule the seasons whatever way she wishes," added King Leafslear.

"Not if we can help it." Josh shot to his feet and lifted his fist in the air.

"The Tree of Seasons and all who dwell within it need your courage," said the queen. "With your help we must find the lost shards and return them to their rightful kingdoms. If you can discover how Gridelda exists in your world we can then take that power from her and force her to abandon the woods," said the queen. "We must find Patina and release King Darkfrost. Only then can we find peace within the Tree of Seasons."

"We'll search her house while our father is discussing business with her," promised Josh. "And if we find any information we'll bring it straight to you."

He heard Beth's trembling sigh but she remained silent.

"Excellent . . . excellent," King Leafslear boomed. "I will inform my people that you have agreed to assist us."

"Is he leaving already?" whispered Michael but the king made no effort to depart. Instead, he closed his eyes and placed his hands on either side of his head. He began to breathe heavily. As he released each breath, a light glowed before his mouth, growing larger then evaporating.

"What's he doing?" asked Beth.

"It's like Forester," said Josh.

"We have the power to communicate with our minds," said Bellatinks. "But it only works when we are making contact with our own people."

"So you can't communicate with elves?" asked Beth.

Bellatinks shook her head. "Only with fairies."

"Just as well you can't communicate with ghouls," said Michael. "Imagine what their minds are like."

After a short time the king opened his eyes. His voice resonated around the throne room. "My people are relieved to hear that you have come to our aid. Trust in the Tree of Seasons. You are undertaking a dangerous task but it will also be the most rewarding and courageous."

"We will do everything we can to defeat her." Josh looked at Michael and Beth. "Isn't that right?"

"Yes we will," they shouted together.

The queen flapped her wings again and rose to her feet. The sun streaming through the stained-glass window bathed her in an amber glow.

"You will not be alone." Once again the queen spoke in her mesmerising voice. "Forester has agreed to guide and protect you. Now that it's summertime, Bellatinks is also free to go with you. She will inform us at all times of your welfare."

Forester cleared his throat at the mention of Bellatinks's name and tried to look impassive. But a telltale blush stole across his cheek.

"It is more difficult for us fairies to go to your world at this time. Gridelda has her ghouls spying on us and they wait until we return to the tree before attacking us," said the queen.

The king sighed and nodded towards his two bodyguards. "I have brought two of my greatest warriors to help you journey back and forth to the tree. As it is not the season of spring, they cannot journey beyond the woods. But once you are within the shelter of the trees, they will come to your assistance immediately. We have brought special gifts for each of you. Please, children, follow me."

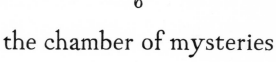

# 6

# the chamber of mysteries

They stopped before a wall, hung with a detailed tapestry on which three fairy children could be seen flying through a rainbow-filled sky. When the queen waved her hand over the tapestry it shimmered then became transparent, allowing them to step through it and follow her into a small room. Their bodies tingled as they felt the silk of the tapestry brushed against them. When everyone was inside the secret room, the tapestry changed back into a solid wall.

Throughout the room, red velvet cushions, fringed with gold tassels, sat on top of small pillars. A glittering object lay in the centre of each cushion: a tiny gold harp, a crown, a ring, a gold rose, and other unusual and distinctive items.

"Josh, Michael and Beth, please step forward," said Queen Glendalock. "I would like you to close your eyes and clear your minds of all thoughts. Our Chamber of Mysteries contains the most magical and wondrous objects once owned by our past rulers. You will each be given one of these precious objects to help you on your mission. But the object must choose you. Hold out your hands and imagine your worst fears."

The children did as they were told. They did not need to share this fear. They had encountered it when they hid beneath the hedge and watched the smoke-like image of Shift transform into a gargoyle. Now he materialised once more before their eyes: he sniffed and turned his red eyes in their direction, then began to pad towards them. His tongue hung loose, saliva dripping from his mouth. The children, frozen in terror, stifled the urge to scream. But just as their fear became almost impossible to bear, the image began to dissolve. It scattered like particles of sand and the picture in their mind was replaced by the calm face of Queen Glendalock.

"Children, open your eyes," she said. "You have shown true courage."

Relieved, they opened their eyes and looked down into their hands. Beth was holding one of the red cushions. On it lay a beautiful necklace, shining with the colours of the rainbow. A small golden scroll engraved with symbols was attached to the centre of it. A golden ring with a sparkling diamond lay on Michael's cushion. Although the ring was too big for his fingers, he felt great strength radiating from it.

Josh held nothing in his hands, not even an empty cushion. He tried to hide his disappointment as he looked enquiringly at the queen. But Queen Glendalock was gazing at his sister.

"Beth, the chamber of mysteries has given you the necklace of our great past queen, Ivy-Rose. She was a powerful ruler and reigned in the Tree of Seasons for many years. The chamber has seen that you are frightened of being caught by Gridelda's evil servant, Shift. This necklace now belongs to you. It holds a great power, the power of invisibility. Wear this, and when you glide your finger across it, you will become invisible, even to Shift."

The necklace opened and floated in mid-air then fastened around Beth's neck. "It's so beautiful, Queen Glendalock," sighed Beth. "Thank you so much."

"You must never take it off," warned the queen. "Wear it under your clothes so that no one suspects you possess it."

"I will," Beth promised.

"Go on, try it," said Michael.

Beth looked towards the queen for her approval.

"Just rub your finger over the ancient symbols," she advised and smiled reassuringly.

When Beth did as she was told, the symbols on the gold glistened and she instantly vanished.

"Are you still here, Beth?" Josh shouted, unable to believe his eyes.

"Yes, I'm here. I can see everything like normal. It's *so* weird . . . .but how do I come back?" Her voice rose in panic.

"Just rub your finger over the scroll again," said the queen and, just like that, Beth, looking flushed and excited, was visible again.

"Michael, you have been given the Ring of Truth." The queen looked towards Michael. "It once belonged to my father. The chamber has seen that your greatest fear is of being captured by Shift and trapped in isolation," she said. "That will never happen while you wear this Ring of Truth. It will tell those you love where to find you. You will know when to reveal this information and bring them to you. While you wear it, you will also know when someone is lying. Then the stone will turn to red. If you state the truth it will change to blue. It will be a useful guide for you on your journey."

Michael thanked the queen and when he placed the ring on his finger it shrank to an exact fit.

"Tell me a lie," he said to Josh, anxious to see if its power really worked.

"OK then." Josh grinned. "Your feet don't smell." The diamond changed to a deep red glow.

Michael blushed. "My feet don't smell," he yelled and the ring glowed even more intensely.

Beth and Josh laughed and King Leafslear said, "My elves advise soaking our feet in tea as a cure. Also, soaking them in vinegar twice a week is recommended, along with a change of socks every day."

"I'll remember that, King Leafslear," said Michael.

Josh was no longer laughing and Beth, seeing his disappointed expression, turned to the queen and asked, "Why did Josh not get a cushion with a magical gift on it?"

"The Chamber of Mysteries does not have anything for him. But it has shown me where to find the one he needs. Your brother's greatest fear is that Shift will harm you and Michael. He needs a weapon to protect himself and his loved ones. The chamber does not possess one strong enough for the courage he will need."

The queen glanced at King Leafslear. "I believe you have the weapon Josh needs."

"I already have it in my possession," replied the king. He pulled out a tiny bow from his pocket and handed it to Josh. "This bow was carved from the only piece of wood ever taken from the Tree of Seasons. It took two centuries of pleading from the ancient Elvin king before the tree gave permission for its wood to be honed into a weapon.

That permission was given with the sworn promise that this weapon would only be used in a time of despair." He handed the tiny weapon to Josh, and continued, "The bow does not work for everyone. Listen carefully and I will train you to fire it with skill."

Josh felt an immediate connection to the bow. "How do I use it?" he asked. "Where are its arrows?"

"It does not need arrows," the king replied. "In your mind I want you to picture the bow growing bigger."

The children watched, fascinated, as the bow began to grow to the size that perfectly fitted Josh's hands.

"Aim it and you will visualise the arrow in your mind," ordered the king. "Then visualise your target and your aim will be true. It never misses. Go on, try it."

Josh pulled back the string on the bow, closed his eyes and aimed at the wall opposite. He took a deep breath and released the string. A magical arrow of light flew from the bow and hit the wall. When Josh opened his eyes, he was astonished to discover that the arrow had struck the exact spot he'd visualised in his mind.

"This is the coolest thing I've ever seen," he gasped. "Thank you so much."

"It will serve you faithfully and protect you from harm," promised King Leafslear.

Josh visualised the bow growing smaller and it immediately shrank to its original size. Queen Glendalock waved her hand over the arrow and it disappeared.

Was there no end to the magic at work inside the Tree of Seasons?

"Before we leave the chamber, I must ask you to take good care of these precious objects," the queen warned them. "Be careful how and where you use them. Ensure that they do not fall into the wrong hands for that will bring tremendous danger to all of us."

"We won't let anyone near them," Michael promised.

"You must leave now," said the queen. "Forester will take you home. King Leafslear's men will guide you to and from the edge of the woods. Now that it's summertime, Bellatinks is able to leave the woods and will assist you when you need help. Call her name three times when you have information and she will bring you to us."

Forester's lips twitched at the mention of the red-haired fairy's name. Try as he would, he was unable to prevent his face breaking into a wide beam.

Once again the shimmering tapestry appeared. "When you return home you must sleep," said the queen. "Time is much slower here than in the mortal world and you have only been gone for a short time."

They entered the grand marbled hall. Bellatinks, accompanied by Forester, walked in front, their heads close together as they whispered to each other. King Leafslear's men followed silently. The children took up the rear.

Just before the door to the throne room closed, Josh turned back. "We won't let you down," he promised.

The queen and king smiled then raised their hands in farewell as the door swung closed.

They crossed the marble bridge where the butterflies waited with Partlant and Bowrain.

"They will take you to the edge of the woods," said Bellatinks. "Once you are there Forester will make sure you arrive home safely. Remember to just call my name three times when you need me. I will be with you in an instant."

The three children thanked Bellatinks then mounted the giant butterflies. Accompanied by Bellatinks and Forester, along with Partlant and Bowrain, the warrior elves, they flew from Brightisdearen.

"Hold on tight, Beth," said Josh, who did not want to see her falling through the air again, no matter how clever her butterfly was at catching her. The butterflies flapped their wings and flew towards the tunnel leading back to Grimsville Woods. They dismounted and bade goodbye to Partlant and Bowrain.

The children entered the flower-scented tunnel and made the journey back to the woods. They stepped out under the sprawling branches of the Tree of Seasons. Standing in the calming glow, it was possible to believe that everything was serene within the four seasons. But with the knowledge they had acquired, the children could see the ugliness that was being inflicted on the tree, especially in the autumn sphere. The air was clammy and a sickly smell oozed upwards from the roots. Josh slipped and, instinctively, touched the trunk to steady himself. His hand was immediately covered in a sticky orange resin. He shook his hand, terrified his fingers would begin to rot or fall off. Forester, seeing his fear, handed him a leaf. Once Josh rubbed it against the resin, it slid like a glove from his fingers.

"What are your names?" Beth turned to the king's warriors, who had not broken their silence throughout the journey.

The two elves looked at each other but made no reply.

"Why don't you answer me?" she asked.

"Request permission to speak, miss," said one of the elves.

"Permission?"

She looked so surprised that Forester said, "Elves need you to grant permission before they can speak to you."

"Of course you have permission to speak." She smiled encouragingly at the elves. "You don't ever have to ask my permission again."

"As you wish, miss," said the second elf, who relaxed his shoulders and stood at ease. "My name is Rufus and this is Rickspin."

"Thank you for coming with us and making sure we get home safely."

"We have orders to protect you in any way we can," replied Rickspin.

As they walked away from the Tree of Seasons, Rickspin moved in front of the children while Rufus moved into position behind them. Darkness enveloped them as they entered the woods.

"We've just left a world of brilliance behind us," said Forester. "In a moment your eyes will adjust."

When they began to make out each other's shapes, they felt more reassured but it was still too dark to move forward. The battery in Josh's torch had died but they had their twigs of light.

Forester stretched his hand outwards and recited the rhyming chants from earlier. Immediately the trees cleared the path to the edge of the woods. When they reached the hedgerow, the elves could travel no further. "I will be back as soon as the children are home safely," said Forester. The two guards nodded and assumed their warrior positions.

The children hurried after Forester, whose ears had disappeared with a loud pop as soon as he emerged from the hedge. Suddenly exhausted, they followed him. At last their house came into view. To their relief, the windows were in darkness. They arranged to meet Forester the following day. Beth bent and flung her arms around him. "Thank you for giving us such a wonderful adventure." She kissed his cheek and giggled when he blushed to the roots of his hair.

Josh was worried about the ivy trellis, which tilted dangerously from the wall. It would never hold them if they tried to climb it again.

Forester, seeing their difficulty, stretched out his hand and spoke softly.

> "*Ivy, reach your tentacles*
> *Towards the children's window sills.*
> *Their eyes are filled with sleep and dreams*
> *So bear them high on leafy streams.*"

The ivy immediately stretched out spidery tentacles and wrapped them around the children. They gasped as they were lifted from the ground and carried upwards towards the window. When they were seated on the window ledge, the tentacles released them. Josh pushed the window open and they collapsed onto Beth's bed. They lay there staring at the ceiling.

"Pinch me," said Beth, after a few minutes.

Michael obeyed her.

"Ouch, not that hard," she protested. "Can I pinch you to see if you're awake?"

"You don't have to," said Josh. "Just look at our gifts."

Michael held up his hand and stared at the ring with pride and wonder. "That was the best experience I've ever had in my whole life," he declared.

"Me too," said Beth and gave a tremendous yawn.

"Better get to bed," said Josh. "We've a busy day tomorrow."

"A dangerous one," said Michael.

"But Josh will take care of us," said Beth. She kissed her brothers goodnight and they slipped across the landing. Swiftly, they undressed. Before lying down, Josh took his magical bow from his shirt pocket. He thought about it growing bigger. It did. Straight away he made it small again.

"Just checking it still works," he whispered to Michael. He climbed into bed and placed it safely underneath his pillow. Within seconds, he was fast asleep.

# 7

# beth's discovery

The following morning Beth was the first to awaken. Another sunny day. She smiled as last night flowed back into her mind. She had always believed in fairies. Even when Josh and Michael had laughed at her and pretended they had seen leprechauns at the bottom of the garden – so that she would make a fool of herself by searching in the bushes – she had held true to her belief. And wasn't she right to do so? She sighed with contentment until she remembered Great Aunt Graves . . . Gridelda . . . evil queen of autumn . . . owner of a gargoyle. She pulled the duvet over her head and squeezed her eyes closed. Good magic. Bad magic. Why couldn't there be just the one kind? Tonight they were going to her grotty mansion. Shift could be there, hanging around like a puff of evil smoke or, worse, in his gargoyle shape. But Queen Glendalock had told her to be brave and she could always call on Bellatinks.

Of all the enchanted folk they had met last night, Beth loved Bellatinks the most. And Bellatinks loved Forester. Beth giggled. She was a girl and she knew about such things. Forester was also in love with Bellatinks but he was so shy . . . so Beth must find some way to bring them together. However, love would have to wait until they found the shards. Suddenly, Beth did not feel like giggling any more. The shards must be in Merryville Manor. Where else could Great Aunt Graves hide them? The thought of exploring the manor was terrifying but Beth touched her necklace for courage and slipped from her bed. She wanted to admire her necklace in the mirror but she was unable to see the sparkling stones with the little golden scroll in the centre. Nor could she see herself. She stared at the empty mirror and realised she had made herself invisible.

Shocked at how easily it could happen, she ran her finger over the ancient inscription and reappeared, her hair all mussed and spiky, her blue eyes still smudged with sleep. She chuckled at her reflection. I must be very careful with this, she thought. No more fidgeting with the necklace. Then, just for the thrill, she made herself invisible once again.

Visible again, she dressed quickly in her dungarees and high-necked pink jumper. It was perfect for hiding the necklace. She was eager to see her brothers and talk about last night. When she entered the boys' room, Josh was sitting up in bed, aiming his full-sized bow at the window.

"Are you going to fire an arrow?" Beth asked.

"No. Just practising visualising," he said.

"He has Shift in his sights," said Michael.

"I wish . . . " Josh sighed and willed the bow to return to its normal size. He slipped it into his pocket and looked at Michael's ring.

"Where will you tell Mum and Dad you got it?" he asked.

Michael jumped out of bed. "I'm going to tell them that I traded all my Top Trumps cards for it."

"Won't it change to red when you tell a lie?"

"I've thought about that. I'm just gonna say it's one of those stones that changes colour with the weather."

"Better make it convincing. You know what Mum's like when she gets suspicious."

Their father was already drinking his morning cup of coffee and reading his newspaper. Mrs Lotts buttered toast and pretended to faint when she saw Michael standing in the doorway.

"What on earth's going on here?" she asked. "Michael Lotts up before noon!"

"We're going to the lake," said Josh. "What time are you going to Great Aunt Graves's tonight, Dad?"

"I'm calling in on her on my way home from work," replied Mr Lotts from behind his newspaper. "Why?"

"We haven't seen her for ages. We'd like to go with you."

"You'd like to *what*?" Mr Lotts lowered his newspaper and stared in astonishment at his three children. "That's a big change since yesterday. What on earth brought that on?"

"We want to find out where she keeps her gargoyle," said Beth.

"Don't be sarcastic, young lady." Mrs Lotts wagged her finger at her daughter. "Some day you too will be an old woman."

"She needs company," said Michael, with such a virtuous expression on his face, Beth wanted to coil up laughing.

"We haven't seen her for ages," said Josh.

"That's because you've refused to visit her," said Mr Lotts.

"We've been talking about that," said Josh. "And we real-ise we should be kinder to her."

"We miss visiting her," said Michael.

"Michael!" Mrs Lotts stared suspiciously at his hand. "Where did you get that red ring?"

Michael glanced at the glowing stone.

"He got it from the queen of the fairies," said Beth. "He was in a chamber of mysteries—"

Mrs Lotts pressed her fingers to her forehead and sighed. "Please, Beth, it's too early in the morning for another one of your tall stories. Answer me, Michael."

"I swapped it for all my Top Trumps cards," Michael glared at his sister. "It changes colour with the weather."

"It certainly shines brightly," his mother replied. "And it looks valuable. I don't want anyone coming to the door demanding that they want their ring back."

"They won't, Mum. They got the best Top Trumps card ever." He slipped his hand under the table to hide the ruby glow.

"About Great Aunt Graves." Josh returned to the most important subject. "Will you pick us up on the way, Dad?"

"If I live to be a thousand and ten, I'll never understand you children." Mr Lotts shook his head, baffled. "But if you insist, I'll bring you with me. What about you, dear?" He glanced at his wife who suddenly busied herself clearing the table.

"Not tonight, dear," she replied. "Maybe another time."

They spent the day by the lake. Unlike yesterday, the weather stayed sunny. Merryville Lake was a favourite gathering place for the young people of the village. But no matter how fast Beth swam – and she was an excellent swimmer – she could not get Shift from her mind. They planned how they would explore the manor. Josh and Michael could not agree on which part of the house they wanted to explore. In the end, Josh wrote the names of the different rooms down on paper and they drew lots. Josh got the downstairs rooms, Michael was going to explore upstairs and Beth had to check out the basement. Josh, seeing her frightened expression, suggested swapping with her but she, determined to be as brave as her brothers, refused to change. She'd been in the basement before. But that was long ago when Great Aunt Graves was nice and filled her basement with boxes of apples and jars of chutney and jam lined on the shelves. It couldn't have changed that much . . . could it?

Twilight was settling and the rooks were cawing above the trees when Mr Lotts drove to Merryville Manor. Beth thought it looked even creepier than usual. She pressed her face to the car window and made no effort to leave the car.

"Come on, Beth," said Mr Lotts. "Stop daydreaming."

Reluctantly she opened the door and stepped out onto the mossy gravel. The garden was so overgrown it was impossible to believe it used to win prizes. Mr Lotts was already mounting the steps and rattling the door knocker. Beth stepped back. The door knocker was new. It was shaped like a gargoyle's head, the mouth open, the tongue hanging loose. She stared at the bulbous eyes, almost expecting them to gleam maliciously, and the tongue to glisten with saliva. The knocker clattered loudly, sending an echoing clamour through the house. The door creaked and opened. Was it Beth's imagination or did Great Aunt Graves look even more sinister than usual? Was her narrow glance even sharper, her smile (which was really more of a grimace) colder and more calculating than she remembered?

"Come in," she snapped. "You're late. And what are *they* doing here?"

"They were anxious to see you, Aunt Graves," said Mr Lotts. He spread out his arms to usher his children into the long, musty-smelling hall. As Beth walked along the hall, she was sorry she had refused Josh's offer to explore the basement. Who needed to be brave? Certainly not Beth Lotts who was only eight.

The hall wallpaper had almost disappeared beneath a film of grime. Beth recognised the familiar pattern of leaves and stems. Now they looked more like wriggling snakes. A narrow table with a telephone, a coat rack, a cubbyhole under the stairs and an umbrella stand were the only pieces of furniture. Beth's eyes were riveted on the cane in the umbrella stand. It was long and sleek, wider at the top and narrowing into a point. It had to be the one . . . had to be. She shuddered and walked a little faster towards the drawing room. This used to be a bright sunny room with chintzy sofas and bookcases and a piano that Beth loved to play. All gone now, just a tall cabinet with lots of drawers and a plain wooden table covered with documents. Instead of comfortable armchairs, six hard wooden chairs were arranged around the table. Not a cushion in sight. Despite the warm evening a fire was blazing. A new oil painting in a gilt-edged frame hung above the mantelpiece. The colours were sombre, dull browns and dark olive greens, a grey sullen sky. A group of people dressed in long, black cloaks and old-fashioned hats stared out from the canvas, their expressions harsh and forbidding. Their eyes seemed to follow Beth everywhere she moved in this dismal room.

"Stay there and be quiet." Great Aunt Graves pulled out three chairs and lined them against the wall. She sat down on a high-backed chair with carvings of snakes on the arms, and gestured at Mr Lotts to sit down.

"What progress have you made?" she demanded.

"I warned you it wouldn't be easy," he replied.

"Your job is to make it easy," Great Aunt Graves snapped back. "Have you spoken to the council again?"

"Yes," sighed Mr Lotts. "But they're not convinced by the report."

"Dr Goyle is a renowned specialist on tree diseases. How *dare* they query his report?" She slapped her hand on the table. Beth kicked her legs outwards in shock and even Josh jerked back in his chair.

"Of course . . . of course," said Mr Lotts. "I'm sure they'll give permission sooner later. Red tape, you know. These things take time."

"I've ordered the machinery and chainsaws. The workmen are ready to start immediately. I cannot tolerate diseased trees. The woods belong to me." Her voice rose.

"It's my choice to get rid of them. How dare those bureau-cratic fools interfere with my plans?"

"The woods are protected by law," protested Mr Lotts. "But as they are diseased, you'll get your way. Just be patient."

Josh cleared his throat. "Excuse me, Great Aunt Graves." His voice rasped slightly. "Do you mind if we go outside and play?"

His great-aunt looked suspiciously at them.

"Play?" She sounded as if she had never heard of the word. "*Play*?" she repeated. "Why on earth do you want to play?"

"They'll be very quiet," said Mr Lotts. "Won't you, children?"

"Yes." Beth also stood up and moved towards the door. "Quiet as mice," she added and opened the door.

"Don't touch anything," their great-aunt warned as they fled to the hall.

Once they were out of sight, Josh ran to the front door. He opened it then slammed it closed.

"OK, this is our chance," he whispered, tiptoeing back to Beth and Michael. "Keep on the lookout for Shift. He's bound to be around here somewhere. Good luck."

Beth stood outside the wooden door leading down to the basement. She must not show her fear. She had the gift of invisibility but still . . . She drew a deep breath and brushed her finger across her necklace. It was still such an amazing feeling to look down and not be able to see her feet, or to see her hands disappearing into thin air. Carefully, she turned the handle, hardly daring to breathe as the door creaked. She was sure the sound would carry to the drawing room but no footsteps sounded, no commanding voice demanded to know what was going on.

As soon as she closed the door the basement darkened, except for a faint, flickering light at the foot of the stairs. This turned out to be a white candle burning in a sconce set into the wall. Guided by this light, Beth climbed down the steps and faced a door engraved with snake carvings similar to the ones on Great Aunt Graves's chair. The flame cast a pallid light over the door as she inspected the engravings. The basement was completely different to what she remembered. The door opened easily and she faced another staircase, a stone spiral one, lit by more candles on the walls.

By now, her heart was pounding. She definitely should have swapped with Josh. She descended the spiral staircase and stood in the doorway of a circular room, filled with blue light. The room was empty except for a large statue. She wanted to walk forward and inspect it but her knees had turned to jelly.

No one can see me . . . no one can see me . . . she kept repeating to herself. After a moment she took one step, then another. The blue light shone directly on the statue. As Beth drew nearer, she realised it was a statue of a man with hooded eyes and a grim, clenched mouth. He was dressed in modern clothes and wore a wide-brimmed hat. He looked important and authoritative. Like a schoolteacher, she thought, no, more like a school principal . . .

or an inspector. Yes, she thought. A school inspector who knew everything and told everyone what to do. Except, of course, that he was a statue.

She noticed a wide pillar, similar to the ones in the chamber of mysteries. A gold chalice sat on top. Beth crept nearer. In the blue light she saw engravings on the outside. Underneath, where the chalice narrowed, she could make out distinct engravings of children's faces. She stared in amazement at the tears on the children's cheeks. How real they looked. But they were real . . . sliding tears that dripped to the floor but dried within seconds.

Suddenly, she heard a sniffing sound. Goosebumps ran along her arms. The hairs on the back of her neck stood upright, or so it seemed as she slowly turned her head. She kept repeating to herself . . . no one can see me . . . no one can see me . . . but the sniffing grew louder. To Beth's horror the statue came to life. The nostrils flared, the mouth opened, the eyes swivelled and rapidly scanned the room for any sign of movement.

No one can see me . . . no one can see me . . . Beth clasped her hand over her mouth to prevent a scream escaping. I can't believe this, she thought. I can't believe I'm going to have a heart attack and I'm only eight years old.

She backed away from the chalice. Softly . . . softly . . . don't even breathe, she warned herself. The statue twisted and turned. Beth thought about the writhing snakes that seemed to be engraved everywhere she looked. As she stood rooted with horror, the shape of Shift in his gargoyle guise began to emerge. He turned his heavy head and sniffed violently.

Move slowly . . . slowly . . . don't make a sound. One step . . . two steps . . . she had almost reached the door when Shift's bulbous eyes fixed on her. But Beth was not waiting around to find out if he could see through invisibility. Fleetly, she ran down the stone corridor, up the spiral staircase, through the carved door that, thankfully, she had left open. She closed it quietly behind her and ran frantically to the top of the stairs. Josh was about to enter the drawing room when she emerged into the hall.

"Josh!" She grabbed his arm to prevent him opening the door. "You'll never guess what I've just seen."

Hearing her voice and feeling her grip, but unable to see her, Josh jerked back from the door.

"Sorry . . . sorry," she panted and rubbed the necklace's gold tag. "It's me, Josh."

"I can see that . . . thankfully." Josh rubbed his hand across his forehead in mock- relief. "But say nothing until we're away from here. I wouldn't be surprised if the walls have ears."

Beth forced herself to calm down. She was anxious to share her information with Josh but he was right. She looked at the wallpaper pattern. Definitely writhing snakes. She wanted to throw up. She placed her hand over her mouth and swallowed. If the basement door opened and Shift appeared, she was definitely going to have a heart attack on the spot.

Michael came quietly down the stairs. From his disappointed expression, it was obvious he had had a fruitless search.

"What happened to you, Beth?" he whispered. "You look like you've seen a ghost."

"Worse," Beth whispered back and rushed towards the downstairs bathroom. She threw up into the toilet and grabbed a towel from a rail.

"Are you all right?" Josh's concerned voice made her weep. She pressed her face into the towel and sobbed.

"What's all this racket about?" The drawing-room door opened and Great Aunt Graves appeared.

"Beth's got a tummy bug," said Josh, blocking the bath-room door. "Leave her alone."

Beth flushed the toilet and gave her eyes a final wipe. "I'm all right now," she said. "I just want to go home."

"Poor pet," said her father. "They spent the day at the lake," he explained to his aunt, who did not look remotely interested. "You've had too much sun today. Lots of liquid and an early night for you, young lady. Say goodbye to Aunt Graves and we'll be on our way."

"Just a moment," said Great Aunt Graves. "We haven't finished our business yet."

"Then please hurry up and do so," snapped Mr Lotts, who looked as if he had had more than enough of his aunt for one night. "Beth is unwell and needs to be in bed."

They trailed back to the drawing room behind their great-aunt. When they were seated, she stared at each child individually, as if reading their minds, then turned back to their father.

"As I've told you, Dr Goyle is quite prepared to provide samples of the disease affecting the trees. I'm not prepared to accept any further delays. If permission for work to begin is not granted within the next two days, I intend taking matters into my own hands."

Beth arose from her chair and stood in front of the painting. Something was different about it. There seemed to be more people . . . which was a silly thought. She'd never counted them before so how would she know? Then she realised what had attracted her attention. There was an extra cloaked figure in the painting. But Beth recognised his dark, hooded eyes, his clenched lips. And he was holding the chalice – she recognised it instantly – in both hands. Great Aunt Graves spun around, as if she knew what Beth had seen.

"Sit down," she snapped. "And mind your manners."

Beth shrank back, longing to clutch her necklace and make herself invisible once more.

Their great-aunt gathered up her documents and placed them in a drawer in the cabinet. "I suppose you're looking for your tea, as usual." She glared at the children, arms akimbo.

"No, thank you, Aunt. That's won't be necessary," said Mr Lotts hurriedly. "I'll be in touch with you as soon as I receive word from the council."

"Then this meeting is over," snapped Great Aunt Graves. "Goodbye."

Mr Lotts was unable to hide his relief as he put on his jacket and picked up his briefcase.

She accompanied them to the front door and slammed it as soon as they stepped outside.

"What an unpleasant and difficult woman she's become," said Mr Lotts as they walked towards his car. "So, who'd like a takeaway?"

"I'm starving," said Michael. "Can we have Indian, please?"

"No. I want Chinese," said Josh.

Beth sighed. Usually she would have joined in the argument and demanded pizza, which was her favourite takeaway. But this evening she just longed to go home. When they reached Jack's Snacks, Josh and Michael were still arguing over what they wanted.

"Fish and chips for all," declared Mr Lotts. "And if you two don't stop arguing in the back, you'll get nothing except the smell of them."

Beth was unable to eat anything. Her stomach still churned at the thought of the statue and something else . . . something that shivered at the edge of her mind but which always shied away when she tried to form it into a thought. The chalice . . . the faces of the children . . . the tears on their cheeks. Her fingers would have been wet if she had touched them.

Michael had seen nothing unusual in Great Aunt Graves's house, nothing except cobwebs, and dank fur coats hanging in a closet, and a walking stick that he had twirled around in the hope that he could do magic with it. But it just remained a knobbly old stick. No flashing green lights, much to his disappointment. Josh had been just as unsuccessful on the ground floor but he reckoned he'd found the magic cane. However, he'd decided to leave it alone . . . just in case. Mr Lotts returned to the car. Soon it was filled with the smell of vinegar and chips. Josh and Michael dipped their greasy fingers into the bags and whispered into her ear. Beth stayed silent. What she had seen could not be whispered between munching fish and chips, and swigging 7 Up.

They rushed to Beth's room as soon as they arrived home and she was finally able to report what she had seen. The boys listened, their eyes widening in horror when she described how the statue had transformed into Shift. When they calmed down she told them about the chalice but they were more interested in the statue. Beth fell silent. Tears on the children's cheeks . . . her brothers would never believe her. She could not believe it herself and yet . . . and yet . . .

She needed to talk to Bellatinks. She closed her eyes . . . Bellatinks! Bellatinks! Bellatinks!

## 8

# how gridelda seized control of duskcanister

As soon as Mr Lotts had driven his family away, Queen Gridelda returned to the drawing room and stood before the fireplace.

"Speak, Shift." She spoke directly into the painting hanging above the mantelpiece.

The image in the painting began to blur and the paint ran in rivulets over the canvas. The people in their dark cloaks disintegrated and a grey shape emerged from the canvas. It coiled in smoky tendrils and drifted in a circle around Gridelda. Then it floated towards the window sill where its smoky appearance thickened to form legs and arms, and the grotesque head of a gargoyle. Carefully, in its claws, it carried the golden chalice. Gridelda reached greedily towards it and drank deeply. When she had satisfied her thirst, her face lost its scrawny appearance and became fuller. Her eyes glittered even more fiercely. Her laughter was youthful enough to belong to a group of playful children but it changed to a furious gasp when Shifted emitted a long-drawn-out hissing sound.

"Are you positive you smelt a child?" she shrieked.

Once again Shift hissed and flicked its tongue at a fly that had flown too close.

"Who was it, Shift?"

The gargoyle shook its enormous head.

"But why couldn't you see it?" Gridelda demanded.

She listened to the sibilant voice, her eyes narrowing.

"I don't understand. You smelled a girl child but could not see her. What can this mean, Shift? I've gifted you with vision to see beyond the shades of darkness and the solidity of stone. Your sense of smell is never wrong."

She walked the length of the room and back again to stand before the gargoyle. "There is only one explanation. Invisibility. Queen Glendalock must have sought the help of those children. They live close enough to the woods to have made contact with that wretched watchman."

She folded her long, thin arms and surveyed the gargoyle. "Power is within my grasp. I will not be thwarted by foolhardy children. They are a nuisance, Shift. An irritant. A fly in the ointment, as those mortals say. But flies are vermin and must be destroyed. Then we will move forward to achieve my final victory."

For as long as Gridelda could remember, she had craved power; not a share of power, but total domination. Even as a child sylph, she had watched the movement of seasons and longed to unite the four kingdoms under her own rule. One crown, one voice, one authority to whom all would bow and scrape. But she was just an autumn sylph, responsible for the turning of leaves and the soothing of earth for its winter sleep.

She had bided her time, knowing that Queen Auburina was old and weakening. Her emerald hair had turned white and her hazel eyes dimmed. She was no longer able to pierce the disloyal thoughts of her subjects. When her time came to die, she retired to her favourite leafy glade and called the guardians of the Shard of Decay to her side. Subfusc, Ecru and Umber had served her faithfully. They swirled before her then placed the precious shard in her hands.

"Gridelda is dangerous." Queen Auburina's voice was weak yet it carried clearly to Gridelda, who crouched unseen behind the trunk of an ancient linden tree. "She intends to rule in my place and control the Tree of Seasons," said Queen Auburina. "Her ambition knows no bounds."

The guardians trembled, their leaves fluttering wildly as the queen outlined her fears. "Already she has gathered her army of ghouls around her and she will seek the help of humankind to achieve her aims. She will not rest until they too are her subjects, bent to her will by the destruction of the seasons."

Gridelda had to admire the queen's insight. Just as well she was breathing her last. Otherwise Gridelda would have to strike her down. But why waste energy when nature would take care of her aging body. Her plans to take control of Duskcanister were well advanced. Among the sylphs, she had sought those who would serve her faithfully in return for power in the kingdom she intended to rule. Those who were weak and selfish, lazy, intolerant, dissatisfied, greedy – and there were many who found the tending of trees and the ripening of harvests to be tedious work – gathered in secret. They donned the leafy hooded garments of ghouls, intent on spreading decay and destroying the power of renewal.

The queen's voice grew weaker as she instructed her guardians. "Bring Patina to my side. On the instant I draw my last breath, a great wind will blow through

Duskcanister. That is when you place the crown of maple on Patina's head. She will lift the shard from my arms and its power will guide her through the flow and ebb of her season. I have passed my ancient lore on to her, as it was handed down to me and to those who went before me. Go to her now and prepare her for my demise. The Tree of Seasons will mourn as I leave. But there will be rejoicing also as a new tree ring encircles its ageless trunk and the crown of maple is placed on the head of the chosen one. Go now. My heart is anxious to rest. Bring Patina to my side."

Gridelda watched them leave the glade, their strands of willow hair streaming in a leafy whorl of orange, yellow, red and brown. Auburina sighed and moved her head towards the linden tree, as if she sensed Gridelda's presence. She clutched the shard more tightly but when Gridelda sprang into the clearing, Aubrina's voice, when she called for help, was too faint to reach beyond the glade.

"Patina will defeat you," the queen cried. Her rich autumn leaves had faded to a dun brown and her once pale-green skin was ashen.

"Patina has been frozen into immobility," crowed Gridelda. "Your guardians will find an empty chamber. But your throne will not be empty for long."

Autumn was in the full flush of splendour when she raised the shard above her head and held it towards the setting sun. Blood-red rays flashed against its gleaming surface and the glade was filled with the sighs of a king-dom about to be vanquished.

Earlier, when Gridelda had invaded Patina's chamber, the young sylph had been taken by surprise. She would have been easy to slay. Gridelda longed to do so. One swift arrow through her heart would remove her forever. But Patina, the chosen one, would take the ancient autumn lore with her. Gridelda needed this invaluable knowledge. As Patina turned, disturbed by a shadow too faint to alert her, Gridelda had laid the spell of decay on her. It was a slow spell and would take many years before Patina's slender body wasted away. By then Gridelda would have drawn the ancient lore from her. Her ghouls removed the young sylph to a hiding place where she would remain until her body reached the final stages of decay.

The guardians of the shard, finding Patina's chamber empty, swirled back to the glade in a panic-stricken flurry of leaves. They realised, too late, that they had been outwitted. Their queen lay dead, her peaceful expression replaced by one of wild despair. The leaves that had brought her such comfort in life had folded in a shroud around her. The shard had disappeared.

A wind gusted through Duskcanister, growing in strength until it seemed as if the entire population of sylphs would take flight and flutter towards the sky. Mourning broke out in the Tree of Seasons but when the crying ceased – as it always does – Gridelda had placed the crown of maple on her head. Her army of ghouls cheered and bowed before their new queen. Without the shard, Subfusc, Ecru and Umber were powerless to defeat her. She sought to destroy them and they were forced to camouflage themselves – along with the other sylphs who had remained faithful to the memory of Patina – deep in the autumn glades of Duskcanister. Hidden between the decaying leaves, they could only watch helplessly as Gridelda increased her reign of terror – and discovered the power to survive outside her season in the mortal world.

Now, within that world that she despised, she paced up and down the drawing room. Those wretched children, how dare they invade her kingdom? Last night Shift had sniffed them out . . . almost. Forester and a lost dog! Was Gridelda losing her wits to fall for such an unlikely story? Her anger grew as she swung round to face Shift.

"Go immediately to their home and stay there until you find out what they know. As soon as you have the information, report back to me. Go at once . . . and do not fail me."

Shift's form began to change again. The thick body and tail become insubstantial, and the hideous features merged into a vaporous wisp that floated from the room, drifted high over the manor wall and out along the road, following the tyre tracks, turning corners, stooping briefly outside Jack's Shack where customers queuing for fish and chips noticed how the mist – drifting past the lighted window – seemed to hover and form an animal-like shape that pressed hard against the glass before the night wind gusted it forward and out of sight.

# 9

# the chalice of elentra

Bellatinks perched on the pillow in Beth's bed and listened fearfully as the young girl described her experience in the basement.

"You have fulfilled Queen Glendalock's belief in your courage," she said when Beth fell silent.

"I *actually* wasn't that brave," Beth admitted. "I ran from there as fast as I could."

"I'm glad you did." Josh put his arm around her. "Otherwise Shift would have caught you."

"He couldn't see me but he knew I was there." Beth shuddered and looked at Bellatinks who had arisen from the bed and was flying around the room. She flitted from the dressing table to the wardrobe, landing here and landing there but unable to stay still for an instant. When she reached the bedroom window, she drew back so suddenly she became entangled in the curtains.

Josh, hearing her cry of alarm, ran to the window. The moon cast a dim light over the garden and revealed a raven perched on the branch of the cherry tree. At least, Josh assumed it was a raven but it was twice the size of any raven he had ever seen. Its beak looked sharp and dangerous, and its eyes, staring directly at the window, had two pinpoints of red in the centre. Josh pulled the curtains and slumped on his bed. He had to be brave. Beth had shown great courage earlier and she was only eight years old.

"Shift is outside," he whispered.

"Shift?" Michael sounded as if he wanted to follow Beth's earlier example and throw up. "What's he doing?"

"Watching us," replied Josh. "He's in the shape of a raven."

Michael opened the curtains a chink and peered out. "He's flying away," he said.

"But he can see through walls," said Bellatinks. "He knows I'm here. I must call Forester at once." She closed her eyes and spoke aloud. "Forester, come quickly to the children's house and escort us to the Tree of Seasons. Bring Partlant and Bowrain with you. Make sure King Leafslear's men are waiting for us in the woods. We are in danger."

She tilted her head, listening to his reply. The children could not hear anything but the fairy's expression relaxed, as if Forester had soothed her fear. She opened her eyes and smiled as they huddled together on the bed. "We must prepare to leave now," she said.

"But what if our parents find out that we're missing?" asked Beth. "They're downstairs. They always check on us before they go to bed."

"Don't worry," Bellatinks replied. "Time within the tree is slower than mortal time so you will be back here before they wish you goodnight."

Just then, they heard a faint tap against the window.

"Who's that?" Michael looked nervously towards the curtains.

"Don't worry. It's our friends," said Bellatinks.

When Josh opened the window, Bowrain and Partlant flapped their wings in welcome. Forester had also arrived and was held aloft on strands of ivy.

"Children, are you ready?" asked Bellatinks.

When they nodded, Forester stretched out his hand and spoke to the ivy.

> *"Ivy stems, we can not tarry*
> *Any longer – so you must carry*
> *These brave children to the ground*
> *Do it please without a sound."*

The ivy immediately crept over the windowsill and along the floor. The children were enfolded in its strong tentacles and lowered to the garden. Swiftly, they ran towards Grimsville Woods where King Leafslear's warriors, their bows and arrows at the ready, greeted them. So far they had not seen any sign of Shift or Queen Gridelda. But everyone was nervous as Forester cleared the path through the woods and onwards towards the Tree of Seasons. Rufus moved fleetly in front and Rickspin guarded their rear.

"We're nearly there," panted Forester but he had no sooner uttered the words than they heard a crash behind them.

The children almost collided with each other as they stopped and spun round. Beth screamed then muffled the sound with her fist. Shift, in gargoyle form, rushed towards them, his eyes blazing in the darkness. Saliva dripped from his mouth and he seemed even taller and more hideous than Josh remembered. King Leafslear's men drew their bows and began firing at him. The arrows streamed a bright blue light as they whizzed through the air.

"Shelter behind the tree," ordered Rufus. "We'll try to hold him off."

They ran towards the tree and hid behind the summer section of the trunk. The light was brightest on this side and Josh watched in horror as Shift picked up Rickspin and flung him against the tree. Rickspin cried out in agony as he collapsed. The other elf continued firing but, as Shift kept transforming from solid form to a transparent mist, the arrows kept passing harmlessly through him.

"Stay under cover," warned Bellatinks, as Josh darted from the shelter of the tree.

But Josh was beyond hearing her. He reached into his shirt pocket and pulled out his magic bow. Let's see how well this really works, he thought, trying to hold his hand steady. He closed his eyes on the gargoyle, who was now so close Josh could feel the heat of his breath and smell the fetid stench of his saliva. Rufus, seeing Josh advancing, held his fire and watched anxiously.

Josh closed his eyes. Suddenly an image of Shift loomed inside his mind. He refused to flinch at the beast's fearsome appearance and visualised exactly where he would strike. In the same instant, he felt the bow lengthen and the string tauten between his fingers. He released the string and opened his eyes. A brilliant stream of golden light exploded from the bow as an arrow flew through the air. Shift had caught Rufus in his paw and was about to fling him against the tree when Josh's arrow struck him in the centre of his stomach. Shift bellowed in pain and outrage. The screech rang upwards through the branches and it seemed to Josh that the ancient tree shuddered with such force that the ground shifted slightly. Or perhaps it was Josh's relief that was causing his legs to collapse. Shift stared directly at Josh then spread his huge scaly wings. With the glowing arrow still embedded in his belly, he shot upwards, circled the Tree of Seasons once, then flew into the surrounding trees. They could hear leaves rustling and branches breaking, the sound growing fainter and finally fading.

Josh, shaking, rose from his knees and ran towards Rufus and Rickspin. The elves were wounded but still conscious. Rickspin tried to rise but his leg was broken. Forester laid him across his shoulder and approached the door to New Blossomdale.

"We have no time to waste," he said. "You must reach Brightisclearen as soon as possible. I will take the warriors to New Blossomdale to be healed by the Shard of Spirit."

"You will make a great warrior some day, Josh," said Rufus.

Josh's chest swelled with pride as he stepped into the Tree of Seasons.

"He's right," said Beth. "You were terrific, Josh."

"Awesome." Michael sounded a little envious. "Would you like to swap gifts?"

"Your ring will serve its purpose when the time is right," said Bellatinks. "Every gift has a purpose and they have chosen to belong to those who will use them wisely."

The children climbed on board the butterflies and were quickly flown to Locksun Castle. Bellatinks led them directly to the throne room where the larger chairs had been placed in readiness around the Meeting Table.

How strange, thought Josh, as Queen Glendalock joined them at the table, that he no longer noticed her size. He had adjusted completely to this miniature kingdom which seemed to expand to the needs of the children who had entered its realm.

Quickly, Beth explained about her encounter with Shift in the basement.

Queen Glendalock's radiant face grew pale when she heard about the chalice. "It must be the lost Chalice of Elentra," she said. "There can be no other explanation." She flew towards Beth and hovered at eye level to her. "In the face of a terrifying experience, you have shown great courage," she said. "Now I must ask you to return in your mind to that dark space."

"No . . . no." Beth hunched her shoulders and stared pleadingly at the queen. "I'm too frightened."

The queen stretched out her slender hand and touched Beth's upper eyelashes. "I will not let any harm befall you. Just close your eyes and try to remember everything you witnessed in your encounter with Shift. I will travel in your footsteps as you enter Gridelda's world."

Beth felt her eyelids grow heavy. They fluttered once then closed. Almost immediately, her breathing slowed. The sounds in the throne room fell away and a deep stillness surrounded her. At first her mind was empty. Blank as the inside of a fathomless well. Then, gradually, shapes began to form. They strengthened and became recognisable. She saw herself standing outside the basement door, hesitating, trying to pluck up courage and enter. The sensation was strange, almost as if Beth was watching herself on television. She knew what would happen next yet she could not prevent beads of perspiration breaking out on her forehead. A low cry escaped as she watched her shadow-self turn the door handle and walk down the basement steps. She was able to see her shadow-image yet she knew that she was under the spell of invisibility. But that did not stop her shuddering when she saw the statue. The same deep sadness swept over her as she approached the chalice.

When the gargoyle emerged from the statue, Beth's fear of this shadow-world was so great that she grabbed Michael's arm, squeezing him so tight that he yelped.

"Stay calm, Beth. There is still much to see." The queen's mesmerising voice forced Beth to remain seated. She heard Shift sniff, saw his puzzlement, and then his fury as he failed to find her shadow-self. She watched as he sniffed and tried to locate her but instead of witnessing her shadow-self running frantically along the corridor and escaping, she remained in the room with Shift. Her breathing became shallow as she watched him approach the chalice and take it in his claws. Beth moved her eyes behind her closed eyelids and suddenly she had a view of Shift from behind. He lifted the chalice and gazed into its depths. Beth could see that it was full of sparkling liquid. It was not fluid, like water, or sleek like oil, but rolled instead like drops of mercury, each drop glinting so fiercely that she had to shield her eyes. Still holding the chalice, Shift began to transform from his gargoyle shape into the man in the painting above the fireplace. In the blink of an eye, Beth moved from the basement to the drawing room. She could see herself sitting quietly between her brothers as Great Aunt Graves and her father discussed the Grimsville Woods. Her eyes moved to the gloomy painting above the fireplace where, cloaked and menacing, Shift stared from the painting, the chalice clasped securely in his hands.

"Beth, you can return to us now," said Queen Glendalock.

Beth seemed to jolt forward. The room with its occupants and the sinister painting disappeared, as swiftly as if a bright light had been cast on shadows.

"Did you see the chalice?" she asked the queen.

"I saw the chalice and more much more besides." Queen Glendalock's voice was laden with sorrow. "We will be eternally grateful to you, Beth. Through your willingness to return to the place of danger, we know it was Gridelda who stole the Chalice of Elentra. She has been using its power to survive in the mortal world."

"I *knew* it," cried Beth. "As soon as I saw that engraving, I knew the chalice was important." She swallowed a lump in her throat and fought back the urge to weep. "I keep seeing the tears on the children's faces and I want to cry with them."

"The Chalice of Elentra is meant to spread joy," said the queen. Her silvery wings quivered as her agitation grew. "It should not send out the essence of sorrow."

"Who is Queen Elentra?" asked Josh.

"Elentra is no longer with us," replied the queen. "She ruled Brightisclearen until she reached a great age. Before she died, she passed her crown to me and I have tried to rule with her wisdom and compassion. During her reign she commissioned our most skilled goldsmith to craft the chalice. The mortal world was in turmoil at the time, torn apart by war and strife. When the chalice was presented to Elentra, she filled it with the essence of joy. This joy was drawn from the four seasons. Each ruler willingly gave her their consent to create an essence that would bring serenity to the world. When the chalice was full to the brim, she cast a spell to ensure it would always be replenished."

"I don't understand what you mean," said Michael. "What is an essence?"

"Essence of Rosebuds," said Beth. "It's perfume. Don't you remember, you gave me a bottle for Christmas?"

"Yuck . . . that smelly stuff." Michael wrinkled his nose. "Did Elentra make perfume?"

"The chalice had a wonderful scent." Queen Glendalock nodded. "But it kept changing. Sometimes it was as fresh as spring, sweet as summer, mellow as autumn, crisp as winter. But this essence was more than a scent. It was the heart, the spirit, the core of the seasons. It was a distillation of pure joy."

"I think I understand," said Josh.

"I don't," admitted Michael. "Is it something like orange juice with water?"

The queen's laughter was a merry tinkling sound. "It's the orange juice without the water, Michael," she said. "Think, children, what is your favourite season?"

"Summer," they chorused.

"It's because of our school holidays," explained Michael.

"I understand the joy of such freedom." The queen smiled at their anxious faces. "But think more deeply about my question. When spring arrives, do you not experience joy? A different kind, perhaps. But joy comes in many forms."

Josh thought about the forsythia growing at the end of his garden. It was always the first to bloom after the long winter and seemed to appear overnight, covering the back wall in bright yellow blossom. Yes, there was joy when he noticed it. A rush of anticipation for the sunny days that lay ahead.

"I feel joy when I see birds building their nests," said Beth. "There's a blackbirds' nest in our back garden. I guard the eggs from the cat next door."

"Tadpoles in the garden pond," said Michael. "I enjoy watching them turn into frogs."

"Daffodils," said Beth. "Easter eggs."

The queen held up her hand for silence. "As you've proved, there is much to celebrate in spring, as there is in summer. And also in autumn, despite the spell Gridelda has cast upon the season. Winter also brings its own joys."

"Frost on glass," said Beth. "It makes such pretty pictures."

"Christmas," said Michael. "Presents."

"Stars," said Josh. "They're brilliant then."

"Log fires," said Beth. "Stirring the plum pudding."

"Eating it, you mean," said Michael and added, "I like snowball fights best of all."

"Each season brings its own joys and you have barely touched the surface of all that nature has to offer," said the queen. "Elentra had no difficulty filling her chalice with the essence of joy."

"But why did the goldsmith engrave such sad faces on the outside?" asked Beth.

"The children were smiling," said the queen. "Their faces were alive with happiness."

"Not any more," said Beth. "Their cheeks are wet with tears."

"Is it possible that when Gridelda stole the chalice from Elentra, she reversed the spell?" asked Michael. "Instead of giving out joy, she traps the joy inside it and uses it to give her human powers."

"But Elentra's essence cannot be trapped," said Queen Glendalock. "Like the unfolding of seasons it can only spread outwards." She tapped her tiny fingers against her chin, her expression growing more thoughtful. "Unless she replaced it with a different essence. One that can be turned inwards and used to her advantage. Let us seek the truth from your ring, Michael."

Michael, pleased to have an opportunity to demonstrate the power of his gift, held out his hand and addressed the ring of truth. "Is Gridelda drawing human joy into the Chalice of Elentra?"

The diamond glittered, cold and translucent. Michael peered closer but he could not see any colour in its translucent depths.

"It doesn't work!" His disappointment was obvious as he tried to pull it from his finger. "It's *useless*."

"It cannot give you information, Michael," the queen reminded him. "It can only distinguish between fact and fiction. You must frame your questions carefully so that it can illuminate the truth."

Michael sank his chin towards his chest and thought deeply. "The essence of human joy is helping Gridelda to survive in the mortal word," he stated.

A faint blue hue glazed the centre of the diamond.

"She draws this essence of joy from children." Michael began to sound more confident as he watched the diamond turn to a sparkling azure.

Queen Glendalock flew to his side and whispered in his ear.

"She steals this joy from the echo of a baby's first cry." Michael repeated her words.

Stronger rays of blue flickered on their faces.

"She strengthens this joy with the echo of children's laughter and song, from their voices at play and at prayer. She has stolen the sounds of innocence, kindness, artlessness, affection, happiness, love?"

As Michael repeated the queen's words, she studied the ring's unflinching blue glare.

"But wouldn't children notice if their joy was disappearing?" asked Josh when Michael fell silent.

"Not at first," replied the queen. "Not if Gridelda just took a small portion from each child."

"We'd just think we were having a down day," said Beth. "Everyone has them."

"That's true." Josh thought about Johnny Welts. Lots of down days and detention, and the feeling that he was worthless every time he received a beating from the bigger boy. Now that he thought about it, there had been a lot of down days recently.

"The joy of children is a potent essence." The queen spoke again. "But Gridelda also needs ancient wisdom to survive outside her season. I do not believe she is gifted with such knowledge. Seek the answer from the ring, Michael."

"Where is Gridelda getting her wisdom?" Michael asked.

The blue hue weakened and became translucent once again. Michael sighed and after a slight hesitation, he said, "Gridelda is using her own wisdom to survive in the mortal world?"

Like a flame flickering into life, a faint red glow deepened.

"She is stealing her wisdom from children."

The diamond continued to redden.

"Ask if she's getting it from Great Aunt Graves?" Josh spoke suddenly.

"But she can't take wisdom from herself," Beth protested, but Josh put his finger to his lip to silence her.

"She is taking wisdom from Great Aunt Graves." Michael's voice was filled with disbelief as he stated this fact and he, like Beth, stared at the ring, expecting the fiery glow to continue blazing. To their astonishment, it turned to blue.

"She is taking it without our great-aunt's permission," said Michael.

Blue . . . blue . . . blue . . . Josh's heart swelled with relief as he stared at the diamond. The truth lay before them. Gridelda was not Great Aunt Graves. Josh had no idea if his great-aunt was alive or dead, if she was bewitched and imprisoned. For now, all that mattered was that his faith in her memory had been rewarded.

"Great Aunt Graves is Gridelda's prisoner," Michael stated, watching the steady blue glow.

"She is hidden in Merryville Manor." As he uttered the last words, the diamond flashed to red.

"We must recover the Chalice of Elentra and force Gridelda back to her kingdom." Queen Glendalock's voice rang with steely determination. "Then we will continue our search for the shards."

"The shards are hidden somewhere in Merryville Manor." Michael stared at the ring of truth but the diamond sent back a blood-red sparkle.

"We must concentrate on the chalice first," Josh said. Unable any longer to sit still, he paced up and down the room. He remembered the terrified expression on Beth's face when she returned from the basement. He could not ask her to venture down there again. This must be his task. But how could he steal the chalice when it was guarded by Shift?

The door to the throne room swung open. King Leafslear, accompanied by Forester, entered. "Gridelda is approaching the Tree of Seasons," he said. "She is accompanied by Shift and her ghouls. They are prepared for war."

"Now is the time to leave." The queen spoke directly to Josh. "While our warriors battle with Gridelda's troops, Merryville Manor will be empty. You have time to take the chalice and return it to us."

"But what if Shift smells us when we're going through the woods?" said Beth.

"I have the power of transportation," said Queen Glendalock. "I use it sparingly as its magic will only work in an emergency. Go now and search wisely. Bring the chalice safely back to us."

The queen's wings fluttered as she flew towards each child and bestowed a kiss on their eyelids. "To strengthen your vision," she said in her gentle voice. Then she spread her arms wide, as if she could embrace them. She still hovered a short distance from them but to Josh's astonishment, he felt himself enfolded in a strong clasp that gathered him closer to Michael and Beth.

"Are you ready to be transported, children?" the queen asked. "Have no fears. You will be quite safe."

"Yes, we're ready," said Josh.

He felt his body tensing, narrowing and growing longer. It seemed as if he was being squeezed through a tiny hole the size of a pinhead yet the sensation was not uncomfortable. He closed his eyes and listened as a faint buzzing noise grew louder, reminding him of bees droning about flowers. And still his body narrowed, his shoulders rose as if they would clamp his head, which seemed to stretch upwards, seeking release from the tension. Then, just when he believed he would cry out – if it had been possible to move his mouth – he felt a great sense of release and his feet touched the ground with a gentle jolt. The buzzing faded. He could hear the distant hoot of an owl, and, closer, a rustling in the bushes. He jumped back as a rat ran across his feet then darted into the undergrowth. He was standing with Beth and Michael in the grounds of Merryville Manor.

Bellatinks glowed faintly in the darkness as she flitted before them and raised her finger warningly to her lip. "Are we clear about what we have to do?" she whispered.

The children nodded.

"I'll check out the house and make sure the coast is clear." She glided around the outside of the manor, checking each window before flying back to them. "I can't see any sign of Gridelda or Shift." She still spoke in the same hushed tone, her wings quivering nervously as the children and Forester approached the manor. The walls were covered in Virginia creeper. At this time of the year the leaves should have been green and glossy but there were only spidery stalks clinging to the brickwork. As Josh drew nearer, he could see candles guttering in the drawing room where they had sat earlier. When they reached the porch, they stopped in front of the locked front door.

"How are we going to get in?" asked Josh.

Forester pulled out a small piece of bamboo cane from his pocket.

*"Bamboo cane, I ask you please*
*Unlock Gridelda's door with ease."*

Immediately, the bamboo began to lengthen and become pliable. Bending towards the lock, it slipped into the keyhole and wrapped itself around the latch. The children waited anxiously until they heard a sharp click. The front door swung open.

"Amazing," said Michael. "Does it always work?"

"Yes." Forester nodded modestly. "But I never take my gift for granted."

"Why bamboo?" Josh asked.

"It grows quickly and is as strong as steel," Forester explained.

Bellatinks checked the hallway then gestured at them to move forward. The air was dense with dust particles and the smell of mould caught against their breath. Beth stiffened as they turned in the direction of the basement. Michael put his arm around her shoulders to reassure her when Forester opened the door leading downwards.

Their twigs of light lit up the engraved door at the foot of the stairs.

When they descended the spiral stone stairs, Josh shivered from the cold. He had glibly told Beth to search the basement, never realising the danger he had placed her in. His admiration for his little sister grew. At the end of the corridor, they stopped at the open door and stared into the room, empty now except for the Chalice of Elentra. Josh was about to walk into the blue light when Bellatinks hissed in his ear, "It's too easy."

"We need it," whispered Josh and took another step forwards.

"I suspect a trap." Her wings flapped so fast they fanned a breeze against his cheeks.

"If that happens we'll deal with it." He took his bow from his pocket, ready for action if anything went wrong.

Suddenly everyone froze as the screech tore along the corridor, rebounding off the damp walls, striking the ceiling, echoing back and forth with such ferocity that Bellatinks fluttered as if she had flown into the teeth of a gale. Higher than Gridelda's shrieks came an inhuman, chanting sound that Josh had only ever heard in his more terrifying nightmares. "Destroy them! Destroy them!"

"It's Gridelda and her ghouls." Bellatinks darted towards the ceiling to check the strength of the advancing army. Panicked, Josh looked around and saw Gridelda rushing towards them, followed by an army of squat, pallid, black-eyed figures dressed in rust-coloured robes. Their open mouths revealed rows of rotting teeth. Open sores oozed from their faces and the stench arising from them reminded Josh of decomposing leaves. The ghouls flowed in a wave along the floor; some ran along the walls, led by the gargoyle. Shift clawed at the walls with his long nails. Saliva drooled from his mouth and his eyes glistened with triumph as the army drew nearer to the small, terrified group.

Gridelda's face was raddled with hatred. She shrieked at her ghouls to stop Josh taking the chalice and he, in that instant, wondered how they could ever, even for an instant, have believed that their gentle great-aunt had turned into this evil husk. Thinking about her gave him courage. He would find her and release her from Gridelda's spell. His mind cleared and his hand was steady as he lifted his bow. Instantly, it grew to the necessary size. He closed his eyes, shut his ears to the ever-growing clamour, and aimed his bow at an approaching ghoul. The ghoul screeched out in pain. Josh opened his eyes in time to see it collapse into a heap of mulch.

"Quick, get the chalice," Josh yelled as he continued firing.

Beth ran towards the chalice but she was too late to escape the green blast from Gridelda's cane. On the instant it struck her chest, she was unable to move. Even her expression, surprise mixed with terror, was frozen. Josh and Michael stared in disbelief as her body became rigid. They felt a chill emanating from her, as if she stood behind an invisible wall of ice.

Bellatinks tapped her fingers then opened them to release a shower of purple sparks, screaming, "*Frezetik stillect timeix*" at the same time. The sparks flew through the air towards Gridelda and scattered over the ghouls. Their clamour was suddenly silenced and Josh, lifting his bow to fire again, realised that Beth's fate had also befallen Gridelda and her army. The saliva dripping from Shift's teeth hardened into icicles and the ghouls' arched hands with their sharp, red talons were as stiff as stone. Only their black eyes moved. They glared at Josh who stepped back, still holding his bow aloft. Unable to hide his panic, he stared at his sister. "Bellatinks, what's happened to Beth?" he cried. "Is she dead?"

"She has been frozen by Gridelda's spell," cried Bellatinks. "Just as I have petrified her army. But her heart beats strongly and blood still flows in her veins. She can hear and see us. She understands that we have no other option but to leave here now."

"No way!" cried Michael. "We can't desert her."

"He's right," said Josh. "We have to take her with us."

"We can't, Josh." Bellatinks spoke urgently. "If anyone touches her, Gridelda's spell will freeze them also. We must leave now with the chalice. My spell will only last a short time. But I promise, no matter what danger we face, we will return and rescue Beth."

Josh's eyes filled with tears. "We won't leave her behind. How will we explain to our parents what's happened? I'm not leaving without her . . . I'm *not*."

"Josh, there are two levels of magic at work. For the moment Gridelda and her army are powerless. We must make haste to the castle and return the chalice to be replenished with the essence of the seasons. Only then will Gridelda's existence in the mortal world be destroyed."

But Josh, closing his eyes, held up his bow and imagined Gridelda in his sights.

"It's no good, Josh," said Forester. "You won't be able to break through the force that surrounds them. We must do as Bellatinks ordered."

133

Josh ran towards his sister and stopped, compelled by the power of Beth's gaze. Within their frozen depths a light flickered, faint but defiant. It commanded him to leave, as clearly as if the words were ringing through his mind. Do not touch me, she warned. The chalice must be returned to the Tree of Seasons. Go now. I'm not afraid.

For all her brave words, Josh knew she was terrified. He moved in a wide circle around her and clasped the chalice, then ran, sobbing, forcing his way through the immobilised ghouls. Michael ran behind him. He could hear his brother panting and the occasional terrified exclamation as they sought a clear passage towards the stairs. The smell of rot almost overwhelmed them. Gridelda's eyes flashed but she was powerless to prevent them leaving and could only watch furiously as they ran past her.

Thick dust motes danced before their eyes when they emerged into the hall. Blinded, Josh staggered and waved his hands to clear the way. Michael, running behind, crashed into him. The boys tumbled to the ground. Michael flailed the air as he fell, his body crashing against a narrow table lined against the wall. The table wobbled and overbalanced, landing on top of the boys.

The edge of the table struck Josh on his head. Stars exploded before his eyes and the breath seemed to rush from his lungs. He lay still, unable to move, as Michael stood up and lifted the table off him. He steadied it against the wall and shoved a narrow drawer that had opened back into position. As soon as he did so, the boys heard a loud click and the outline of the drawer was no longer visible.

Josh staggered to his feet. The hall swayed then steadied. Blood trickled from his forehead. His foot kicked against something. Still groggy, he bent to look. A piece of parchment, rolled up in a tight scroll, lay on the floor. It had obviously fallen out of the drawer.

"Wait," said Forester when Josh bent to pick it up. "We must not be deceived by appearances. Gridelda will have laid spells and charms all over her house. This could be an enchanted scroll." He removed the piece of bamboo cane from his pocket.

*"Bamboo cane, please do unroll.*
*Test the truth within this scroll."*

The bamboo lengthened and curved around the scroll before lifting it and placing it in Forester's hand.

"Let's go," he shouted. "Queen Glendalock is ready to transport us back to Brightisclearen."

Despite his fear for Beth, Josh was unable to prevent a thrill of excitement as his body tautened and lengthened. In the twinkling of an eye, he was transported from the grim manor to the ancient Tree of Seasons.

He had to believe Bellatinks. He trusted her. She would not allow his sister to come to any harm.

# 10

# beth is imprisoned by gridelda

In Locksun Castle, Queen Glendalock's relief at their safe return with the chalice was immediately replaced by anxiety when she realised Beth was missing. Quickly, Bellatinks related all that had occurred in the basement.

"We need to move fast," said Josh. "Use the chalice to end Gridelda's reign in our world."

"First we needed to ensure that it is the real chalice," replied the queen. "Gridelda is cunning enough to have made a replica. Michael, you must come to our assistance."

Michael stepped forward and placed the chalice on the Meeting Table. With each question he asked, he could feel his confidence growing.

"You are not the Chalice of Elentra," he said and sighed with relief when the ruby hue glowed in the centre of his ring.

"You *are* the true Chalice of Elentra," he stated. In the surge of blue light, he handed it to Queen Glendalock.

"Thank you, Michael," she said. "You wear the Ring of Truth wisely." As she bent forward and stretched her arms towards the chalice, her long silvery tresses brushed against the gold rim. Suddenly, before she could touch the chalice, the gold whitened and became as dazzling as the winter sun on a frosty morning. Heat radiated from the chalice and the smell of singeing hair filled the throne room. Queen Glendalock stepped back from the heat but not before the ends of her hair had shrivelled. Tears gathered in her eyes. She covered her face with her hands. Queens were not supposed to display weakness. The heat of the chalice also blasted towards Bellatinks when she flew too close to it.

"Gridelda has placed a spell on the chalice," Bellatinks cried, her wings whirring as fast as a hummingbird's. "We cannot replace the essence of seasons until her magic wears off."

"When will that be?" shouted Josh. "You promised Gridelda would be destroyed when we brought the chalice back."

"Why can't we do it?" asked Michael. "We're able to hold the chalice without being burned."

"Only the reigning queen can create the essence of seasons," said Bellatinks. "In your hands the chalice is a useless vessel. I should have realised it would not be so easy to defeat Gridelda."

Queen Glendalock rose to her feet and flew to her gilded chair at the head of the Meeting Table. Once seated, her distress was replaced by determination. "Beth has placed her trust in us and we will not betray her. Our minds have connected and I'm relieved to tell you she is still protected by Bellatinks's magic. We have time to mount a campaign to rescue her." She gestured towards Forester who had been silent since they entered the throne room. "I sense you have important information for me, Forester."

Forester laid the parchment on the table and unrolled the scroll. An ancient map had been drawn on it and Josh, leaning closer, read out the words at the top of the scroll: *An Exact Survey of Dublin Including all Public Buildings,*

*Dwelling Houses, Gates and Doors, Arches and Gateways, Churches and Meeting Houses, Workhouses, Alehouses, Schoolhouses, Warehouses and Stables.*

He stared at the names. Some were familiar: Inchichore, Kilmainham, Stonybatter, Cabra, Kilmainham. Mrs Lotts's parents lived in Dublin so he recognised Howth. He knew Howth Head and had often climbed to the summit with his grandparents. He noticed an image on the parchment. At first he thought someone had drawn a fragment of broken ice with razor-sharp angles and painted it with an ice-blue glaze. He noticed a similar drawing on another section of the map, only this one glowed like amber.

"The shards." Queen Glendalock uttered a soft cry as her attention was drawn to the images. She leaned closer to the map and gasped. "Children, not only have you brought us back the chalice but we now know the whereabouts of the shards."

"Are they the shards?" Josh was unable to hide his disappointment. He'd had no idea what exactly a shard was but had imagined something powerful like a burnished shield or a massive sword with a jewelled hilt. Not these tiny triangular drawings that he could have drawn when he was in High Infants. But as he watched, the images lifted from the parchment. At least that was what it looked like. He half expected them to fly away but, instead, they began to beat like a regular heartbeat, and the colours deepened, each shard reflecting the many shades of autumn and winter.

"Howth is where our grandparents live." Michael was equally fascinated by the beating shards. "They know

Howth really well. We can show them the map and they'll lead us to the first shard." The ice-blue shard beat even faster, as if it understood that help was finally on the way.

"The other one is in the Phoenix Park," added Michael, who was excellent at geography. He pointed to the second shard. This shard was not as sharply angled as the blue one. Its outline was indented, leaf-shaped, but with the same razor tips. "That's where Dublin Zoo is. But Phoenix Park is massive," he warned. "And Howth is full of cliffs. Where do we start looking?"

"Now that the hiding places of the shards from Icefroztica and Duskcanister have been revealed to us, I will ask the shrubs and trees in the park and along the cliffs to guide us," said Forester.

But no sooner had he spoken than the shards disappeared from the map. The city also changed. Suddenly they were looking at an ancient map of Kerry. Josh and Michael were familiar with the Dingle peninsula, having spent three holidays there with their parents.

"Remember the drive through the Connor Pass?" Josh said. "The time Dad was driving the caravan."

Michael nodded and rolled his eyes upwards. "It's the highest mountain pass in Ireland," he explained. "And it's really rugged . . . especially if you're trying to pass a caravan coming the opposite way." He pointed to the exact location where the autumn shard was beating. "That's a really deep valley with lakes. Everyone stops to admire it but we'd never be able to climb down there."

"Perhaps with the butterflies ... " Josh sounded thoughtful but even as he imagined flying down into the emerald green valley the heading on the map had changed to Galway.

"Gridelda mocks us." The queen's anger flashed across her face. "This map has been bewitched. The truth is hidden behind her spell. Michael, we need your assistance once again."

Michael drew the parchment towards him and placed his ring finger in its centre.

"The shards are hidden in Galway," he said. Instantly the ring reddened.

"The shards are hidden in Cork." The colour remained the same as he began to list the thirty-two counties on the island of Ireland.

"Try Wicklow," suggested Josh. "Gridelda may not have travelled far from the Tree of Seasons."

Michael nodded and addressed the ring again.

"The shards lie hidden in Wicklow," he said and grinned when the ring changed to blue.

"It's near the Tree of Seasons," he said but the ring turned red again.

As he kept asking questions, the search narrowed to a half-moon bay called Echo Cove for the blue shard. The autumn shard was hidden in a nearby country village called Eleven Oaks.

Queen Glendalock rolled up the parchment and locked it in a metal chest. One of the fairies immediately entered the throne room and stood guard beside it.

"Gridelda has no idea that we have this information," said the queen. "We will begin our search as soon as we have rescued Beth."

Bellatinks sighed and uttered a low moan. Her face grew pale, even her lips lost their lustre, and her fiery hair dulled to a mousy brown. "Gridelda has defeated me." She raised her hand and pressed it to her chest. "She has broken my spell and captured Beth."

# 11

# trapped in merryville manor

Beth had once had a nightmare. It had seemed so real that she had awoken and screamed for her parents to protect her. Her father had rushed into her room and hugged her, told her it was only a bad dream and she was now awake, safe in his arms. After a while, she had stopped shivering and had gone back to sleep. The next morning she could only remember some of the details of her nightmare. Mainly she remembered the sensation of trying to reach somewhere safe, and the dragging sensation as her legs refused to move. No matter how much she tried to force them forward, they remained stuck to the ground. The danger, the unknown force that was trying to harm her, drew ever nearer. Now her dream had come true.

Earlier, when Gridelda's green beam struck her chest, the sensation had seared through her body. At first she had imagined heat but almost instantly she realised it was the sting of ice piercing her flesh. She had remained frozen to the spot, unable, like her nightmare, to force her legs to move. She could hear everyone speaking. The despair on her brothers' faces when they were forced to leave her behind had been awful to watch. But Bellatinks flew as closely as possible and smiled reassuringly at her.

"I know you have the courage to survive this danger, Beth. As soon as we have returned the chalice to Queen Glendalock, we will defeat Gridelda and set you free. Until then, my magic will prevent her from harming you."

Gridelda and her fearsome army looked as if they could break free from Bellatinks's spell at any moment and devour her. But she had to believe in Bellatinks. She had forced herself to gaze confidently at her brothers and encouraged them to leave.

Sadly, Bellatinks was wrong. Her magic was not strong enough to keep Gridelda at bay. As soon as the front door of Merryvale Manor slammed closed, Gridelda's face moved. She lifted her sharp chin upwards until she was staring at the arched ceiling above her. She raised one arm, then another. With both arms upraised, she moved her body sinuously and with this snake-like movement she was free. But Shift and the ghouls remained frozen.

She pointed her cane in their direction and released blasts of light but they stayed in the same rigid position. When Gridelda realised that her power was not strong enough to break Bellatinks's spell, she turned her attention to Beth. Once again, the blast of light seared through the young girl. This time the icy sensation slowly began to melt. Her limbs relaxed. As the increasing heat brushed against her skin, her heart began to quake. Her legs trembled so much she sank to the floor.

"On your feet immediately," commanded Gridelda.

Beth struggled to her feet and raised her hand to touch the necklace of invisibility.

"Ah, now I understand why Shift was unable to see you." Gridelda was even faster. In one swift movement, she ripped the necklace from around Beth's neck. "Move," she ordered, slipping the necklace into her cloak pocket.

Beth had no idea where she gained the courage to walk towards the frozen army. She tried not to look at their faces but Shift's gaze was compelling. It warned her that he was waiting to tear her apart as soon as Bellatinks's magic wore off.

Beth was led to the drawing room where, earlier, and it seemed like another lifetime ago, her father had discussed Gridelda's determination to raze Merryville Woods. Gridelda pointed towards one of the wooden chairs. "Sit," she said, as if Beth was a dog. "Speak only when I demand an answer."

Gridelda stood before the fire. The flames flickered on her face, revealing her thin, clamped lips, her narrowed eyes.

"So, Beth, it appears that you and your brothers have been busy with matters that do not concern you." At last she turned and spoke directly to Beth. "Children should be seen and not heard. They should not meddle in powerful magic. When they do there is only one way to deal with them."

"What are you going to do with me?" Beth began to sob.

"That is for me to decide," replied Gridelda. "Tell me what you know and I may be lenient. But hide any information from me and you will know the full force of my wrath."

"I don't know anything." Beth wanted to sound brave and strong but her voice wobbled as her tears continued to fall.

"You were about to steal the Chalice of Elentra yet you claim to know nothing." Gridelda's voice grew shriller. "Do you take me for a fool?"

"No . . . but I don't understand what's going on," sobbed Beth. "Please . . . please let me go home."

"But first you will tell me everything, Beth. If not, you will be punished. I have spells so powerful you cannot imagine how destructive they can be."

"Bellatinks is powerful too." Beth's breath shuddered. "She is going to rescue me."

"You really believe a pathetic fairy can interfere with my plans." Gridelda laughed harshly. "Before you invaded my home, I drank deeply from the Chalice of Elentra. That draught has freed me from the magic of those who would try and thwart my plans. Soon the fairy's paltry spell will weaken and my army will be freed. Then there will be a reckoning. Yes, indeed, then there will be a great reckoning."

"Where is my great-aunt?"

"She is of no importance. I will not waste my time discussing her."

"But she's important to us. Have you . . . " Beth stopped, afraid to ask the question.

"Killed her? Is that what you want to know?"

"Have you?" Beth sobbed louder. Her pet cat had died last year and Beth had cried for two days. But that was the only time she had thought about death. Since Michael's ring had revealed the truth about Great Aunt Graves, Beth kept remembering nice things about the elderly woman. The stories she used to tell Beth – and she had believed, like Beth, in fairies and elves. She had told Beth about fairy raths that farmers were allowed to cut down because it destroyed fairy kingdoms and brought back luck. She had shown a fairy rath to Beth. It was a raised circle of grass with a tree growing in the centre. She and Beth had pressed their ears into the grass and Beth had been convinced she heard music and dancing feet. But she had forgotten those special times . . . until now. The woman who was discharged from hospital the day after her accident had been so crotchety and scary that all the pleasant memories had simply flown from Beth's mind.

"Tell me what you know."

"Why are you doing this?" Beth had no idea where she got the courage to ask the question. Maybe it was the warm, wonderful memories about Great Aunt Graves – or Lily-May, as she used to be called – that now flowed through her mind. Josh had puzzled many times over the changes in their great-aunt but Beth had just seen a bad-tempered, ugly woman with terrifying hands. Now, she remembered those hands stroking her face when she was a little girl, singing her to sleep at night, soothing her tears when she fell from her bike or from the wonderful swing she and the boys had made in her garden.

Gridelda moved from the fireplace and grabbed Beth's hair, jerking it so violently that the young girl's face was tilted upwards.

"There have always been four seasons," Beth said. "Why do you want to control all of them?"

"Oh, such a brave child." Gridelda mocked her. "Such brave questions." She snapped Beth's head back even further. "I ask the questions. And demand the answers. I repeat for the last time, *tell* me what you know."

Beth was forced to stare into her eyes. She saw her own reflection in Gridelda's pupils and heard herself speaking. Beth wanted to stop. Her voice was a monotone as she revealed everything that had happened since she and her brothers saw the first bolts of light arching over Grimsville Woods. She wanted to stop talking but she had no control over the words that spilled from her mouth. When she had revealed everything she knew, the pupils in Gridelda's eyes grew opaque and Beth's image faded. She was left with an empty, shamed feeling. She had betrayed those she loved and the new friends who trusted her.

"So they plan to return the shards to the Tree of Seasons." Gridelda laughed grimly. "Fools! They have no hope of penetrating my hiding places and getting their hands on them. But now they have discovered how I exist in the mortal world." Gridelda mused aloud as she stroked her chin. "Hmmm . . . that does give them a slight advantage but they are unable to touch the chalice. I need to recover it and drink the essence of joy if my plan is to succeed. I must get the chalice back but the kingdom of Brightisclearen is well protected and King Leafslear will fight to the bitter end by her side. But it –" She broke off and stared at Beth. "What is the value of a mortal child to them? Let us put it to the test."

Beth listened as Gridelda outlined her plot. Beth would be a hostage. She would be exchanged in return for the chalice. What would Bellatinks do if she was in the same situation? Beth wondered. She would certainly not sit here crying her eyes out. Beth looked at the distance from the chair to the door, which was unlocked. She was a fast runner. On sports day before school broke up, she had won first prize for sprinting. Gridelda was once again staring into the flames. Beth rose and took one step forward, then another. Still the queen of autumn paid no attention. She sprinted across the room towards the door. Her heart thumped so loudly she was sure Gridelda could hear it. But there was still no movement from Gridelda. Beth reached towards the doorknob but before she touched it, she saw it turn. Someone was outside and about to enter the room.

The door swung open. A boy stood facing her. His solid body blocked her escape. Beth recoiled and ducked to the other side of him but he moved just as swiftly. He smiled, mocking her. As Gridelda's harsh laughter sounded across the room, Beth's shoulders slumped. The gloating sound convinced her that Gridelda had heard every step she had taken. She had been playing with Beth, a cat and mouse game, and now the boy had joined in the fun.

He was well built with broad shoulders and large hands. His short black hair was shaved close to his scalp and emphasised his tough, square chin. He raised his hand and pushed her back into the room.

Johnny Welts. She recognised him immediately. Josh's arch enemy. She remembered the times Josh had arrived home late from school, his eyes or his cheeks ballooning, and how the bruises would spread over the following days, turning from purple to a muddy yellow before finally fading. She felt the force of his hand on her chest.

She tried to stand firm but staggered backwards when he pushed her again.

"You came quickly, Johnny," said Gridelda. "Well done. We need to talk urgently. But first things first. A fly is harmless but irritating, and must be controlled."

She pointed to the chair and turned to gaze at Beth. "Sit," she said, angrily.

Beth sank into the chair.

Gridelda pointed her cane at the chair. Immediately, slim, rope-like vines emerged from the wood and lashed Beth to the seat. The chair's grip tightened when she tried to pull her arms free. With every movement she made, the vines tightened.

Johnny Welts watched, still smiling. His dark eyes were deep-set, too small for his large face. They disappeared into slits when he laughed.

"Sit down, Johnny." Gridelda switched her attention to him. "I have an important task for you to undertake."

"Do you need more joy?" he asked and shadow-boxed the air with his fists.

"Not for the present," replied Gridelda. "You will have ample time to fight your enemies when this task is done. My chalice has been stolen. More essence is needed but first I must recover the chalice so that it can be replenished. I am disarmed for the moment so I need to act urgently. Watch over this girl while I am engaged on my task."

Johnny looked dismissively at Beth. "That's it? You want me to mind a stupid girl?"

"Yes. It is imperative that she does not escape." Gridelda walked to the press where she had flung the necklace of invisibility. She removed a small bottle filled with green liquid. "This will pay for your time," she said.

Johnny accepted the bottle and removed the cap. He tilted his head back and drank deeply before placing it on the table. His body began to shake violently. But he remained unperturbed by the uncontrollable movements. Gradually, the movements became less violent until they ceased altogether. He walked over to Beth. Before she had time to brace herself he lifted her and the heavy chair with one hand. He held it as lightly as a feather and smiled at Gridelda.

"Don't worry, she'll not escape," he said. Even his voice had a deeper, more powerful ring to it.

Beth held onto the arms of the chair as she was lowered to the floor. No matter what happened, she would not let Johnny Welts know she was terrified.

"This is what will happen if you try to escape," he warned and walked towards the statue of the horned centaur in front of the window. He clenched his fist and drew back his arm. The movement was so swift it reminded Beth of the speed with which Josh's enchanted arrows flew to their target. The centaur lay on the floor in tiny fragments.

Beth struggled with this new knowledge. Johnny Welts was not as frightening as Shift or the army of ghouls but he was just as dangerous. He brought the joy of children to Gridelda so that she could create the powerful essence that made her mortal life possible. She wondered how this was possible. She listened carefully to the conversation between Gridelda and Johnny, trying to glean as much information as she could.

"Well done, Johnny," said Gridelda, capping the phial and replacing it back in the cabinet. "You have been rewarded for your faithful service."

She gestured to Beth. "Come with me, Beth. We must make haste to the Tree of Seasons."

Beth tried to understand what was happening. How could Johnny Welts mind her if Gridelda was bringing her to the tree? But when she tried to move from the chair, the grip of the vines held her even tighter. Below her, she heard a rumble. At first it was so faint she hoped it was her imagination but then it was repeated, louder this time. The sound growled up between the floorboards, a voice making unintelligible noises, but there was no mistaking the anger seeping from it. Other voices joined in, the sound becoming more distinct and blood-curdling. Gridelda and Johnny smiled at each other.

"All magic spells run their course," said Gridelda and raised her voice commandingly. "Make haste, Shift. We have no time to dally."

Beth heard another sound, like a gale rushing through the woods. The door of the drawing room burst open and Shift, in his smoke-like form, entered, followed by the ghouls. At once, the room was filled with their ghastly stench. Johnny held his nose and grew pale while Beth, gagging, wondered what would happen if she threw up as violently as she had earlier this evening. And still the vines held her more securely than the strongest rope.

"To the woods," said Gridelda. "Defend my kingdom." The air cleared as ghouls flitted from the room. "Are you with me, Beth?" asked Gridelda. Her voice lilted over Beth's name. "Come with me to the Tree of Seasons and I will offer your life in exchange for the chalice. It will be a fair exchange, do you not agree?"

She watched Beth struggle and laughed. "Don't waste your strength," she said. "You will never leave this room alive."

She pointed towards Shift whose smoke-like form blurred and deepened to a shade of charcoal grey. His hot red eyes were still visible as he became even more form-less. Then a shape began to appear, a small pair of arms and legs, a head and shoulders, a slim body wearing dungarees and a pink jumper. Beth gasped. Nothing she had experi-enced since this incredible adventure started had been as horrifying as the sight before her eyes. She could have been staring at her own reflection. She was bound head to toe, yet a girl who looked like her in every detail was walk-ing freely around the drawing room. The only trace that remained of Shift was his dangerous red eyes. With one blink of his eyelids they disappeared and were replaced by Beth's wide-set cornflower blue eyes.

"Are you ready, Beth?" Gridelda addressed Shift. "It is time to regain the chalice and claim the remaining shards."

"You won't fool my brothers." Beth found the courage to speak. "They will know immediately that Shift is an impostor."

"Will they?" asked Gridelda. "Did you believe your great-aunt was an impostor? No," she answered the question herself. "You were quite prepared to forget the kindness she had once bestowed on you. You failed to remember the good times and accepted me in her place. Your brothers will do the same when they see Shift."

"Please tell me where she is?" she cried out, knowing that Gridelda spoke the truth. "Where is Great Aunt Graves?" she repeated and jerked her body so hard that the chair rocked back and forth. But Gridelda laughed and beckoned to Shift. When he reached her side she lifted his blonde hair with one hand and smacked him firmly across his face with her other hand. She repeated this act three times. The marks of her hand were clearly visible on Shift's face. Suddenly, he looked frightened, bruised and worn-out.

"Always strive for authenticity," said Gridelda.

Shift whimpered, but it was obvious he was unhurt. He stretched out his hand – and how like Beth's it looked – and clasped Gridelda's bony fingers. Together they walked from the room.

"Remember, Johnny, don't let her out of your sight," she warned as Shift opened the door and they disappeared from view.

# 12

# gridelda's journey to
# brightisclearen

Fools . . . such fools, Gridelda gloated as she left Merryville Manor and turned in the direction of Grimsville Woods. The shock of being caught by Bellatinks's magic still rankled but pride was not important when there were more urgent matters to consider. The Chalice of Elentra had fallen into enemy hands. She had drunk deeply from it before those foolhardy children had invaded her house and now, if she did not replenish it, she would lose her power to survive outside her season. And that, thought Gridelda, quickening her pace, was where the danger lay. She had worked too hard, plotted for too long, and with the end in sight, she would not be defeated by three children who had strayed from their natural world into kingdoms that were normally invisible to the human eye.

Beside her, Shift sighed. Such a deep heaving sigh, as if the burden of being Beth Lotts was difficult to bear, even for a short time. He too must be shocked by the power of a minion fairy to freeze him, render him and the ghouls helpless, render Gridelda, Queen of Autumn, rigid as granite, unable to do anything except glare helplessly as the boy, Josh, escaped with the chalice. Not that it would be of any benefit to the queen of Brightisclearen. Gridelda chuckled as a ghoul emerged from the trees, leading a snow-white stallion. Swiftly, she mounted the stallion and waited for Shift to settle behind her. Such a light child, hardly any weight at all, her blonde hair streaming behind her as the white horse spread his powerful wings and rose above the trees. Yes, indeed, Shift was playing his role to perfection. Gridelda sighed with satisfaction as she stared down on the crowns of tall, ancient trees. Soon the woods would cease to exist, felled by chainsaws, their roots poisoned or ripped from the earth by mighty machines. And that was only the beginning. So much work still to do. Gridelda urged the stallion onwards towards the Tree of Seasons.

Seizing control of Duskcanister had been easy compared to her battle with King Darkfrost. At first, although taken by surprise, when Gridelda's ghouls had hurtled along the tunnel leading to Icefroztica he had rallied his goblins to his side. Sitting astride his powerful snow-white stallion, he had urged them to fight for their kingdom. But Gridelda had been busy. She had the Chalice of Elentra to bribe those goblins who, like her ghouls, were prepared to betray their king and sip from the chalice. Immortality, she promised them. Riches and power in the mortal world. Goblins were like children, so easily charmed by her promises. They sipped from the chalice. Just a drop, that was all they needed to be filled with the joy of conquest.

The chalice had been easy to fill with the essence of joy. Johnny Welts was the first. His desire for strength without discipline made him a willing victim. He was willing to exchange his joy for strong, ropy muscles and fists that crashed his victims to the ground. The children called him Johnny Warts, he told her. Some called him Wartface or Warthog or just Warts. When he tried to fight them, they laughed at his puny body and flung him into the bushes or shoved his head down the school toilets. Not any more. Johnny's fame as a fighter had spread throughout Merryville and no one challenged him now. Other children were equally content to exchange their joy for dreams. They demanded fame, friendship and popularity without effort, money without labour, knowledge without thought. It amused Gridelda to grant their wishes. To know that when they achieved what they most desired, they wondered why it brought no happiness. Why joy had been replaced by a gnawing dissatisfaction and why the sky always seemed grey. Yes, indeed, it was easy to fill the Chalice of Elentra ... almost. To fill it to the brim Gridelda had needed to mingle human wisdom with the joy of youth. And so she came to Merryville Manor, to the home of the old woman who owned the woods and knew that in its centre there was a mystery no human being should penetrate. The old lady never knew what hit her. All that was necessary was a bolt from Gridelda's cane. Poor fool. She now rested with Patina in the dark hollows of Duskcanister and slowly, drop by glistening drop, Gridelda was acquiring the wisdom of age, the wisdom of autumn and, more swiftly, the joy of children. What a powerful essence.

No wonder the goblins guarding the entrance to Icefroztica had allowed her to pass unchallenged into their kingdom.

King Darkfrost was defeated after five days of war. Triumphant and confident, Gridelda turned her attention to New Blossomdale, a pale, weak kingdom, peeking shyly, or so she thought, through the rime of winter. But she had reckoned without the ferocity of the elves. Defeated at the entrance she had turned her attention to Brightisclearen, believing that the frail fairies guarding the kingdom would be easily overcome. They too proved fierce and brave in battle, and she had still not managed to capture the shards.

She needed them before the felling of the woods began. Humankind had the power to lay waste the forests, poison the sky, pillage the earth, and disturb the cycle of the seasons. But they could not bring her the shards of spring and summer. For that purpose she needed her ghouls and the goblins who had betrayed their king. Soon she would unleash all her forces against the Tree of Seasons but she, and her army, needed to drink deeply from the chalice. No more time to waste.

She urged the white stallion onwards. She felt him shudder, unable to disguise his hatred for her. What matter? King Darkfrost would never again gallop across the wintry plains of Icefroztica astride his strong, broad back.

How had those hideous children stumbled on the Tree of Seasons? There must be a link between them and the old woman. Gridelda had no idea what it was. Not knowing made her nervous. An unfamiliar emotion and one she had every intention of controlling. She was within reach of her goal. Soon the children's father would bring her the permission she sought to level Grimsville Woods. The woodcutters would come with their machines to rip the roots from the earth, to reduce the proud trunks and branches to sawdust, to move ever closer to the centre of the woods where the greatest tree of all, the centre of the universe, would shudder and fall by the hand of humankind.

She tightened her lips as she dismounted from the stallion outside Locksun Castle. She walked with Shift across the marble bridge. His resemblance to Beth Lotts impressed Gridelda, who believed she had lost the power to be awed by anything. She stiffened as two fairies in loin-cloths blocked her entry. They stood perfectly still, their arrows aimed directly at her heart. Shift growled low in his throat, the cornflower blue of his eyes reddening with fury when he recognised Bowrain and Partlant.

"Be careful," hissed Gridelda. "Do you want to be unmasked at this early stage? They will not hesitate to fire and alert our enemies."

"Stand aside immediately." She approached the fairies, who remained in the same position, their aim unswerv-ing. "I have come to barter with Queen Glendalock." She shoved Shift forward.

Shift squirmed and fell to his knees, sobbing loudly. "Please bring me to my brothers. Gridelda is evil. She will kill me if she does not get the Chalice of Elentra. I'm frightened . . . oh, I'm so frightened."

Gridelda resisted the urge to laugh aloud. Her gargoyle was excelling himself.

"Do not touch a hair on that child's head." A voice thun-dered through Shift's sobbing. Gridelda, looking towards the entrance to the castle, recognised Forester. Such a minion, she thought, who believes he has the power to guard the woods. Let him enjoy his illusions for a short while longer.

"You may have every hair on her head in exchange for

the Chalice of Elentra," she said. "Otherwise, she will die by my hand and I will throw her body to my ghouls. They are seething with fury after Bellatinks trapped them in the spell of immobility and they are anxious for revenge."

Shift's sobbing reached such a crescendo that Gridelda wondered if he was overdoing it. But Forester and the fairies were fooled. At Forester's command they lowered their bows and stood aside. Gridelda roughly grabbed Shift by his arm and stepped inside the sweetly scented castle.

# 13

# beth confronts johnny welts

Beth was trussed as tightly as a fly in a spider's web. She needed to escape. Every moment that passed brought Gridelda nearer to Brightisclearen. Twice tonight she had watched herself from a distance, once through the power of her mind, but the second sighting had terrified her. As Shift departed, Beth's mind had been petrified by fear but now, watching Johnny Welts as he paced up and down the room, she wondered how he had become caught up in Gridelda's schemes. She had met him for the first time when she was five years old and in High Infants. He was skinny then, smaller than the other boys in his class, who called him Johnny Warts. She had forgotten that until now. Johnny Warts instead of Johnny Welts. They used to chant it in the schoolyard. Once, on the school bus, sitting between Josh and Michael, she had seen the bigger boys beating him. Sheila, the bus driver, had stopped the bus and threatened to throw off the next person who made a noise above a whisper.

No one would call him Johnny Warts now. He towered over Beth and flexed his muscles, testing them with his fingers, as if unable to believe the bulging biceps belonged to him.

"They're not real muscles." Beth blinked, afraid she was going to cry. He scowled so menacingly she believed he would hit her with his mighty fist. If he did so, she would collapse unconscious, or maybe she would die. "They're fake," she added. "If I stuck a pin in them they'd burst."

"Is that what you think?"

"They look stupid. Like warts."

"What did you say?"

"Like big fat warts."

"Shut your face, Beth Lotts," he roared. "You're in enough trouble already."

"All I said was that they look like warts."

"Feel them, you little squirt." He knelt down before her and flexed his arms. His muscles rippled and bulged alarmingly.

"How can I feel them?" snapped Beth. "I'm tied hand and foot."

"So you are," he said. "Ha ha *ha*."

"Johnny *Warts* . . . ha ha *ha*." His eyes flashed angrily but she held his gaze, challenging him. "Even I could beat you in a fight and I'm only eight."

"You and what army, squirt?"

"With my fists. Johnny Warts . . . Warts . . . *Warts*."

"I'll break your face, Beth Lotts, if you don't shut up!" He slammed his fist towards her face then pulled back at the last second. "I'll be strong forever." He lowered his voice and leaned closer to her. "Call me Warts once more and you'll see what I'm talking about."

"You'd fight me when I'm tied up? Oh, that's brave," she taunted him. "That's so *very* brave."

Without replying, he walked to the cabinet and flung open the door. He reached inside and removed the phial. She watched as he tilted back his head and swallowed the green liquid. Almost immediately, his body shuddered even more violently than the first time. The vibrations travelled along the floor and up the legs of the chair that was holding Beth prisoner. She gasped as the vines tightened, knocking the breath from her body. After a moment, the vibrations ceased and Johnny Welts stood before her again. She tried to steady her voice but still she sounded hoarse and trembling when she said, "*Wart*face."

He grabbed the vines and snapped them one after the other . . . snap . . . snap . . . snap, freeing her arms, then her legs, snap . . . .snap . . . snap . . . she was on her feet and facing him, her fists raised. She looked beyond his shoulder towards the window and screamed, "The ghouls . . . the ghouls. They're *back*."

He spun around, his expression suddenly fearful. Beth fled towards the cabinet where, earlier, Gridelda had carelessly flung her precious Necklace of Invisibility.

"Where are they?" Johnny shouted and laughed when he turned from the window and saw her standing by the open cabinet door. "You think you're so clever, don't you? Clever little Beth Lotts. But you don't escape that easily." He advanced towards her, his arms swinging loose. How unhappy he looked, she thought before she disappeared. How lost and unhappy and uncertain. His expression changed to bewilderment as he floundered around the room, calling her name over and over again. She ducked away from him and when his back was turned she grasped the door handle. He spun around in time to see the door closing and rushed towards it. He raced up the hall, yelling furiously. She waited until his footsteps faded before quietly stealing across the drawing room and slipping out the window.

Once she landed outside she clapped her hands and called softly, "Bellatinks. Bellatinks. Bellatinks!"

The door of the throne room swung open and Gridelda entered. She held Beth roughly by the scruff of her neck and Josh, seeing the red marks on his sister's face, and her terrified expression, wanted to fling himself at Gridelda and wrestle her to the ground. But that would be a futile gesture. At the very least, Gridelda would toss him aside or she would bewitch him, as she had earlier bewitched Beth. He forced himself to stand still as Beth was shoved forward and forced to her knees. She bent her head so low that her hair fell over her cheeks, hiding her terrified expression.

"Give her the chalice," Beth sobbed. "She will kill me if you don't obey her."

"You heard the child." Gridelda addressed the queen. "She knows the fate that awaits her if you do not return what is rightfully mine."

"The Chalice of Elentra belongs to all who dwell in the Tree of Seasons," said Queen Glendalock. "You have used it for your own ends and destroyed its purpose."

"No speeches, please." Gridelda spoke mockingly. "I have no time to waste. Make the exchange or I will carry out my threat."

"I'm frightened . . . so frightened." Beth gasped and pressed her hands to her chest. Tears dripped from her eyes and splashed on the floor.

"Be silent, child." Impatiently, Gridelda bent and pulled

Beth's hair, jerking her head backwards and exposing her long, slim neck. "Do you want me to break her neck?" she shouted. "I can do so with one twist."

"We have to give her the chalice." Josh could hold still no longer. He picked up the chalice and held it out towards Gridelda.

But at that moment Bellatinks, who had left the room just seconds earlier, pointed her finger towards him. "Put the chalice down, Josh," she ordered.

"No," he shouted. "I want to save my sister."

In response, Bellatinks tapped her fingers and released a shower of purple sparks. Josh froze in mid-motion, his arms outstretched. Now he understood how Gridelda and her army must have felt when they struggled in vain against the force of Bellatinks's spell. He stared at her in astonishment, silently demanding to be freed. But Bellatinks ignored him.

"Break her neck," she said in a shrill, tinkling voice. "See if we care. You shall never again possess the Chalice of Elentra."

Josh heard Michael's gasp, felt his brother's outrage blasting towards the fairy, whose hair had returned to its usual fiery shade. Her green eyes gleamed mockingly at Beth. "Go on, Beth. Sniffle and snuffle. Our hearts will not be moved."

Gridelda drew a razor-sharp blade of grass from inside her cloak and touched Beth's throat with it. A trickle of blood oozed from the open cut. "I will slay her this instant if you do not obey me." She sank the blade deeper. Michael, unable to contain himself any longer, lunged towards the chalice that Josh still grasped. As soon as he touched it, his fingers froze and he was gripped by the spell of immobility.

Bellatinks arose in a graceful movement and flew from the room. Queen Glendalock and King Leafslear watched impassively as Gridelda, desperately reaching for the chalice, was forced to draw back before her fingers stiffened. She snarled and kicked Beth, who collapsed on the floor. Josh and Michael could only stare helplessly. Blood flowed from Beth's wound. But she was no longer crying. A glaze had settled over her eyes. When she lifted her head and peered at Queen Glendalock through tendrils of blood-soaked hair, Josh thought her eyes were also bleeding. But then he realised they were dry. No tears, no blood, just filled with fury, a blasting fury that she directed at the queen. Her hands, as she pushed herself from the floor, had turned to scaly claws. As realisation dawned on Josh, the door to the throne room opened. Beth, the real Beth, his courageous, breathless sister, entered. Bellatinks flew above her, spinning in delirious circles of excitement. Josh wanted to run and scoop his sister in his arms but Bellatinks appeared to have forgotten him and Michael. Gridelda looked stupefied. As for Shift . . . he was morphing back to gargoyle form with dizzying speed.

How could Josh have been so easily fooled? He should have known Beth would never whimper and plead and grovel. He was filled with admiration for her as she ran towards him, stopping just in time when Bellatinks called out a warning. Josh realised that Bellatinks had not forgotten him. As long as he was under the spell of immobilisation, Gridelda could not touch the chalice.

Queen Glendalock flapped her wings. He had always thought of them as silvery scraps of gauze but now, as they moved back and forth, they created great waves of air and claps of thunder. Suddenly the throne room was filled with warrior fairies, tiny men and women armed with bows and arrows. Some carried rods, slight as water reeds, over their shoulders but when they pointed them towards Gridelda and Shift, they cowered back as bolts of blue light exploded from them. The lights danced harmlessly around the throne room, creating incredible shapes in the air, but Josh suspected that one command from Queen Glendalock and their aim would be deadly. Gridelda, realising she was outmanoeuvred, whistled. A magnificent white horse flew through the open doorway, gracefully swerving to avoid the blue shafts.

"Go back to your kingdom, Gridelda," commanded Queen Glendalock. "Leave us in peace."

Gridelda snarled and leapt on the stallion's back. The horse shuddered, ripples running across his broad back. Pain shone from his dark brown eyes. With a wide sweep of his wings, he took flight, veering away when Shift flew too close.

"Why did you let her go?" Beth cried out as the fairies silently withdrew. "You should have kept her prisoner."

Bellatinks flung purple stars in the direction of the boys who immediately felt life returning to their limbs.

"Beth's right," said Josh. "She's evil and dangerous. Why is she free?"

"She has placed Queen Patina, the rightful ruler of autumn, under the spell of decay," said Queen Glendalock. "And the whereabouts of King Darkfrost remain a mystery. If we keep her prisoner her ghouls will rush to attack the castle. We must try and outwit her without anymore loss of life. However, for now, we have the upper hand."

"How?" asked Michael. "She will return to steal the chalice. Otherwise she can't survive in the mortal world."

"It will be guarded with my life," said Forester.

"And mine," said Bellatinks.

"Now you must return to your home and rest, children," said the queen. "It has been a long and dangerous night. Tomorrow, the search for the shards will begin. You have proved to be true friends to the Tree of Seasons."

The butterflies were waiting to escort them from Brightisclearen. Swiftly they rose into the air. From the turrets of Locksun Castle, ranks of fairies cheered. Their voices faded and the butterflies flew a straight course towards the tunnel of flowers. The trees were still and silent when the children emerged under the Tree of Seasons. They greeted the warrior elves guarding the entrance to the ancient kingdoms. The moon washed the sky with silver and in the dark night the silence was broken by a faint but distinct whinny. It was the loneliest sound in Grimsville Woods.

# 14

# strange weather forecasts

"Snow!" Mrs Lotts shouted in disbelief. "Snow in summer? What is happening to this country?"

Mr Lotts opened the front door and stared at the drifts of snow covering his car. It had fallen heavily during the night and reached the halfway mark on the garden wall. The children rushed down the stairs and joined him at the door. Even in the middle of winter there had never been such snow.

Mrs Lotts had turned on the television to see the weather forecast but it seemed as if the snow was also falling inside the television. White dots filled the screen and the weather forecaster's voice was distorted or, thought Josh nervously, increasing the volume, it sounded frighteningly like Gridelda's high shrieks. The same sound emerged from the radio.

"It's going to be impossible to leave the house today," said Mr Lotts, sitting down to breakfast. "I'd better ring the office and explain the situation." But the house phone and his mobile had stopped functioning. "We're marooned," he groaned. "Trapped."

"Somehow, I don't think so," said Mrs Lotts, keeping watch by the kitchen window. "The snow has stopped and the sun is coming out. Crazy weather."

Sunshine spilled into the kitchen. Soon all the windows were open and the snow outside melted so fast it looked like the road outside the gate had turned into a crystal stream. Steam arose from the damp earth and formed dark clouds. A wind began to blow. The clouds heaved and clashed and created great peals of thunder.

"It's Gridelda's doing," said Josh, watching the rain falling. "She's demonstrating what will happen when she controls the seasons."

"Do you think she suspects we've found the map?" said Michael.

"Not unless she checks the hidden drawer," said Josh. "And Forester put the table back in exactly the same position."

"I give up," said Mrs Lotts, slumping into her chair and buttering a bagel. "I'm emigrating to the Caribbean."

As she always said this when the weather did not suit her mood, her children paid no attention, and their father continued to read his paper.

"Well, it looks like my aunt can begin work on the woods soon," he said, folding his paper and laying it on the table beside his plate. "I expect she will shortly have a phone call from the county council giving permission for the felling of the woods to begin."

Josh picked up the paper and read the opening sentence: *Dr Goyle, a world-renowned specialist in tree diseases, fears human contamination from diseased trees in Merryville Woods.* A photograph had been inserted underneath the headline.

"Can I see that?" Beth snatched the paper from his hand then jerked her thumb upwards.

Her brothers followed her upstairs to her bedroom.

"Dr Goyle is the man in the painting," she hissed. "That means he's Shift."

"I'm off, children," Mr Lotts shouted up the stairs. "Better make haste before the weather changes its mind again."

"Bye, Dad." Josh and Michael leaned over the banisters and waved at their father.

"Bye, Daddy, bye." Beth ran down the stairs and hugged him.

His mobile phone rang as he was opening the hall door. "Yes . . . yes, Aunt Graves." He made a resigned face at Beth and held the phone away from his ear for a few seconds before continuing his conversation. "When do you expect work to begin? Tomorrow morning. I see . . . I see. . . Yes, Aunt Graves. I'm already late for work due to the snow. Goodbye." He clicked off his phone and sighed. "That dreadful woman. What difference does a day make? The work can't begin until tomorrow and she's carrying on as if there was going to be a six-month delay."

The boys were already running down the stairs to join Beth in the hall.

"Quick, before the weather changes again, we'd better get to the woods," said Josh. "We're going to play," he shouted at his mother, who popped her head out from behind the kitchen door.

"Stay close to the house in case it snows again," she warned. "Take your scarves and hats just in case." But the children were already running down the garden path. This time they did not bother going the long way round to the woods. It didn't matter who saw them. Soon there would be no woods for trespassers to be prosecuted. As soon as they came within sight of Merryville Manor, Josh yelled, "Bellatinks! Bellatinks! Bellatinks!"

She came immediately and tapped her fingers. A mist

descended over the manor and hid the children as they ran past the grim walls. When they reached the hedgerow, Forester was waiting for them.

"Gridelda has declared a great war," he said. "She is assembling her army of ghouls to fight us for the remaining shards. The disloyal goblins in Icefroztica are also assembling behind her. Come quickly. Queen Glendalock needs you now."

The butterflies were waiting to carry them to the castle. As they flew over Brightisclearen, the children could see how the usual peaceful countryside had changed. Fairy children were inside their houses, the doors locked. Ranks of soldiers, wearing padded armour made out of leaves and twigs, were gathering in the castle courtyard. There was silence amongst them, as they concentrated on the battle that lay ahead.

The queen greeted them sadly and invited them to sit at the Meeting Table.

"Tomorrow morning the chainsaws begin their work," said Josh. "Permission has been granted to cut down every tree."

The queen nervously flapped her wings and gazed deep into the eyes of each child. "Josh, Michael and Beth, we are depending on you."

She clapped her hands and the fairy guarding the metal chest unlocked it and removed the scroll. At the queen's command he handed it to Josh. "Search for the shards of Duskcanister and Icefroztica while we do battle to defend the Tree of Seasons," said the queen. "You will be protected by your three gifts. Once the shards are recovered, and the rightful rulers restored to power, Gridelda's reign is at an end."

They bid the queen goodbye and flew from her kingdom, escorted by Bellatinks and Forester.

"We need to act fast," said Bellatinks. "As soon as we reach the woods, I'll use my magic to transport us to where the first shard is hidden."

They walked through the door leading into the woods. The air was heavy and still, as if the trees had taken a deep breath and were afraid to release it. A mist lay everywhere, making it difficult to see.

"The calm before the storm," said Forester.

"I'm going to use my powers of transportation," said Bellatinks. "When you open your eyes you will be in Echo Cove. Let the search begin."

In Merryville Manor, Gridelda opened the door of a gardening shed where once the tools for digging, hoeing, pruning and clipping hung from hooks, and potting plants had lined the long trestle table. Now it was occupied by the white stallion and Johnny Welts. The whites of the stallion's eyes were visible and he nickered nervously, jerking his head to one side when she touched him with her cane.

"Johnny Welts, crawl out now," Gridelda hissed.

The boy crawled on his hands and knees along the floor. He looked skinny and sickly as he raised his pallid face to Gridelda. Dark shadows ringed his eyes.

"Please, let me drink the strength potion," he whispered hoarsely. "I'm weak and ill."

"You are weak." Gridelda pulled him to his feet and shook him so hard his head jerked backwards. "You allowed the girl to escape and destroyed my plan to recover the Chalice of Elentra."

Johnny staggered backwards when she released him and joined his hands together. "Please, Gridelda, I'll do anything you ask. Just give me the potion."

"You must earn your rewards, Johnny Welts. Protect what is mine and then I will reconsider." When she had given him his instructions and he had been whisked from sight on the back of the white stallion, she called for Shift.

"Carry me to my kingdom," she said. "It is time."

From the balcony of her grey stone castle, Gridelda addressed her army. "Carry your weapons proudly," she shrieked. "You are fighting for a splendid victory. To rule the seasons is the ultimate power we can achieve. Be merciless. Seize the Chalice of Elentra! Seize the Shard of Spirit! Seize the Shard of Light! Strike down anyone who moves from the doorways of Brightisclearen and New Blossomdale. Tomorrow, when the Tree of Seasons is reduced to a pitiful, useless stump and its roots wither in the grip of poison, we will be invincible."

Her voice rang throughout the land that had once gleamed with the rich colours of autumn but now lay in the final stages of decay. Her army cheered, ghouls standing shoulder to shoulder with goblins, each sharing only one thought. Victory.

# 15

# an encounter with a sea witch

Michael loved the seaside. Brittas Bay, Bray, Silver Strand: these were just some of the beaches he visited every summer to swim and play football with Josh on the sand. But this beach did not belong to the summer. For a start, the weather was freezing. Snow fell on the sand and the sea looked as if ice was forming on the waves. But that was ridiculous because the sun was shining high in the noon-day sky.

Steep cliffs rose above them and seaweed-covered rocks bulged from the sand. "Quick, keep close together," said Forester, catching Bellatinks in his arms just as the fairy was about to be blown towards the sea. To protect themselves from the biting wind, they followed him to the shelter of an overhanging rock at the foot of the cliff. Josh sat down on the sand and unrolled the map.

"We need your help, Michael," he said.

By now, Michael was a confident wearer of the Ring of Truth. Without hesitation, he said, "We're close to the stolen shards."

The ring glowed red.

Josh muttered under his breath as the wind frisked around the rock and almost tore the map from his hands.

"The shard is hidden under rocks," said Michael. The red hue deepened. He sighed and glanced along the half-moon bay. Rocks, cliffs, lashing waves, seagulls diving into the wind, nests snuggled into every chink of the cliff face.

"The shard is hidden in a seagull's nest." Michael was relieved when the ring remained red. The idea of climbing the cliff and inspecting each nest did not appeal to him.

186

This was a small beach, nothing more than a half-moon cove with steep steps leading down to the sand. Michael suddenly remembered being here once before. It must have been two summers ago when he came with his family for a picnic. The cove had been crowded with families then, noisy with children splashing and swimming in the sea. He had explored a cave with Josh. Beth had come with them as far as the entrance then ran away when Josh made ghoulish noises. The eerie sounds had echoed back at them. Peering through the swirling sand, he tried to remember exactly where it was.

"The shard is in the echoing cave," he said. He watched the red glow flicker and die. For an instant the diamond shone as clear as glass before turning blue.

"Hurray . . . hurray," he shouted, jumping up and down with excitement. The wind blew him over and the snowy sand rose in a great spray, almost blinding him. But he struggled to his feet and took off down the beach, running close to the cliff face. He stopped and consulted the ring again.

It was like the game he used to play when he was younger. Josh would hide something and Michael would have to find it.

"Am I hot?" he'd shout as he searched for the hidden object and Josh would shout, "You're cold! Freezing! Warm! Warmer! Hot! *Boiling* hot." Then it would be Michael's turn and the game would go on until they grew tired playing it. But today he was the only person playing Hot or Cold with the Ring of Truth. He was the only boy in the whole world with such an extraordinary ring and it was up to him to use it wisely.

"I'm close to the echoing cave," he shouted above the wind. The ring flashed red and Michael changed direction, heading back to the opposite side of the cove. As he drew near an outcrop of rocks, the blue rays flashed off the cliff face, sending out a powerful signal. Michael clambered over rocks, his feet slipping on brown slimy seaweed, his knees and hands grazed by shale. He jumped down from the last rock and stared into the open mouth of the cave. The ring cast a blue light into its dank, dark depths. The cave was a lot larger on the inside than it had looked from the outside. Water dripped from the entrance and clumps of brown, bubbly seaweed burst beneath his feet.

He cupped his hands together and yelled back to the others. "I've found it." His voice echoed back, bouncing off the walls and ceiling in the most terrifying way possible.

The sand and snow blew dangerously along the beach as they emerged from shelter and ran towards him. Bellatinks, still unable to fly in the gale, clung to Forester's neck. The small, sturdy man forced his way through the sandstorm and was the first to reach Michael.

"It stinks something awful," gasped Michael. "*Sttttt . . . stttt . . . awwww . . . awwww . . . fullllllll,*" the cave echoed back.

Forester placed Beth in the shelter of the cave and handed out twigs of light to everyone. Now that they could see where they were going, this made walking a little easier. Michael tried to remember how far he and Josh had gone into the cave.

"Not very far," said Josh. "The stink drove us back."

"I can understand why," said Michael, holding his nose. "We're close to the shard," he addressed the ring and the blue hue remained strong. They reached the end of the cave. Nothing to see except gleaming brown walls and the rocky ceiling curving above them.

"Look!" Bellatinks flew close to the wall and vanished from sight.

"Where's she gone?" shouted Forester, holding his twig of light close to the wall.

"*Goooonnnnne*," echoed the cave.

Bellatinks reappeared through a slit in the wall so narrow that none of the others had noticed it.

"I can see an icy-blue sheen beyond the wall," she whispered. "I think it's the Shard of Frost."

Immediately Forester began to chant.

> "*Cave of echoes, if you will,*
> *Please bestow no harm or ill*
> *On those who've worked so long and hard*
> *To find the precious winter shard.*"

Immediately the clumps of seaweed clinging to the wall began to move. They pressed their slimy suckers deep into the chink Bellatinks had discovered. The rock groaned and the echo rumbled so loudly that the children, their hands over their ears, crouched down, terrified the cave was going to collapse on top of them.

"Don't be frightened," said Forester. "The seaweed is our friend."

Michael looked up and saw that the chink had widened to allow them passage into an interior cave that was filled with a pulsating silvery-blue glow. Their footsteps echoed even louder as they moved forward. In the distance, a more intense light flowed from a small pointed object that throbbed like a heartbeat. It reminded Michael of a piece of broken glass, with sharp edges and a pointed tip.

"The Shard of Frost," breathed Bellatinks. "At last."

Michael was about to run forward when Forester grabbed him by his arm.

"Wait, Michael. Be careful," warned Forester. "Remember what Queen Glendalock told us. Now that we are within sight of the shard, we face grave dangers. We must stay close together and watch out for traps."

Even as he spoke, Michael fell forward, his hands sinking into piles of mulching seaweed. He thought he was going to keep sinking, that he would disappear beneath the rotting kelp and nobody would ever find him again. Forester grabbed his tee-shirt and yanked him to his feet. For such a little man he had powerful strength. Michael's heart pounded as he rubbed the mulch from his hands and knees.

"Thanks, Forester," he gasped. "I thought I was going—"

Forester, interrupting him, put his finger to his lips. In the distance they heard a noise. They drew closer together, straining to hear.

"It sounds like someone is crying," whispered Forester.

"Then it could be someone who needs our help," said Michael. "Someone in danger. Come on. Let's find out."

"Or someone has set a trap," said Bellatinks. "Be careful." She tilted her head to one side and listened again. "I have a plan." She nodded to Beth. "The sound is coming from the direction of the shard. Let's get closer and hide behind that corner." She pointed towards a section of rock that jutted out from the wall. "Then Beth can use her power of invisibility to find who's crying."

They moved as silently as possible towards shelter then, when they were out of sight, Beth clutched her necklace.

Michael only had a fleeting glimpse of her face, frightened but resolute, before she disappeared. It still startled him, the way she could become invisible in an instant. He wanted to shout out, "Beth, come back. Let me see that you're safe," but all he could do was huddle beside Josh and hope that his sister would once again survive Gridelda's evil magic.

Nothing could be as scary as being a prisoner in Gridelda's house. Beth moved forward from the protection of her brothers and the enchanted people. The icy glare from the shard was now so fierce she had to shield her eyes. She had thought the shard was floating in mid-air but as she drew nearer she realised it was positioned on the edge of a rocky ledge. The weeping grew louder, a high echoing keen that sent goosebumps running along her arms, especially when she realised a beautiful young girl was crouching before the shard. The girl was trying desperately to pull away from it but it seemed to have a magnetic power that drew her ever closer to its pulsing light. Ice radiated from the shard and the silvery glow revealed the girl's terror. Her glossy, black hair fell to her waist in a plait. Her face was heart-shaped with wide-set blue eyes. They were filled with tears. Beth was reminded of the children's faces engraved on the Chalice of Elentra and how their tears had coursed just as violently down their cheeks. Beth reckoned that the girl was about her own age. If they went to school together, Beth just knew they would be best friends. She longed to run forward and drag the girl to safety. But the shard could trap them both and she knew enough about Gridelda's cruelty not to take risks. Had Gridelda taken the girl's joy and turned it into an essence for the chalice? Anything was possible. The girl's sobs grew louder.

"Help me . . . someone please help me," she pleaded.

Beth forced herself to turn away from her cries and run back to the group.

"Whew!" Josh's expression turned from anxiety to relief when she clutched the necklace and reappeared. "I'm always frightened you won't come back."

"It's not a trap," she told them. "There's a young girl beside the shard. It's drawing her nearer and nearer to the edge. She needs our help. We have to rescue her."

Forester called on the children to wait but they ran from cover. The girl's cries were louder. They rebounded off the walls and the roof, creating a petrifying echo.

"Don't worry," Josh called out to her. "We're going to rescue you."

The girl wiped her eyes in amazement and looked

towards them. "Help me," she sobbed. "I'm trapped by the shard. Please help me to escape."

Bellatinks flew close to the girl. "What's your name?" she asked.

"Hannah." The girl continued sobbing. "A woman took me from my home one night and left me here. She promised to come back and bring me to her castle but no one came back . . . until now."

"Did she take your joy?" asked Beth.

"Yes." Hannah sucked in her breath and said, "She told me she had a magical potion I could drink. I would become the cleverest girl in my class. I always wanted to be clever but I'm not . . . and now I'm stuck here and that stone is going to burn me."

"It's the Shard of Frost," said Bellatinks. "It can't harm you."

"You're wrong. It's sharp and dangerous. Please . . . please, pull me away from it before I die. Come nearer . . . please come nearer . . . all of you must help me to escape." Her voice became soft and restful. Like soothing waves lapping off the shore, Beth thought. Everyone moved towards the ledge where she crouched. But Michael stopped and stared at his ring. It was shining brighter than ever, shining with a bright and dangerous crimson.

"Nobody move," he shouted. "Hannah is a trap set by Gridelda. The Ring of Truth never lies." He held it up so that everyone could see its crimson hue.

Everyone froze. Even Bellatinks suspended her wings in mid-flight.

"It must be wrong," cried Beth, who started to run up the rocky steps. The desire to rescue the girl before the shard could harm her was the only thought in her mind.

"Ask it again," shouted Josh.

"Hannah is lying!" Michael stared frantically from the ring to the girl. "She wants to prevent us taking the shard."

Once again the ring sent out its warning signal.

"We can't ignore the ring," said Josh. But Beth – drawn forward by the sorrow in Hannah's deep blue eyes – was unable to stop. She had almost reached the ledge when Josh grabbed her. She struggled fiercely when he carried her back down the steps.

"Come to me, Beth," crooned Hannah. "Don't leave me here on my own. I'm so frightened . . . so frightened."

At the foot of the steps they paused and looked upwards.

"Let me go, Josh," Beth begged. "I have to protect her."

But Josh's arms were hard around her.

"Help me, Michael," he shouted as Beth continued to struggle.

Michael ran forward and held her securely. "You must trust the ring," he panted. "It has never let us down. We're in danger."

As they dragged her further away from the girl, the atmosphere in the cave changed. Hannah's voice was no longer melodic. It began to rise to a wailing chant. "No one gets the shard," she shrieked. "No one gets the shard! No one gets the shard!"

As she chanted, her blue eyes clouded. They turned black as ink, cold as stone. Beth watched horrified as a split appeared in the girl's beautiful face. It ran from her throat all the way up to her glossy hair. Except that her hair was no longer glossy or black. It uncoiled from its plait, becoming a greenish-brown shade that swayed like fronds of seaweed under water. The split in her face widened. Another face lay underneath the shrivelling skin. Her dainty hands swelled, first one finger, then another, her arms becoming puffy, the flesh stretching, as if it could no longer contain her body.

Everyone wanted to look away. What they were witnessing was revolting. The most disgusting thing they had ever seen. But they were rooted to the spot, forced to watch as the skin peeled away from Hannah and another person . . . thing . . . creature . . . emerged.

"It's a sea witch!" Through her terror, Beth heard Forester shouting.

A sea witch. The most dreaded thing Beth had ever imagined *really* existed. The sea witch was old. As old as legends. Her skin was green and glistening, like the ocean when the sun was shining on it. Her black eyes bulged with fury and her straggling seaweedy hair fell like a cloak to her feet. The remains of her skin lay in shreds along the rocky ledge. As she stared at the horror-stricken group, her scornful laughter echoed through the cave. Before anyone could move, she leapt from the ledge and landed beside Beth.

"I've been in your nightmares," she hissed. "But there will be no awakening from this nightmare." She gripped Beth's arm with her scaly hand. Her touch was cold and slimy.

"Josh, your bow!" yelled Forester. "Remember your bow. Use it now."

The sea witch rose in the air with Beth in her arms and perched her on the ledge. Beth was so close to the shard, she could have touched it. She could feel its chill, feel the vibrations of its beat within the rocks. The sea witch held Beth in front of her. The fetid smell from her body was unbearable. Down below Beth could see Josh, the bow in his hand. But he was unable to fire for fear of striking her. He ran from one side to the other but the sea witch swung Beth in the same direction.

Beth remembered something Josh had once told her. Sea witches feasted on human hearts, particularly young hearts. She had chosen Beth because she was the youngest. But when she had torn Beth's heart from her body, she would attack Michael, then Josh. No wonder Gridelda had called on a sea witch to protect the shard.

Beth thought of clutching her necklace and becoming invisible. But that was not a good idea. The sea witch would still hold her captive and Josh would not know where to fire. The shard, as if aware of the tension and fear in the cave, pulsed ever faster. Beth had a sudden longing to touch it. It was the same feeling she had experienced earlier when she thought the sea witch was Hannah. Now she realised that it was the shard that had attracted her, not, as she had believed, the beautiful girl. Suddenly, before the sea witch could stop her, Beth leaned to one side and touched the shard. It was not cold, as she had imagined, nor was it sharp.

As soon as she touched it, the scent of spices was released, nutmeg, cloves and cinnamon. She could smell pine and cedar, and Christmas trees hung with lights. Other smells arose, parsley, sage, thyme, cranberries, roasting turkey, candles burning in the window on Christmas Eve, log fires. So many different smells filled the cave that they banished the fetid smell of the sea witch.

She shuddered and released her grip on Beth. Her breathing was harsh, as if the fresh winter smells had attacked her lungs. She screamed and scrabbled after Beth, chanting at her to stop. When Beth kept running, the sea witch's greenish-brown hair flowed across the ledge and tangled around Beth's legs, tripping her. As Beth fell face down, Josh raised his bow. She knew his eyes were closed and she buried her face in her arms, hoping his aim would be true.

Josh held his arm steady as he drew back the string. Time was precious but he did not rush. Their lives were at stake if he missed. Beth whimpered as the sea witch's slimy hair wound around her legs and held her still. She looked up as the golden arrow flew upwards, almost touching the ceiling before it swerved with unerring accuracy towards the sea witch, who watched, unafraid, as it sped towards her. She held the palm of her scaly hand towards it. Her gaze defied it to come any closer.

At first, the arrow seemed to obey her command. Despite its great speed, it stopped in mid-flight and hovered in mid-air. Beth watched the arrow, expecting it to fall like a stone to the floor. The sea witch's triumphant laughter rang out. The arrow twitched. Instantly, gaining speed, it flew twice around her body then buried itself deep into her heart.

Silence filled the cave. The sea witch's eyes widened. She touched the arrow, her withered face filled with disbelief. Her hair loosened and unwound from Beth's legs. Her huge dark eyes filled with water. Black tears ran down her cheeks. She collapsed to her knees, still clasping the arrow. Her body shuddered violently then her hands fell limply to her side.

The putrid smell had disappeared from the cave and the smells of winter grew stronger. As the life faded from the sea witch's eyes, she looked down at Josh and sighed.

"You have vanquished me," she gasped.

"You would have killed us," shouted Josh.

She nodded slowly. "I would have devoured your hearts . . . and still have wanted more." Her breath whistled harshly as she struggled to continue speaking. "In my long life, I have always hungered for the next victim. But I have never been satisfied." Her voice grew fainter as her head drooped forward, her face almost covered by her dank hair. She parted the strands and stared for the last time at Josh. Her gaze was filled with sorrow. "I have longed for peace but it has never been mine . . . until now. You have recovered the shard. Carry it safely to Icefroztica and release King Darkfrost. Otherwise, you will all perish in the great battle to save the Tree of Seasons." Her face twisted with pain as she ground out her final words. "Gridelda is the enemy of mankind and magic. Don't let her win."

Beth lifted the Shard of Frost and carried it down the steps. Forester accepted it from her and placed it in his satchel. They walked quietly from the cave. Beth looked back once. She held her twig of light upwards. The sea witch was no longer visible. Except for a hank of seaweed slowly rotting on the rocky ledge, she might never have existed.

# 16

# the dragon's egg

When they returned to the beach, the weather had changed. Sunshine danced on the waves. Seagulls swooped over the waves and a tern gazed steadily at them from a rock. The sand had settled into soft drifts and was warm underneath them when they sat down to consult the map. The Shard of Decay was still in the same location.

"Eleven Oaks." Josh read out the name of the village. It sounded vaguely familiar. He tried to remember if he had ever been there. A garden centre . . . yes, he thought . . . there was something about a garden centre. Then he remembered. Before Great Aunt Graves's accident, he had gone there with her and his mother. They bought young trees for their gardens and he had helped to load them into a trailer attached to the car. The village was small, he remembered, with a main street of shops, a petrol station, and the garden centre on the outskirts. After they bought the trees, they'd had coffee in a café. He'd eaten an enormous blueberry muffin. Thinking about the muffin made him realise he was starving. But he mustn't think about earthly things. Not when he was in a mythical place with enchanted people. Try telling that to his stomach. It rumbled loudly. He coughed to cover the sound and it rumbled louder. Bellatinks laughed and tapped her fingers together. Tiny squiggles of light played around her hands.

"Humans have a wise saying," she said. "An army marches on its stomach."

As soon as she stopped tapping her fingers, the children heard a tinkling tune and a van appeared at the far end of

Echo Cove. A large fake cheeseburger was attached to the roof, along with a sign reading, *Wally's Burgers and Chips*. With one accord, the children leaped to their feet and ran towards the van.

"We've no money," wailed Josh, but the jingling in his pockets told him otherwise.

"Thanks, Bellatinks," he shouted back. "Can I get you anything?"

She shook her head and turned her attention back to Forester who kept removing the Shard of Frost from his satchel and staring at it, afraid it would disappear before his eyes.

Wally had a shaved head and tattoos on his arms. He wrapped the chips and burgers in sheets of white paper and took three bottles of 7 Up from the chiller cabinet. "I don't usually stop off in Echo Cove," he said as Josh counted out the money. "Too rocky on the wheels, man. But today the steering wheel kept turning in this direction and the rocks at the entrance are gone. Weird stuff, man. Enjoy the nosh."

"We will, Wally . . . we will," said Beth, lifting the bottles from the counter. Michael grabbed the food. Unable to wait any longer, he tore off the paper and sank his teeth into a juicy cheeseburger.

Josh studied Wally's tattoos. He recognised the Superman emblem.

"You and me, man," said Wally, glancing at Josh's tee-shirt. "Stay cool, man."

Forester was still holding the Shard of Frost when they

returned. "I'm afraid Gridelda will disappear it again," he explained. "Her power is greater than mine."

"That shard is going back to Icefroztica," said Bellatinks. "Did you see how it glowed when you held it? You are the keeper of the Tree of Seasons. The shard trusts you to bring it back to its rightful kingdom."

Forester blushed as he replaced the shard. Everytime Bellatinks spoke to him, he had the same reaction. Josh felt sorry for the little man. With all the magic whizzing around the Tree of Seasons, it was a wonder no one had yet found a spell to prevent blushing.

When they finished eating and had dumped their left-overs in the beach litter bin, Bellatinks gathered them in a circle around her. "We have to find the Shard of Decay before Gridelda discovers what has happened in the cave," she said. "Concentrate on Eleven Oaks. Repeat the name over and over again while I cast my relocation spell."

Bellatinks touched the map. The tiny shard winked urgently. Before Josh closed his eyes, he had a last impression of waves gently rolling towards the shore. Then the stretching sensation dragged against his body and he heard a low humming sound, as if something was moving at great speed. That something was himself and, he hoped, his brother and sister.

When he opened his eyes he was standing in a country lane. The weather was colder but not like the freezing temperatures they had encountered on the beach when they first arrived. This was the cooler air of autumn. The settling in months before the chill of winter settled. The bushes were ripe with juicy blackberries and the overhanging trees filled with russet apples. On either side of the lane, fields of wheat and corn swayed. But with each step they took the ground become more swampy. Their footsteps squelched. Stagnant water oozed upwards between the dead leaves under their feet. Blackberries rotted on the stems. Withered apples fell to the ground. Josh was reminded of the Duskcanister entrance to the Tree of Seasons. The feeling that autumn had moved too quickly from ripeness to decay.

They stopped at the end of the lane. The village of Eleven Oaks lay in front of them. People walked along the main street. They entered shops, emerged again, stopped to talk, parked their cars, lolled on benches. Everything was so normal.

"We're going to attract attention." Josh stared across at Bellatinks, who was perched on Beth's shoulder. He glanced down at Forester. "What should we do?"

"Leave it to Bellatinks," Forester replied.

The fairy flew to the ground and stepped lightly over the decaying leaves until she stood in front of Forester.

"Are you ready?" she asked.

He nodded. "I don't want a moustache this time," he said. "Promise there'll be no moustache."

"If you insist." With a soft tap of her fingers, she and Forester disappeared. Josh jumped back with shock when his parents appeared on either side of him.

"Oh, no, I'm in big trouble now," he muttered, knowing he would be grounded forever for allowing his younger brother and sister to become involved in such a dangerous adventure.

"What do you think, Josh?" His mother spoke with Bellatinks's voice.

"I said *no* moustache," muttered his father. "You always do this to me, Bellatinks."

"But it suits you," said his mother. "Don't you agree, Josh?"

Josh clasped his hands over his ears. "You can't do that, Bellatinks," he protested. "Please be someone else. It's too weird trying to find the Shard of Decay with our parents by our side."

"Just teasing." Bellatinks laughed and tapped her fingers again. Immediately, she turned into a graceful woman with red hair and green eyes. She looked exactly like herself, but without wings. Forester was clean-shaven and over six feet tall. He stared down at his feet, moved one foot, then the other. Satisfied that he was not going to fall over, he strode down the lane, followed by the children and Bellatinks.

Forester consulted the map and pointed across the road towards a small bookshop. "It's over there," he said.

The bookshop was the first building on the main street. Compared to the other shops with their brightly lit windows, the bookshop had a grimy, neglected appearance. Paint had peeled from the window frames and the front door. They stared through the grimy windows. Only a few ancient books with dusty green leather covers were on display.

The bookshop was called Spooky Books. Josh loved spooky books, ghost stories, horror stories, fantasy. He would have remembered if that bookshop had been on the main street when he was here before. When he looked closely at the wall next to the supermarket next door, he realised that there was a narrow lane running between the two buildings. The space was slight. His father would have called it "a hair's breadth". He stared fearfully into the interior of the bookshop, knowing they had come to the right place. What new threats awaited them inside?

The thought of the dead sea witch troubled him. It had been necessary to slay her to save Beth. But he kept thinking about her eyes and the black tears running down her cheeks. She had welcomed death. He hoped she was peaceful now, free from her unending quest for human hearts. Would he have to slay other enchanted creatures to recover the Shard of Decay? The bow quivered in his pocket each time he touched it. He drew courage from its strength.

"Well, I guess we have to go inside and investigate," he said. His voice shook.

"Don't be afraid, Josh." Forester placed his hand on Josh's shoulder. "We have powerful magic on our side."

"I know." It was strange looking up – rather than looking down – at Forester. But his height made no difference. Tall or small, Josh trusted him completely.

They peered through the window. In the dim light Josh could make out a high, old-fashioned counter. The walls were lined with shelves of books. A candle burned in a holder on the counter, throwing a shadowy light over an old man. He sat on a high stool behind the counter, a large book open in front of him. He turned a page and bent his head closer to read the words.

"This is my plan," said Josh, drawing back from sight. "Forester and Bellatinks will pretend to be our parents and tell the old man they want to buy second-hand school books. But we'd better be on our guard. The old man looks harmless but after what happened in the cave we can't trust appearances. Beth, you must become invisible again. When we enter the shop, you come with us and take a good look around for anything suspicious. But stay close to us. Promise."

"I promise," said Beth and touched her necklace.

Josh wished she would give some warning. She disappeared so utterly, it always unnerved him. He felt the warm clasp of her fingers and gripped them tightly as they walked towards the entrance. A bell tinkled when Forester pushed open the door. The old man looked up. He seemed so shocked to see the two adults and two children that he nearly fell off his chair.

Bellatinks cleared her throat and smiled politely at him. "Can you help us, sir? We're looking for second-hand school books for our children. Here's the list." She produced a sheet of paper from her handbag and placed it on the counter.

"I don't sell school books," he said. "My books are rare and expensive. I have nothing here that would interest you."

"But I'm very interested in old books," said Forester in his gruff, manly voice. "Do you mind if I look around?"

Beth squeezed Josh's hand. He wanted to keep holding her but he knew it was time for her to use her invisibility power. Reluctantly, he loosened his fingers and she slipped away. The old man glared suspiciously at Josh and Michael as they walked around the shop, pretending to examine the titles on the books. They stopped in front of a cabinet, not unlike the one in Gridelda's drawing room.

"Make him look the other way," whispered Beth, who was obviously following in their footsteps. Michael grabbed a book from the shelf and returned to the counter. "How much is this?" He leaned over the counter to attract the old man's attention.

The doors rattled slightly as Beth tried to open them. They were locked, except for one on the bottom of the cabinet. A large, white orb, almost translucent, lay inside. Faint red lines were visible through a pearly glaze. It reminded Josh of an old-fashioned gaslight. He thought he heard a sound coming from within it. Checking that Michael was still holding the old man's attention, he bent down to listen.

"It's like a heartbeat." Beth put her lips close to his ears and whispered. "What can it be?"

"I've no idea," Josh whispered back. "Have you seen anything else that's suspicious?"

"No. But there's a door marked *Private*. I'm going to check what's inside."

Josh looked beyond the cabinet and saw the door. The old man looked impatiently at Michael and shook his head. "Put that book back," he shouted. "It's not for sale."

"I was only asking—" protested Michael.

"You heard," snapped the man. "This is my shop. Do as you're told." His voice sounded different, not so quavering or so old. In fact, it sounded so familiar it was like an itch at the back of Josh's mind.

As Michael lifted the book from the counter, he jogged the candleholder and knocked it to one side. The flame went out. As the shadows deepened in the shop, the door marked *Private* opened and closed. The old man was becoming increasingly twitchy. "I'll have to ask you to leave," he said. "I'm closing up for the evening."

"Closing so early?" asked Forester. "But I haven't had a chance to see all your books."

"You have to leave now," snapped the old man. He slammed the large book closed and sneezed when a cloud of dust arose from the pages. "I've got to look after some very important business."

Forester glanced across at Bellatinks, who nodded thoughtfully.

"Do you hear me?" the man snarled. "Leave my shop *immediately.*"

"We hear you," said Bellatinks. "But we won't heed you." She tapped her fingers and released a shower of purple sparks. "*Riffitix parolix spilix,*" she chanted.

Instantly, the man froze. Only his eyes moved. They grew wide with astonishment as Bellatinks changed back to herself and flew behind the counter.

"*Enchanted Spells of Deceit.*" She read out the title of the book the old man had been reading. "Now what can all that be about?" she asked. "Time to take a look inside."

The book opened at her command. Dust arose from the yellow pages. "*How to Deceive a Dragon*," she said. "That's a very ancient spell indeed. Speak to us, old man. Explain why you were so interested in dragons?"

"You'll never get the shard," the old man snarled. "Why do you think my book lay open on the dragon spell?"

"A dragon," gasped Josh and ran towards the door Beth had opened. "Are you telling us there's a dragon guarding the shard?"

"Yes." Beth suddenly reappeared in the doorway. She slammed the door closed but not before a coil of smoke had escaped. It floated upwards and whirled above her head as she ran forward.

"An ancient spell but one that still works powerful magic," said the old man. His gleeful laughter filled the shop. Bellatinks tapped her fingers and silenced him. If anything, he looked even more frightening with his crinkled laugh lines frozen and his mouth hanging open. But his eyes glinted fearfully as he watched Josh turn the door sign to *Closed*. Forester, still in his man guise, lifted the old man and placed him on the floor behind the counter.

"There can't be a dragon down there," gasped Michael as a dark puff of smoke seeped from underneath the door. "How could a dragon get through such a tiny doorway?"

"Spells, I suppose," said Beth. "Anything's possible when there's magic about."

"Indeed," said Bellatinks. "But dragons usually do no evil. Normal magic doesn't work on them. There's something suspicious going on here. What did you see, Beth?"

"It was so dark I had to use my twig of light," said Beth. "But there is a dragon down there. It's fast asleep so I was able to get really close. Strange thing is . . ."

She stopped, puzzled.

"Go on," said Bellatinks.

"The dragon seemed to be crying in its sleep."

"A dragon crying?" Michael scoffed. "Dragons breathe flames. They don't *cry*."

"This one was," said Beth. "It was lying in a pool of tears."

"Like Hannah?" asked Josh.

"Hannah's tears fooled me so I don't know if the dragon was only pretending to be sad."

"We'll have to find out," said Forester. "Keep close behind me."

He opened the cellar door. Holding his twig of light aloft, he descended a rickety staircase. The others followed, their eyes stinging as smoke floated towards them. A scorching smell filled the air, catching in their throats and causing the children to cough loudly. But above the sound of coughing, they heard the dragon's sighs and hiccupping sobs.

"I can't breathe." Josh gasped and wiped his eyes. He smelled cinders and ash on his clothes. When Bellatinks tapped her fingers the air immediately cleared. They walked from the foot of the stairs to the end of the cellar where an enormous reptile-like creature lay stretched on the floor. The dragon's skin was orange with spiky scales running from its head to its tail. Two horns grew from either side of its head. Fat tears oozed from under its leathery eyelids.

Bellatinks flew so close she was almost blown off course by the dragon's breath. "This is a female dragon," she said, pointing to the breasts of the dragon's chest. "And you're right, Beth. She is lying in her own tears."

"The dragon guards the Shard of Decay," said Michael and nodded, satisfied, when the Ring of Truth shone blue. He stepped closer to the sleeping dragon then jumped back in horror when he saw the Shard of Decay clamped between her front claws.

"How are we going to get it back?" Josh whispered nervously.

The dragon stirred, opened one eyelid, then another. She shifted her position and began to rise on legs as wide as tree trunks. Her crinkled skin flapped when she took a step forward. Her eyes still swam with tears. She flung back her powerful head and bellowed. The staircase began to shake so violently it seemed in danger of collapsing.

"Don't move," ordered Bellatinks. "I'm going to try the spell from the old man's book." Her wings twitched nervously as the dragon's eyes narrowed and swivelled in her direction. "*Dragtatious opendom mindintrim sedatious,*" she intoned.

Instead of charging towards her, the dragon sank down again and stared mournfully ahead.

"It's like she's lost something precious," said Josh.

"I'll ask the ring." Michael held out his hand. "The dragon has lost something really important." The ring shone blue but did not offer any clue as to what that was.

The children tried to think of things that might be important to a dragon. Michael suggested magical wings, a dragon cave, fire breath, titbits to eat like lions and tigers or even humans, but the ring flashed red each time.

In desperation Josh stared at the dragon. The colour of her skin reminded him of a full moon in autumn. An orange moon that looked close enough the touch the rooftops. He whispered in Michael's ear.

"The dragon wants her egg," shouted Michael and grinned as the ring spread its blue light over the dark, tear-filled corner.

Josh ran back up the stairs. He glanced over the counter to check that the old man was still tied up. His eyes seemed different, not so old and rheumy any more. But there was no time to think about anything other than his mission. He opened the cabinet door and carefully lifted out the pearly orb. It filled his arms. The faint orange lines had deepened and the throbbing heartbeat was louder than before.

It's her egg, he thought. That's why she was bellowing. Gridelda must have taken it from her and forced her to guard the Shard of Decay instead.

"You think you're so clever, Josh Lotts." The old man's voice came from behind Josh's shoulder. Except that, like his eyes, his voice no longer quavered. It was strong and gloating, and no longer tugged at Josh's memory. It was so annoyingly familiar that he carefully placed the egg back into the cabinet before spinning round, his fists raised. As he suspected, the old man no longer existed. Johnny Welts stepped back on his toes and swayed, his left fist reaching out to catch Josh on his jaw. Josh stumbled back against the cabinet. The egg wobbled and almost fell to the floor. Recovering, he aimed at Johnny's cheek and landed a blow that almost knocked the bigger boy to the ground. They were used to fighting each other. Usually they fought surrounded by other boys yelling encouragement, knowing they only had a short time to fight before one of the teachers arrived and dragged them apart. Now, there was no one to yell or drag them apart – and this added an extra urgency to the fight. Breathing heavily, they punched the air and sometimes each other, stepping in and stepping out, each one determined to land the knockout blow.

Bellatinks flew from the cellar and gasped, taking in the scene in an instant.

"No magic," shouted Josh, as she began to tap her fingers. "This is between him and me."

Johnny, noticing the fairy, dropped his guard for an instant. It was enough for Josh. Suddenly Johnny Welts lay sprawled on the floor. He tried to rise, swaying on his hands and knees. He shook his head. Blood dripped from his nose.

"Gridelda will destroy me," he gasped before his arms gave way and he collapsed, unconscious. Josh had no time to feel triumphant, nor any desire to do so.

"Let's hope he stays out cold until we escape," he gasped.

"I'll make sure he does," Bellatinks replied and scattered a shower of purple sparks over Johnny's sprawled body.

"Check the dragon spell of deceit," said Josh as he once again lifted the egg and carried it down the cellar stairs.

"I'm going to place the egg beside her," he said to Michael. "Get ready to snatch the shard from her claws."

"Who, me?" Michael gulped and looked in horror at the dragon's massive paws.

"Yes, you," snapped Josh. "Unless you want Beth to do it."

Michael stiffened with indignation and took a step towards the dragon. She snorted, breathing smoke from her nostrils. Michael leaped two steps back as flames licked along the floor.

Bellatinks flew around the dragon and muttered something into her scaly ear. The dragon roared once more, a sound so powerful it almost lifted them from their feet.

The stairs began to groan. Cracks appeared in the cellar wall. "If she roars again, the shop will collapse," cried Beth.

"Michael, stand behind me," ordered Josh. Cautiously, he approached the dragon, the egg held out before him.

The dragon's eyes opened wide and fastened on the egg. She glanced down at the winking shard and lifted it in her claw. Josh and Michael ducked as the shard flew over their heads and smashed against the opposite wall.

The dragon arose on all fours and lowered her head, her horns pointing directly at Josh. He held her gaze as he bent down, gently placing the egg between her two front paws.

Michael ran to the shard and lifted it. Immediately the

cellar was filled with the smell of ripe apples and plums, juicy blackberries, woodsmoke, and the drifts of autumn leaves slowly starting to decay.

"Run," shouted Forester as the dragon clutched her egg and bellowed with joy. The cracks widened in the walls. Loose plaster showered them like snow. They raced up the steps. Behind them, they heard the staircase collapsing. The windows fell in, shattering glass across the floor. The front door fell off its hinges. The roof lifted and took off across the sky. The dragon, her egg clutched firmly between her paws, spread her wings and flew upwards.

The walls began to buckle. Cement dust flew everywhere, making it almost impossible to see.

"Forester, take the book of spells," shouted Bellatinks and watched anxiously as Forester shoved the book into his satchel.

Josh had reached the open doorway when he remembered Johnny Welts. He ran back and found him still unconscious, his body covered in falling debris. Staggering under the weight of the bigger boy, Josh lifted him on his shoulders.

"Hurry, Josh," screamed Beth. "The walls are falling down."

Josh coughed, dust clogging his throat. He collapsed on his knees. He was aware of voices calling him but there was no strength left in his legs. Michael ran back into the shop and grabbed Johnny. Together they carried the unconscious boy outside and laid him in front of the supermarket entrance.

"What's happened to him?" A woman stopped on her way into the supermarket. She stared at Johnny, unaware that a bookshop was collapsing right beside her, stirring up clouds of dust and creating a pyramid of bricks. She also seemed unaware – as were all the other shoppers gathering around Johnny – that a dragon, clutching her egg and breathing great flames of relief, was flying directly overhead.

"Call an ambulance," someone shouted.

"It's on its way," a second voice shouted back. Within seconds Josh heard the faint wail of a siren drawing closer.

"Time to go," said Bellatinks.

When they opened their eyes, the scorching smell had disappeared from their clothes and they were lying in a field of sweetly scented lavender.

Bellatinks flew towards a stem of lavender and perched on the flowering head. "I'm going to break the good news to Queen Glendalock," she said.

The slender lavender stem swayed as she closed her eyes and made mind-contact with her queen.

Forester, back to his normal size, took the shard from Michael and placed it in his satchel. "We must make haste and return the shards to the Tree of Seasons," he said. "Now, the most dangerous task of all lies before us."

"The most dangerous?" moaned Josh, thinking about the sea witch and the dragon. What could be more dangerous?

"We have the shards but Gridelda still reigns over Duskcanister and Icefroztica," said Forester. "We have to free the rightful rulers and place the shards in their keeping. But for now, we must rest amongst the lavender and recover our strength."

In a low voice he said,

> *"Lavender blue, please help us renew*
> *Our vigour and strength to pursue*
> *Gridelda who breaks all nature's true rules*
> *Helped by Shift and her army of ghouls."*

As soon as Forester finished his verse, the children's eyes grew heavy. Michael yawned and lay back with his arms behind his head. Beth curled in a ball and stuck her thumb in her mouth, a habit she had finally broken when she was five years old. Josh closed his eyes and breathed in the fresh scent of lavender.

Why did he feel sorry for his sworn enemy, Johnny Welts? He was in Gridelda's power and would be severely punished for not protecting the Shard of Decay. But that was not Josh's business. Still and all . . . the idea of being in trouble with Gridelda was terrifying. His eyes closed. He thought of the time he had watched Johnny Welts being beaten up by bigger boys on the bus. He had wanted to stop the fight but he had been afraid to stand up to the bullies. The next time anyone had tried to bully Johnny Welts, they had landed in a heap on the ground. No one understood how he suddenly became so strong. Mystery solved. Gridelda had taken his joy and exchanged it for strength. Beth had told her brothers everything that had taken place in Merryville Manor. Johnny Welts was Gridelda's slave and on two occasions he had let her down. Guarding the shard had probably been his last chance. Josh watched the lavender stem swaying as Bellatinks reported to her queen. When would the battle begin? Could they possible save the Tree of Seasons from destruction?

The sky was streaked with peachy clouds and twilight shadows were settling over the lavender fields when Josh awoke. Beth and Michael stirred shortly afterwards.

"I feel as if I've been sleeping for days," said Michael. "I could climb a mountain and run down the other side."

"I could swim across the Irish Sea," boasted Beth.

"I could race fifty of the fastest lions in the world and win." Josh joined in the boasting competition and the three of them laughed when Michael's ring flashed red . . . red . . . red.

Beth whispered urgently in Forester's ear. He shook his head violently but she persisted. Whatever did she want? Josh could just imagine her pleading, "Please, Forester, please . . . please . . . *pretty* please . . ."

Finally, Forester, knowing he had met his match, shrugged, and said:

> "*Oh, Rose that blushes with my love*
> *Please help me to compose*
> *The words I wish to speak aloud*
> *To one who' d make me proud*
> *If she would hold her hand in mine*
> *And both our hearts entwine.*"

the dragon's egg

Immediately, a tiny rose bush thrust upwards through the lavender and filled the air with a heady scent.

"Go on." Beth nudged him firmly. "Do it now."

Josh and Michael threw their eyes upwards in disgust as Forester picked the most beautiful red rose and presented it to Bellatinks.

"That is *so* cheesy," groaned Michael.

"Pass the vomit bucket," agreed Josh.

But they kept their voices low because it seemed a shame to dim the pleasure in Bellatinks's eyes as she accepted the rose and raised it to her lips.

Beth smiled, well pleased with her matchmaking skills.

But the time for love games was short. Bellatinks had grave news. "Queen Glendalock's faith in you has been rewarded. She is relieved and happy that the shards are now in our possession. But the armies are assembling and she needs me by her side."

"We'll go with you." Josh frowned and touched his bow, anxious to defend the kingdom of Brightisclearen.

"I must go along," said Bellatinks. "Gridelda does not realise you have recovered the shards. Queen Glendalock requests that you return the Shard of Frost to Icefroztica. When King Darkfrost is freed, he will gather his army around him and help defend the tree."

"But how will we manage without your magic?" asked Michael.

"Forester has a powerful book of spells in his satchel," said Bellatinks. "He will use them when the time is right. But now I must protect you from discovery when you move through the warriors who are now raging a fierce battle around the Tree of Seasons."

She removed the book from Forester's satchel. Her eyes skimmed over the pages and stopped when she found the spell she wanted. As she spoke her enchanted language, a metallic light ascended from the book and hovered above the children's heads before disintegrating and falling like shimmering rain over their heads.

"You are protected," Bellatinks declared as the silvery grains disappeared. She picked up her rose and spread her wings. "Are we ready to be transported to the Tree of Seasons?"

The children nodded. "I won't be with you when we reach our destination," said Bellatinks. "But I'll be watching over you and we will soon meet each other again."

With one accord, everyone looked at the lavender fields for the last time. How serene and safe they'd felt as they lay in that waving sea of blue. As the sweet fresh scent wafted around them, they drew it into their nostrils. Then they closed their eyes and were swept towards the tree by the spell of relocation.

# 17

# danger in icefroztica

The woods had turned into a battlefield. Everywhere they looked, they saw small, fierce warriors fighting. Gridelda's ghouls fought side by side with goblins. Facing them, the fairies and elves flew from branch to branch, or landed lightly on the ground, their weapons clashing or silently gliding through the air.

No one paid any attention to them as they approached the entrance to the tree. Nor were any arrows, flaming twigs or axes aimed in their direction. Josh longed to join in the fight. His hand was hot from holding his bow but Forester's calm voice urged him to hurry. Beth was weeping, her hands over her eyes as a fairy warrior was stabbed with a stake. Immediately, two elves ran with a stretcher, gauzy as a spider's web, and lifted the fallen warrior onto it.

"The elves will heal him," Forester comforted her and glared across at the goblin who had inflicted the blow. "His name is Crush," he said. "He helped Gridelda to steal the Shard of Frost and imprison his king."

"Why can't they see us?" she asked.

"It's Bellatinks's spell," Forester explained. "Each side sees us as one of their own. Hurry . . . we're almost there."

The children kept close to Forester as they approached the Tree of Seasons. Two goblin guards with scarred faces, and armed with axes, stood to attention at the entrance to Icefroztica.

"I'll do the talking," said Forester. "Don't show any fear. Remember, they are seeing us as goblins."

The goblins looked suspiciously from Forester to the children then lifted their axes, clashing the handles together and criss-crossing them.

"Where do you think you're going?" The goblin who spoke was slightly taller than his companion. A thick scar ran from his eye to the edge of his chin.

"We have been ordered to protect the castle of Icefroztica," replied Forester. "Commander Crush has received a report that an attempt will be made to free King Darkfrost."

The goblins looked at each other and lifted their axes even higher. "Commander Crush has not relayed that information to us."

"Commander Crush is leading a battle charge against the enemies of Icefroztica," Forester calmly replied. "If you wish to contact him, I'm sure he will explain the situation to you."

The goblins shifted uneasily and glanced towards the battlefield. The smaller goblin raised a bushy eyebrow at his companion, who shrugged. They uncrossed their axes and the taller goblin unlocked the door into Icefroztica. Once they were inside, the door was abruptly slammed behind them.

The tunnel they entered could not have been more different than Brightisclearen. Transparent icicles, large as stalactites, hung from the ceiling. Their feet skidded on ice and they had to walk cautiously, holding on to each other, towards the end of the tunnel. No scented flowers, or rose bowers, nothing except a chill wind that whistled so fiercely it was almost impossible to move through the tunnel at times.

"Come on," said Forester, "We need to keep going."

"I ca . . . ca . . . *n't* go any fu . . . fu . . . *further.*" Beth's teeth chattered so much she was hardly able to finish speaking.

"It's time for the ice charm," said Forester and delved into his satchel. He removed the spell book and quickly scanned the pages. He cleared his throat and said, "*Warmenta insidentra sunnelfa withinstat.*"

A ball of light, similar to a tiny sun, shone from the page then lifted into the air. As it began to grow, its rays moved in every direction before splitting into four circular sections. Each threw out rays of heat so hot that the icicles began to melt. Suddenly, and without warning, the miniature suns flew rapidly towards the children and Forester, slamming into their chests and flinging them backwards onto the icy ground.

Josh was the first to rise. He offered his hand to Beth who struggled to her feet.

"Well that certainly did the trick," she said. Already, the colour was returning to her lips and her teeth no longer chattered. Everyone hurried towards the brighter light at the end of the tunnel.

"Wow." Josh's mouth opened in astonishment at the scene that greeted them. They were surrounded by enormous mountains of ice and the gales, blowing through the kingdom, whirled the snow into strange, eerie drifts. Their footsteps were muffled as they walked forward but when Josh looked back, they had left no footprints in the snowy wastes. Nothing else stirred, no tree or bush, no startled reindeers or prowling polar bears. The warmth of the lavender fields seemed like a dream but the spell kept them warm. Josh shielded his eyes against the glare of snow and stared into the far distance. The sun was hidden behind a covering of white cloud. Looking towards the horizon, it was impossible to see where the earth ended and the sky began. At first, Josh was unsure if shadows were playing over the highest mountain top. But as he continued to stare, the shape became clearer. Was it a castle? he wondered, before it disappeared, hidden by a drifting cloud. Then he saw it again. Definitely a castle, tall and splendid with round towers and tall pointed roofs where pennants flew. The curved walls shimmered, as if carved from a single block of ice.

"Is that where we have to bring the Shard of Frost?" Josh pointed upwards towards the castle.

One by one the others noticed it. Beth's eyes shone with excitement as she stared upwards, taking in this wonderful sight.

Forester nodded. "It was once the home of King Darkfrost and the rulers that reigned before him. Gridelda and her ghouls, and the goblins who turned traitor, occupy it now."

"Did all the goblins betray their king?" asked Michael.

"Many remained loyal but they were forced into hiding," Forester replied, his footsteps dragging in the snow. Sweat rolled down his forehead and his cheeks were red with exertion. Sometimes the snow was so deep that he almost disappeared under it and had to be helped forward by the children.

"This was once a welcoming kingdom," he panted. "Winter blossoms grew wild and free. Spruce and pine covered the mountain slopes. The goblins and their king created a season that brought warmth to the hearts of humans but now, if Gridelda wins this war, this bleak vision is your future. We must reach the castle before the battle ends."

"But how are we supposed to climb up there?" Josh stared in dismay at the sheer, steep mountainside.

"Gridelda's magic is at work here," said Forester. "When I visited Icefroztica in the past, the steps leading to the entrance were carved into the ice and entry to the castle was easily gained."

"See if there's a spell," said Beth. "Maybe we can summon the butterflies."

"They'd perish in these conditions," said Forester. He removed the spell book from his satchel. No sooner had he opened the book than a gust of wind snatched it from his hands. The children tried to run after it but it skittered like a kite and rose into the air.

"What now?" sighed Beth.

"Let me think . . . let me think." Forester lifted his cap and scratched his head. For the first time they heard uncertainty in his voice. He was in an alien land where trees or plants could not survive, or respond to his magical verses.

"I saw something move," whispered Beth. She pointed towards the valleys of snow but nothing stirred except their breath puffing before their faces.

"It's your imagination," said Michael. "There's nothing here but snow and ice."

"Look." Beth pointed towards a mound of snow. "I'm sure there's someone looking at us."

They walked closer to the mound and discovered a low dome-like shape. It barely rose above the level of the snow yet when they looked closer, they realised there was an entrance with steps leading downwards into darkness.

"Is it an igloo?" asked Josh. "I though igloos sat on top of the snow."

"This one wants to be unnoticed," said Forester. "Curious. Very curious indeed."

As they stood staring, a goblin's head appeared.

"Who are these mortals?" he demanded, mounting the last steps and standing before the entrance. He was dressed in a fur cloak with leather trousers and a shaggy wool jumper. His boots reached his knees and an axe was strapped to his side. He showed no fear as he walked towards the children then glanced enquiringly at Forester. "How do they possess the power to survive in Icefroztica?"

The goblin could see their true identity. Bellatinks's spell of deceit must have worn off. Josh pulled his bow from his pocket and felt it fit securely into his hands. He raised it and aimed it at the goblin. His fingers quivered. If he closed his eyes and visualised the goblin's heart, the golden arrow would fly straight to its target, as it had done in the sea witch's cave. He shuddered and shied away from the memory.

The goblin made no effort to reach for his axe. Instead, he raised his hands in a gesture of surrender. He did not look frightened. Nor did his eyes carry the anger or fierceness the children had earlier witnessed when they passed the battling goblins.

Forester stood in front of the children and spoke quietly. "Put the bow away, Josh. The goblin sees our true identity. I suspect he is friend, not foe." He glanced at Michael. "Let the truth be known, Michael."

"The goblin standing before us is our friend," said Michael. "He will not harm us." The diamond flashed a blue haze across the frozen drifts.

The goblin's eyes widened as he stared at the ring. "I've heard of this ring," he said. "It is only presented to those who are courageous and truthful. You are welcome to Icefroztica, although there is little warmth or welcome to be had in this desolate kingdom."

"The children are on a mission to save the Tree of Seasons," said Forester. "What is your name?"

"Griten," answered the goblin. "One of King Darkfrost's most loyal subjects."

"King Darkfrost's subjects are fighting alongside Gridelda's ghouls," said Forester. "How many have remained loyal to him?"

"A sizable number," said Griten. "But we live in hiding, outnumbered by Gridelda's ghouls and the traitor goblins." He gestured towards the igloo. "We have built a snow fort for protection and have been forced to watch our kingdom become trapped by ice and wind." He gestured towards the entrance. "Come with me and I will tell you my story."

Forester looked from the dome to the high, unreachable castle. "Time is not on our side. We need to reach the castle and rescue King Darkfrost before darkness falls."

Faintly, over the snow, they heard voices shouting, cheering, the clash of steel, the thud of wood.

"Quick!" Griten ushered them towards the igloo. "The entrance to Icefroztica has been opened. Our enemies approach."

He led the children and Forester down the steps into a cavernous room with a network of snow tunnels leading off in many directions. The room was lined with rows of benches carved from ice and arranged in a semicircle. It was obviously a meeting room and the benches faced a high platform. Griten removed his fur cloak and hung it on a curved icicle protruding from the wall.

"Please sit and tell me how you reached Icefroztica," he said. "I have served King Darkfrost for almost a hundred years but in that time I've never seen mortal children in his kingdom."

"Our story can wait." Forester swept his arm around the room. "Is this where the loyal goblins gather?"

"This is our assembly point since our council chambers were taken from us," said Griten. "I was King Darkfrost's chief advisor and we had many loyal council members. We worked in harmony to bring the season of winter to the mortal world. We tried to choose wisely, although mortals often interfered with our decisions. The climate we ordained was not always what we planned. One evening during a meeting about the distribution of snow we were attacked by Gridelda's army. We had no prior warning, no time to defend ourselves. Our guards at the entrance to the castle were slain and the doors to the council room burst open. A monstrous thing entered. We would later discover his name was Shift. Smoke billowed from his nostrils and he kept changing shape. We could not tell if he was dragon or gargoyle. He was followed by Gridelda. She flung her cloak over her shoulder and marched straight up to the king's throne. When his guards moved to defend him, she froze them to the spot. She informed King Darkfrost that she had achieved the power to exist outside her season in the mortal world. We were astonished. No one, no matter how powerful, can survive outside the Tree of Seasons when their season has ended. She tempted the king, promised to share her power with him if he would hand over the Shard of Frost.

"When he refused, knowing she lied and had no intention of sharing power, she laid waste to his kingdom. Shift set fire to the forests, and her ghouls ransacked our homes. Our goblins, men and woman alike, fought bravely. But others betrayed us, tempted by Gridelda's promises of riches and lands in the mortal world. Foolish goblins. Since then, many have died in battle as they fought to possess the last two shards."

"What has happened to your king?" asked Forester.

"He is frozen in the depths of his castle," replied Griten. "We have tried to rescue him but without the Shard of

Frost we do not have the power to break Gridelda's spell and assail the castle."

The goblin's eyes filled with tears. "My wife Dritin fought bravely by my side. But she was slain by Shift. As she lay dying, she begged me to continue the fight. I have tried to honour her last wishes. Those of us who survived Gridelda's attack hide out in this snow fortress and wait for what . . . ?" He shrugged and spread his hands, helplessly. "Hope? Victory? Vengeance? I will not rest until I avenge Dritin's death. But we are outnumbered and attacked as soon as we emerge into the open. Without the Shard of Frost, we are powerless."

"Not as powerless as you think, Griten." Forester smiled and reached into his satchel. "We have undergone great danger to return this shard to its rightful ruler."

Griten stared in wonder as the shard's blue light reflected off the walls of the igloo. "Can this be true?" His voice shook with joy as he raised his fists in the air and released a triumphant roar.

"As true as we stand before you," said Josh. "But how can we return it to the castle?"

"Come with me." Suddenly Griten no longer looked old and defeated. He grabbed his fur cloak and wrapped it around him. His shoulders straightened and his eyes filled with determination as he mounted the steps. The wind wailed around the mountains but the sounds of battle had died away. "Our enemies are out of sight." Griten beckoned them forward. "It is safe to emerge."

When they were standing in a circle around him, he raised his fingers to his lips and whistled. At least, Josh assumed it was a whistle. The goblin's lips were pursed but no sound emerged. He repeated this action four times then buried his hand back in the folds of his cloak.

"Were you whistling?" asked Beth. "I couldn't hear anything."

"The note is too high for human ears to hear," replied the goblin. "But those who come to our aid have been alerted." Unable to control his joy, he flung off his cloak and turned a perfect cartwheel in the snow. Beth laughed and lunged forward, her head disappearing into the snow as she followed the goblin's example. Josh longed to do the same but such behaviour seemed too childish for a twelve-and-a-half-year-old. Michael, being only ten, did not hesitate. Josh, unable any longer to watch his brother and sister tumbling through the snow, decided that thirteen was the perfect age to become dignified. With a whoop and a holler, he plunged into the snow, surprised to find it as light as thistledown.

Griten straightened up, snow melting on his beard, on his eyelashes, on his mop of curly grey hair. "Listen carefully," he said. "They are coming."

At first, Josh could hear only the wind but gradually the ground began to vibrate. Another sound became more distinct . . . *dud dum dud dum dud dum*. It grew louder until it filled his ears, drawing ever closer.

"What is it?" he asked but Griten just winked and smiled smugly.

"Look!" cried Michael. All eyes followed his pointing finger. Four shapes galloped towards them through the swirling snow. One moment they were indistinguishable then slowly their shapes emerged. Josh could not decide if they were white horses or enormous St Bernard dogs. Their heads were thrown back and their hooves . . . or were they paws? . . . pounded against the snow.

"What are they?" Beth squinted.

"They're cats," said Michael, checking his ring. "Cats," he repeated. "Giant cats."

"Sabre-toothed cats, to be exact," said Griten. "Extinct in the earthly world since the last ice age but we are fortunate to have them in Icefroztica."

The great big cats slowed down to a gentle trot. Their white tusks gleamed and their muscles rippled beneath thick, glossy coats.

"We saved this tribe from extinction," he explained to the children. "Since then, the great sabre-toothed cats have been our friends. When Gridelda invaded our kingdom they camouflaged themselves against the snow and she has been unable to find them. Now they are ready to help restore the natural order to Icefroztica."

The leader of the cats let out such a mighty roar that Josh nervously fingered his bow.

"Have no fear," said Griten, walking towards them. "She is anxious to begin the journey to the castle." At his command, the cats sank down on all fours. The goblin looked small and defenceless beside their massive height. They meekly bowed their heads and allowed him to pat their faces.

"What now?" asked Michael.

"You climb aboard," replied Griten. "They will carry us safely to our destination."

"Wow! This is fantastic." Michael lost no time climbing onto the cat's back. Josh was relieved when Griten told Beth she could sit behind him. Butterflies were nimble enough to catch a falling child but he was not so sure a fleet sabre-toothed cat would notice if she tumbled off and landed in the snow.

"OK everyone," ordered Griten. "Hold on tight to their fur. These cats really know how to travel."

Josh gripped a hank of long, white fur. He jerked backwards as the cat rose and padded across the snow. Griten and Beth led the way but as the pace quickened they soon blended into the frozen, empty landscape. Did it ever stop snowing in Icefroztica? Josh wondered. Was this what his world would become under Gridelda's rule? His fear must have transferred to the big cat who gradually increased her speed. The passing ice sculptures blurred before his eyes. Would anyone believe him if he told them he had ridden bareback on a sabre-toothed cat that was supposed to be extinct since the Ice Age? Would they believe he had slain a sea witch, reunited a dragon with her egg, and travelled through two enchanted kingdoms located inside a tree that was hidden in the centre of Grimsville Woods? Just thinking about it made his head spin.

The cats travelled lightly, silently. No telltale beat or vibration betrayed their whereabouts. Fleetly they raced across the mountain slopes. The peaks loomed above them, glistening high and unassailable. But not to the cats. They dug their claws deep into the snow and bounded upwards, seeking shelter from the lookout guards behind glaciers or sinking out of sight into deep ravines. As they neared the summit of the mountain, the castle was visible in all its splendour. But they had no time to admire its fine lines. The guards continually circled the outskirts, their eyes scanning the slopes for any sign of intruders. The mountain ended on a plateau, smooth and slick as a tabletop.

The cats slowed and silently moved from sight behind one of the turrets. At Griten's low command, they sank on all fours and waited for everyone to dismount.

"Wait here for our return," he said, his eyes constantly searching for the lookout guards. "We have to move forward on foot from now on." He still spoke softly. "I know the layout of the castle inside and out. I also know its secrets."

He walked towards a high wall of ice with icicles glinting as sharp as spears along the top. His fingers moved confidently over the ice blocks. "It's here somewhere," he muttered. "It's a long time since I've used this entrance but I'm sure my memory will not betray me."

They watched anxiously as he continued probing the wall. They could hear voices, harsh and commanding, and marching feet. The sounds seemed very close. Josh looked towards the sabre-toothed cats. Even though he knew where they were lying, he could not see anything, no paw prints, no flashing eyes or gleaming tusks. He wished with all his heart that he could blend just as easily into the snow. Griten was still fumbling among the ice blocks.

"I've found it!" The goblin touched an ice block that had a slight bulge in the centre. He pressed the bulge and a door in the ice wall silently began to swing open.

"Move quickly," the goblin commanded and stepped through the doorway.

Josh was the last to enter. He closed the door behind him and followed Griten along a narrow corridor of thick ice. After a few moments, the goblin stopped in front of a section of wall. He gestured at Forester and the children to stand on either side of him then touched the wall with the tip of his finger. Immediately, as if a window of clear glass had appeared, they could see into a large, high-ceilinged room. It reminded Josh of the assembly room in the igloo, except that this one was far more magnificent. Instead of rows of benches, there were seats with plump cushions and high padded velvet backs. The ceiling was supported by pillars and the walls flickered with an icy-blue light. Like the grand hall in Brightisclearen, sculptured busts of previous goblin kings were on display. These figures were carved from ice and their eyes seemed to stare coldly at Josh, as if they were aware he was staring through the wall. At the end of the room, ice steps led upwards towards a dais with a pillar in its centre. From where Josh stood, it looked as if the pillar was on fire. As his eyes grew accustomed to his surroundings, he realised that the flames were contained within a cage woven entirely from fine strands of ice. Six goblins stood to attention, guarding the dais.

Forester opened his satchel. "Beth, this is the most dangerous task you will have to perform," he said. "The shard belongs in the cage of frost. Use your power of invisibility to restore it to its rightful place."

"We will distract the guards," said Girten. "When their attention is elsewhere open the cage and place the shard within the flames."

Beth swallowed and glanced nervously at Josh.

"But she'll be burned," Josh protested. "Give me the necklace. I'll do it."

Forester shook his head. "The gifts chose their owner, Josh. The necklace knows that Beth has the courage to perform this last task."

"The flames are controlled by the ice," Griten reassured them. "Even when she places her hand directly into the flames, she will only feel a sensation like cold feathers brushing against her arm."

"But what about the goblins—"

"What about your bow?" Griten interrupted him. "You would not have hesitated to use it against me if you thought I meant to harm your brother or sister."

"He's right, Josh. I know you'll keep me safe." Beth swept her finger over her necklace and faded from sight.

Instantly, as if they had responded to an inaudible command, the sabre-toothed cats began to roar.

The goblins spun round and raised their axes, their

ferocious expressions turning to terror as the roars of the giant cats shook the castle.

"Won't the goblins guarding the castle attack them?" said Michael.

Griten shook his head. "They are phantom sounds," he said. "Distractions." He turned a doorknob and edged the door open.

"Be extra careful," whispered Michael as she brushed past him and entered the assembly room.

"I will," she whispered. Already she was moving away from them, invisible except for the Shard of Frost fluttering like a heartbeat in the palms of her hands.

Forester reached into his satchel and drew out the piece of bamboo he used for picking locks. It looked pathetic in his hand compared to the glinting axes Josh could see through the ice window. But he had learned to respect anything Forester carried in his satchel so he listened to the sing-song rhyme.

> "As danger stalks this child who gave
> Her courage bravely in the cave
> Of echoes – where the sea witch dwelled.
> Grant now that evil be expelled.
> Bamboo! Expand to battle length.
> Bamboo! Unleash your mighty strength.
> Bamboo! Strike at those who'd dare
> To touch one strand of Beth Lotts's hair."

Suddenly, Forester was holding a mighty cudgel in his fist. Griten nodded in approval then turned his attention back to Beth. They watched as she walked slowly towards the flaming cage. The goblins huddled together, unaware that she had passed close enough to touch them. The shard plunged once, as if she had slipped on the icy floor, but she managed to keep her balance. As the phantom roars of the cats continued to reverberate through the assembly room, the goblins gathered together. They gesticulated, swinging their axes so violently they looked in danger of bringing them down on each other's heads.

"Sabre-toothed cats," Josh heard one goblin mutter. "Commander Crush will destroy them. We can't desert our posts."

As if the cats could hear the goblins' nervous mutterings, they roared even louder. The drumming beat Josh had earlier heard when they were bounding through the snow . . . ded dum . . . ded dum . . . ded dum . . . sounded faintly in the distance but quickly grew to a deafening pound, drawing nearer . . . nearer . . . until it seemed as if the cats were outside, ready to rip the door open. The goblins, their backs turned to Beth, their axes now purposefully raised, rushed towards the entrance and braced themselves for the attack.

Beth was almost at the pillar. Josh could hardly contain his anxiety as the Shard of Frost fluttered wildly and reached towards the ice cage. She's almost there, he thought. Just a few more steps, Beth. Keep your nerve. You'll do it!

When she opened the lock on the cage, the flames sprang outwards towards the shard. Blue shadows wavered across the ice ceiling. One of the goblins glanced upwards and noticed the flickering pattern. He shouted a warning to the other guards. Instantly, they spun round and stared in astonishment at the door of the ice cage swinging open. They stared, stupefied, but making no sound as the Shard of Frost seemed to float on a breath of air towards the flames. Their astonishment only lasted for an instant. They were seasoned warriors, familiar with enchanted spells and the power of magic to defeat the unwary. The goblin who had first noticed the shadows gave an ear-splitting whistle as he raced towards the cage, his axe slashing through the air. The phantom howls from the cats died away to a piteous meow. Commands were shouted at the end of the corridor, followed by the tramp of marching feet. As a freezing wind blew towards them, Griten did not hesitate. He drew his axe and flung open the door of the assembly room. Once his companions were inside, he pressed an icicle lever and the door closed with a loud click.

"We're locked in," he shouted. "No one else can enter."

Josh's bow was already in position. He closed his eyes and visualised the goblin racing towards Beth. The golden arrow flew straight to its target. The goblin gave a blood-curdling scream as he collapsed on the steps. Forester stood in front of the ice cage, his cudgel raised. He made no attempt to attack anyone and the goblins seemed unable to bring their axes down on his head. Josh remembered something Forester had said on the night they saw Shift and Gridelda for the first time. "I do no harm to living things and no living thing can harm me." He was a watchman and a protector, and so he stood before the ice cage, daring any goblin to approach.

Michael, unarmed, pulled the twig of light from his pocket. It looked frail and useless as a weapon. Nothing for it but his fists. He was on the youth club boxing team and that had to count for something. He ducked as a goblin lunged at him with his axe. White-faced with fear, he saw Josh draw back his bow. Once more, a golden arrow arched through the air and struck the goblin in his chest. Another goblin reached the steps and flung his axe towards the ice cage where Beth was placing the shard.

"It's going to hit Beth," he yelled as the axe hurtled towards her. Forester calmly raised his cudgel and the axe bounced harmlessly off it before falling to the ground. Michael immediately grabbed it and swung round, ready to attack the nearest goblin.

The last goblin still standing raced towards the unpro- tected side of the dais. Before Forester could swing round, he charged up the steps, brandishing his axe. Griten flung himself fearlessly in front of him. The goblin's axe sank into his back and he collapsed on the last step. But not before he too had landed a fatal blow on his attacker.

The door of the ice cage closed and Beth became visible again.

"Griten's hurt," she screamed as she knelt before the wounded goblin. Forester gently eased the axe from the goblin's back and flung it to one side. He removed Griten's cloak and inspected the wound. Blood poured from the open gash. Quickly, Forester removed a jar of salve from his satchel and rubbed it over the wound. When the bleeding stopped, he carefully turned Griten on his back. Blood trickled from the side of his mouth. His eyes were beginning to glaze. It was obvious to those gathered around him that his life was fading away.

"We will carry you to New Blossomdale," Forester said. "The healing elves will help you."

Griten coughed and raised his hand to draw them nearer. "No time," he gasped. His hand trembled as he pointed towards the ice cage, which began to shake violently. The flames raged so fiercely within it that it seemed as if the pillar and everything surrounding it would ignite. In the centre of this inferno, the blue shard pulsed, drawing the flames into its centre. As the flames raced to the heart of the shard, it throbbed more fiercely, drowning out the growls of the warrior goblins, who were marching along the corridor and attacking the locked door with their axes. Suddenly the shard blasted outwards, splintering into particles of energy that surged beyond the room, beyond the castle, beyond the great cats waiting in the snow. They surged towards the snow fortress – filling those who waited inside with hope and joy – and surged down into the dark dungeons of the castle where King Darkfrost stirred and opened his eyes to stare in awe at this wondrous haze.

Griten, knowing all this, smiled through his suffering and gripped Beth's hand.

His lungs had been punctured by the axe and his breath wheezed as he struggled to speak. "You have done great service to the kingdom of Icefroztica," he said. "King

Darkfrost will soon be restored to his throne but only if Gridelda is defeated. That will not happen until the Shard of Decay is returned to Duskcanister. I have played my part in this mission but my time here is at an end."

"No . . . no . . . I don't want you to die." Beth's voice was muffled with sobs. "You saved my life, Griten. Let us carry you to the elves. They will heal you."

"I would not reach New Blossomdale in time." He looked at each of the children and smiled through his pain. "I fought Gridelda's forces in this room," he said. "Dritin fought beside me and died bravely in my arms. Soon I will be by her side again. So do not grieve. I have lived my life to its full cycle and I leave it behind me without regret." The glaze had vanished from his eyes. They shone with a bright blue light as he gazed for the last time at the waves of energy pulsing from the shard. "The sabre-toothed cats are waiting to carry you through the snow. Go swiftly, my friends. May good luck travel with you."

When his last breath was silent, Forester gently closed the goblin's eyes.

"We must leave him now," he said. "Time is not on our side."

"I'll never forget Griten." Beth covered her face, unable to look at his sturdy body lying so still on the ice.

"Look at his expression," said Michael. "He's smiling."

"He's with Dritin," said Forester. "He is at peace. Unlike those of us who must battle on to save the tree."

"How are we going to escape?" said Josh. "There are so many goblin warriors outside."

"Not any longer," said Forester. "Listen."

"I can't hear anything," said Josh.

"Exactly," said Forester. "Now that the shard has been returned, the traitor goblins have retreated from the castle. They know the natural balance within the kingdom has been restored. But word will soon reach Gridelda. With every moment we delay, the danger increases. We need to reach the entrance to Icefroztica before she discovers what has happened. Then you must return home. It is late and your parents will soon begin to worry."

"But the Shard of Decay," said Josh. "How will you manage to return it without our help?"

"That remains the most dangerous task of all. But we now have King Darkfrost on our side. You have seen Gridelda's ruthlessness. She will not spare your lives in this final battle."

"But we want—"

"Silence, Josh." Forester interrupted his protest. "You have to think of Michael and Beth. And what about your parents? How would they feel if their children disappeared and were never seen again? You were tasked with finding the shards and this had been accomplished. Queen Glendalock does not wish you to be exposed to any further danger."

They reached the sabre-toothed cats who stared unblinkingly at the children and Forester, then looked beyond them, searching for Griten. Forester spoke quietly into the leader's ear. Her green eyes grew luminous with tears as she growled softly to the other cats. They began to weep, their tears flowing down their noble faces to the snow.

"Look," said Josh, pointing into the distance at dark shadows swaying in the wind. "Something's moving."

"It's life," Forester shouted and flung his cap in the air. "The pine trees are growing once again on the slopes."

"And look at the crocuses," said Beth as the snow melted under the tears of the sabre-toothed cats and uncovered a carpet of purple and yellow flowers, peeking shyly from the ground.

The lights in the castle windows blazed but this was not the ice diamond glare they had seen earlier. The glow was mellow, welcoming and warm. From the courtyard King Darkfrost sat astride a magnificent white stallion. He lifted a crown of mistletoe from his head and waved it at the children. The stallion pawed the snow and whinnied, anxious to be on his way.

The king flung his ermine cloak over his shoulders and urged the stallion forward. The horse galloped across the snowy plains, and the king's voice rang out mightily as he broke the news to his loyal subjects that Icefroztica belonged to them once more. He was followed by the sabre-toothed cats, pounding the melting snow into a shimmering rainbow.

# 18

# gridelda battles for the
# remaining shards

But what of Gridelda and her army? What evil had been unfolding as the Shard of Frost was restored to the kingdom of Icefroztica? All day long she had encouraged the ghouls and goblins to fight viciously. Now, as twilight fell and the sun sank in a blood-red sky, she surveyed the desolation surrounding the Tree of Seasons. The woods had suffered almost as badly as her army. Everywhere she looked she saw felled trees, hacked trunks, slashed branches, broken boughs. But the Tree of Seasons stood proud and unscarred. Fairies and elves . . . who would have believed they would fight with such might and determination? The warriors of Brightisclearen and New Blossomdale had protected the entrances to their kingdoms and Gridelda's army had not moved one step closer to victory. The shards of spring and summer had remained in the possession of their rulers and the Chalice of Elentra was still protected by Queen Glendalock's guards. Gridelda's spells, no matter how powerful, had been resisted by fairy magic that proved equally as potent as her own. But she was confident of victory. Tomorrow morning at dawn, before the village of Merryville awakened – and busybodies could protest – the witless humans would come to level the woods with their chainsaws and diggers. The Tree of Seasons would no longer exist. Gridelda would claim the last two shards and the Chalice of Elentra would be in her possession once again.

Suddenly, the smack of wood and the clash of metal ceased as an icy blue mist drifted over the battleground. It thickened and became so dense that the warriors could not distinguish between friend and foe. They retreated to their kingdoms and the mist lifted, allowing the healing elves to emerge and search among the fallen bodies for the wounded. They carried them on stretchers, the goblins and ghouls as well as the fairies and elves. The dead were already returning to the earth, their bodies dissolving into the bloodstained grass. The rain fell and the grass was washed clean. Strong new shoots began to stir and push upwards between the winter roots of the ancient tree. Soon, only the sighing wind in the leaves broke the silence in Grimsville Woods.

Gridelda and her army returned to Duskcanister to regroup. But she was growing weaker with each hour that passed. Each time she entered the mortal world, she walked more slowly. The knowledge she needed to survive outside her season was ebbing from her mind. The old woman slept beneath her spell, but without the magical chalice Gridelda could not drink the essence of her wisdom. A ghoul entered her chamber and cringed at the sight of her furious features. Gridelda shuddered with disbelief as she listened to his report. The Shard of Frost had been returned to Icefroztica. An unbelievable victory had been achieved within the kingdom she called her own and King Darkfrost had reclaimed his throne. He sat once again astride his magnificent white stallion. An assembly of faithful goblins had gathered around him. Their cheers rang throughout Icefroztica as the defeated goblins and ghouls defending his castle fled to Duskcanister.

How could this have happened? She raged as she listened to the cowering ghoul. His leaves trembled so violently she could hardly hear his whimpering report. According to a goblin who had survived the assault in the assembly room, the Shard of Frost had floated in mid-air and entered the ice cage of its own accord.

"Nonsense!" Gridelda roared. "The witless goblins were hoodwinked. It was the child with the gift of invisibility. But how did she acquire the Shard of Frost? If she had entered the sea witch's cave, her heart would not have survived the witch's hunger."

The ghoul stepped back from her fury. And, indeed, it was a fearsome anger to witness. Her breath blew the ghoul against the wall where he collapsed in a flutter of decaying leaves. He lay still, hoping she would forget his existence. But she dragged him to his feet and forced her face against his.

"Tell me what else you know," she hissed.

The ghoul flapped his hands and his head shook so violently he was afraid the thin stem of his throat would snap. "The goblin died without revealing anything else, Your Gracious Majesty. Except . . . " He paused, trying to decide if the truth was more terrifying than a lie. One look at Gridelda's face helped make up his mind. "The Keeper of the Woods known as Forester did battle with the goblins. He had a satchel. The goblin saw a light shining inside it. He believed it came from the Shard of Decay."

Gridelda staggered backwards and pressed her hand against her chest. The blood drained from her face. She glanced across the room as a whorl of smoke thickened and moved menacingly towards the ghoul.

"Leave him be, Shift," Gridelda snapped. "We have no time to waste on this pathetic bundle of leaves." She dismissed the ghoul who fluttered swiftly from her sight. But not before he had seen the terrifying sight of Shift morphing into his gargoyle guise.

When she was alone with Shift, Gridelda paced up and down her chamber. Her feet sank into the amber sludge that was taking over her kingdom. "We must act immediately and vanquish those wretched children," she announced. Was it her imagination or did her voice sound fainter? As she weakened, her fear grew. If the dying goblin's report was true, she had lost everything. What had happened to the sea witch? And what about Johnny Welts? And how did the children know where to find the shards? All those questions made her head ache. She had never had a headache in her long life. Now her temples throbbed with pain and she was finding it difficult to lift her feet from the decaying sludge.

"Seek out the sea witch, Shift," she ordered. "And the wretched boy with his puny muscles. Report back to me immediately. But first, carry me with all speed to Merryville Manor."

Within minutes, Gridelda had entered the manor. She opened the secret drawer in the hall table. Empty! As she had suspected. Furiously, she flung the table to the floor. Shift tore at it with his long sharp claws and flittered it into matchsticks.

Without delaying any longer, he flew into the night, heading towards the sea witch's cave. Gridelda stood before the mirror in her bedroom. Was it her imagination or did her reflection look fainter? Hurry, hurry, she ordered herself. No time for fear. You are the most powerful ruler in the Tree of Seasons and you will not be defeated by weaklings and fools.

She walked swiftly towards the Lotts's house. Lights were shining in the bedroom windows. The girl moved to the window and drew the curtains. Gridelda gritted her teeth at the sight of her, remembering how Beth had outwitted the foolish Johnny Welts, and outwitted Gridelda too, just as the chalice was within her grasp.

A flapping noise distracted her. Shift landed beside her. He hissed his information, drooling with fury when he described how he had found a golden arrow in a centre of a hank of rotting seaweed. As for Johnny Welts . . . Shift hissed so violently that Gridelda held her hand to her face to ward off his spittle. The wretched boy was in hospital surrounded by tubes and bleeping machines and doctors who told him he would be strong again as soon as they discovered the cause of his illness. As soon as he saw Shift, he had pressed an alarm bell and screamed for a nurse. She had pulled the screens around Johnny Welts's bed and told the weeping boy that she would sit with him until the bad dream faded from his mind.

"Enough . . . enough!" Gridelda could not bear to hear any further bad news. She watched as the girl's bedroom light switched off. The boys' room was now also in darkness, the window open.

When time had passed and she knew they would be sleeping, she moved. "Now is the time to strike." She breathed heavily as she climbed onto Shift's back. "Carry me to their bedside."

Shift flew through the open window. Both boys lay sleeping. The magic bow lay beside the older boy, his fingers curled around the string. The other boy lay on his back, his diamond ring sparkling in the darkness. Gridelda touched his forehead with her cane. Immediately Michael was surrounded with a green light. His eyes opened. He tried to pull away from her but he was unable to move. His terrified gaze told her he understood everything that was happening. She tried to pull the ring from his finger. It stung her finger, the sting sinking deeper each time she touched it. Unable to bear the pain, she pulled her hand away and lifted Michael in her arms. He was heavy, a dead-weight, forcing her to stagger as she flung him across Shift's back. Definitely, she was growing weaker. Time was running out.

"Quickly," she hissed, climbing up behind the immobilised boy. "Carry me to my castle then bring a message to Queen Glendalock. The Chalice of Elentra for the life of this wretched boy. This time I have his living flesh in my possession. There has been no transformation, no trickery. Much blood has been spilled today. But it is nothing compared to the mortal blood that will be shed before this night is out."

# 19

# gridelda's revenge

The wind awoke Josh. He'd left the window open and the bedroom blind kept tapping against the glass. Grumbling to himself, he left his bed and crossed the room. Michael must have gone to the bathroom. He climbed back into bed and pulled the duvet over his shoulders. It was cold in the room and there was an unpleasant smell. It was familiar yet he couldn't decide what it was. Maybe the window should have been left open to clear the air. He'd tell Michael to open it again when he came back from the bathroom. He closed his eyes and thought about the tree.

They'd slipped unnoticed through the battlefield, the spell of deceit still working. Their mother had scolded them for staying out so late. She'd driven to the lake and through the village searching for them. Their dinner was ruined, she said, and they could like it or lump it. She'd slapped their plates on the table and demanded to know what they'd been doing all day.

"Oh, this and that," said Josh.

"Just messing about," said Michael.

"Slaying sea witches," said Beth and grinned when her mother flipped the tea towel at her and ordered her to stop telling whoppers.

"It's all very well messing about," she grumbled. "But bad things happen. Johnny Welts is in hospital with a black eye and is suffering severe memory loss. His mother is worried sick about him. But the doctors say he's going to be fine."

It had been a relief to escape to their bedrooms and collapse into bed. Josh turned and looked towards the door. No sign of Michael. The smell was really disgusting, like burning hair or rotten eggs. Josh suddenly lay very still. Hardly daring to breathe he waited for Michael to return. Minutes passed. The silence was unbearable. He jumped from his bed and rapped on the bathroom door.

"Michael, what's keeping you?" He kept his voice low, afraid of awakening his parents. No answer. He opened the door. The bathroom was empty. There was no sign of Michael in any of the downstairs rooms. He opened his parents' bedroom door, knowing that Michael was not there but he had to check every option before he allowed his dreadful suspicions to surface. His parents were sleeping and did not stir when he quietly left their room.

Beth awoke as soon as he shook her shoulder.

"Michael's gone," he whispered. "I think . . ." He stopped, unable to continue, and buried his face in his hands.

"What do you mean?" Beth lifted herself on her elbow. "Where's he gone?" She prised Josh's fingers from his face and forced him to look at her. "Tell me where he's gone."

"I think Shift's been here." He had to say it out loud. "I smell him in the room."

"Oh, no . . . *no.*" Beth looked fearfully around the room. "Please please *please* don't tell me he's taken Michael with him."

"I don't know . . . I can't find him anywhere. I never heard anything . . . and I had my bow beside me. What are we going to do?"

Beth pushed her hair from her eyes and jumped from her bed, whispering as she ran to the boys' room, "We have to call Bellatinks."

"You're right." Josh closed his eyes and three times, in his firmest voice, he called the fairy's name. "This is an emergency," he added. "We need immediate relocation."

Queen Glendalock and King Leafslear were conferring at the Meeting Table when Josh and Beth entered the throne room. One look at the expressions on the rulers' faces confirmed the children's worst fears.

"Children, we have received word from Gridelda." Queen Glendalock gestured at them to be seated. "She demands that we travel at once to Duskcanister, carrying the shards of both our kingdoms, along with the Shard of Decay. She also demands the Chalice of Elentra. If we do not obey her, Michael will be slain."

"Slain," whispered Beth. "What does that mean?"

"She will kill him," Josh's anguished cry shivered from him. "But I won't let her . . . I won't." He waved his bow in the air. "Give her the chalice and the shards. I don't care. I want Michael back."

"So do I," cried Beth. "Bring him back to us."

Bellatinks flew in a frenzy from Josh to Beth, trying to calm them down. She only succeeded in making them more anxious and Beth, agitatedly fiddling with her necklace, kept appearing and disappearing.

"Hush, children . . . *hush*." Queen Glendalock's murmuring voice forced them to sit still and listen. "Do not forget that we also possess strong magic. Have faith in us. We will travel to Duskcanister and confront her with our own powers. Remember, without the essence of joy, she is weak. Her weakness is our strength."

"I'm going to Duskcanister with you," insisted Josh.

"Me too," said Beth and touched her necklace. "We'll trick that cruel, wicked witch." Her disembodied voice was filled with determination.

"Then let us make haste," said King Leafslear. "Gridelda's mortal strength may be weakening and that makes her even more vicious."

When they emerged from Locksun Castle, the courtyard and the land beyond were thronged with fairies. Word of Michael's kidnapping had obviously spread through the kingdom. The queen's guards, Bowrain and Partlant, flew to her side. Rufus and Rickspin fell into step behind their king. Forester emerged from the crowd, his eyes seeking and finding Bellatinks. The faces of those who had battled Gridelda's forces were lined with weariness but they raised their voices in a cheer when they saw the children. The full-throated roar lifted Josh's spirits, quickened his step.

No time to dally. His body stretched and tightened and, almost instantaneously, he was standing in darkness with the others under the Tree of Seasons. As always, the tree spread its calming light over them. Beth had already vanished. She held his hand as they walked around the tree and approached the entrance to Duskcanister. Their feet sank into dead and decaying leaves. The smell of mould almost overwhelmed them. A half-open wooden gateway was stuck in mulch. Resin that had been dripping from the leaves had petrified and hung like a glistening amber web beyond the gate. When Josh tried to push the gate, a gluey fungus crept over his fingers and along his forearm. He shook his hand, desperately trying to remove it.

"Don't worry." Forester plucked a moist oak leaf from the summer section of the tree and handed it to him. "It's unpleasant but not poisonous, and will wipe off easily."

"It's *disgusting*." Josh frantically rubbed the leaf across his hand, relieved to see that Forester was right and the fungus was easily removed. "I used to love autumn but this is like a maggoty compost heap. How are we supposed to get into Duskcanister and rescue Michael if we can't even open the gate?"

Forester threw back his head and addressed the gate.

> "*Gateway to Patina's world,*
> *Where gold and amber leaves once swirled,*
> *Must Gridelda's curse destroy*
> *All the wonder and the joy*
> *That comes when autumn casts her cloak*
> *Across the chestnut, elm and oak*
> *And lays her hand upon the land*
> *To bid it rest at her command?*"

The gate slowly creaked open but the petrified resin remained intact. Not even a ripple indicated that Forester's words had been heard. He frowned, shaking his head.

"It is as I suspected. The energy of this wood is not living, so it can't respond. The cycle of decay had reached the midway point when we recovered the shard. Now the rot has stopped but the land is stuck between growth and decay. If we do not succeed in returning Patina to her throne, the cycle of decay will begin anew. Hurry, children, *hurry*."

Beth squeezed Josh's hand. He looked down, startled, as always, to be unable to see her. "That amber stuff hanging over the entrance could turn us into fossils," she whispered. "We learned about it in school. I'm afraid, Josh. I want to rescue Michael but what if we become fossils?"

"Listen, Beth, you've faced down Gridelda, ghouls, goblins, dragons and sea witches. This is nothing compared to what you've been through." And sounding far braver than he felt, he tightened his grip on her hand as they followed Forester through the clinging resin. To his relief, it fell away from them, as the fungus had done, and they were able to enter the tunnel. It was guarded by four ghouls who made no attempt to stop them. Their eyes gleamed when they saw the chalice in Queen Glendalock's hands. One of the ghouls beckoned at the group to follow her. She led them through a dank corridor, her soggy leaves trailing behind her. A pale sheen covered the walls and brown moss was like a thick carpet beneath their feet.

They reached a courtyard filled with shrivelled grass and leafless trees. Unlike the bare trees of winter, these trees had no sap within them, nor buds that would unfurl in the spring. Their footsteps slowed when they saw a castle surrounded by a moat. Green scum floated on the stagnant water. Dead fish floated, belly up. The ghoul led them across the drawbridge and into the castle. Rot had attacked the door of Gridelda's chamber. Flakes of wood fell to the floor when Queen Glendalock knocked on the door.

"Come in! Come in!" Gridelda sounded cheerful, which made Josh even more fearful. He reached out and touched Beth, just the tiniest touch to know she was still there.

Queen Glendalock entered, followed by King Leafslear. Their guards stood behind them, their weapons at the ready. The walls and ceiling were made from the same black, mouldering wood.

"Where is Michael?" shouted Josh. "What have you done with my brother?"

The atmosphere in the room was electrifying as Gridelda beckoned them further towards her. "First things first." Gridelda smiled and held up a silver goblet. "Your Majesty, would you be kind enough to fill my goblet from the Chalice of Elentra and allow me to quench my thirst?"

"Gridelda, do not toy with us," snapped King Leafslear. "You know why we are here. Where is the boy?"

"Ah, the boy. The piteous boy." She replaced the goblet on a table by her side and clicked her fingers, the sound as sharp as snapped wood. The door opened and the ghoul who had led them to the chamber entered, followed by Michael. His hands were tied behind his back and his ashen face was bruised. It was obvious he had struggled fiercely with his captors. His pyjamas were rumpled, the jacket ripped down the front, the buttons missing. He staggered, hardly able to stand as Gridelda pushed him forward.

"Take him," she hissed at the queen. Her thin lips drew back in a mirthless smile. "Now give me what I desire." She stretched her hand towards the chalice and snatched it from the queen's hand. In her anxiety to possess the chalice, she tilted it too far and spilled some drops of essence of joy on the floor.

Josh recoiled as a familiar smell rushed towards him. As the ghoul pushed his brother towards him, Josh looked closer at Michael's eyes. It was only a blink, almost imagined, yet Josh saw it clearly. That red hot glint of fury could only belong to one thing. The *thing* he feared most of all. Beside him, he heard Beth's sharp intake of breath and knew she had also guessed the truth. Their brother was not in the chamber. But it was too late to prevent Gridelda lifting the Chalice of Elentra to her lips.

## 20

# prisoners in the crypt
# of duskcanister

At first, Michael had found it impossible to see anything. It was darker than the cave of the sea witch, darker than the woods at midnight, so dark that he felt it would feel like velvet if he could touch it. But he was forced to lie motionless on a bed of mulching leaves. The smell of decay was everywhere. How awful it would be if Gridelda had her way. The earth would smell like this the whole time. Nothing would grow. Nothing would breathe. No seasons, just endless decay. He wanted to howl but his throat refused to work. As he stared into this void, he heard something: a sighing sound. As if someone was breathing softly in their sleep. He listened, his ears picking up the rhythm. Then he heard a soft snore. It did not belong to the sighs. Two people were in this space with him.

Then, floating ever so faintly over the smell of decay, he smelled lavender. He thought about the lavender field and how Beth had slept beside her brothers, her thumb in her mouth, and Bellatinks had swayed on a lavender stem. Forester had plucked a rose for her. Michael had thought it was the silliest thing he'd ever seen but it seemed different now. He would have watched it forever, knowing it was a gesture of love, and that they were safe and secure in that beautiful place.

Lavender blue . . . lavender blue . . . he knew a song about lavender. Great Aunt Graves used to sing it to them. She had always smelled of lavender. On her dressing table she had had a bottle of lavender water with a rubber bulb attached to a tube. When she squeezed the bulb the perfume sprayed over her throat and wrists. Was she beside him now?

He moved his eyes, attracted by a chink of light, a glittering diamond. But what use was it when he could not speak? Unless . . . He thought of the enchanted people, how they used their minds to communicate. Would the Ring of Truth work if he thought the question?

*Great Aunt Graves is in a bewitched sleep beside me.* Michael imagined this thought reaching the ring. It glowed, sending out a sudden shaft of blue. In the instant before it faded he saw his aunt. She lay on her back, her eyes closed, her lips fluttering gently every time she breathed out. Beside her, a small sylph-like figure was also sleeping. Long tresses of emerald hair trailed over the edges of her bier and her slender hands were crossed on her chest. She was dressed in leaves of bronze and copper, of burnished gold and a radiant yellow.

*She is Patina, the true queen of autumn.* No sooner had his mind released the thought than his ring once again glowed with truth. It lit up the space where they were lying. Tiny stuffed animals, birds and insects, similar to those who roamed the real world, were displayed on stone shelves. A baby polar bear stood between a wallaby and a whale. Tiny butterflies and bees were stuck to the walls. A stuffed bald eagle and a falcon looked as if they were suspended in mid-flight, their dead eyes staring blankly ahead. Michael recognised them as species in danger of extinction. Clumps of dead foliage hung from the ceiling. Each of those plants would face the same fate, he guessed.

Before the light faded, Patina opened her eyes and turned her face towards him. Her amber eyes implored him . . . *Help me . . . help me*. But how could he help her when he was unable to move? What good was a Ring of Truth when he needed ranks of marching soldiers, led by Josh with his magical bow?

The ring flashed, not red or blue, as he expected, but with the flush of a harvest moon. As Michael watched the ring illuminate the dark space around him, he remembered the advice Queen Glendalock had given him when the Ring of Truth chose him.

"The chamber has seen that your greatest fear is of being captured by Shift and trapped in isolation," she had said. "That will never happen while you wear this Ring of Truth. It will tell those you love where to find you and will advise you to reveal this information when the time is right."

Josh! Beth! Michael closed his eyes and focused on his brother and sister. Josh! Beth! He repeated their names, chanting them firmly in his mind as the orange rays drew them onwards towards him.

"What is this?" Gridelda screeched as the flame-coloured light flowed through the windows of her castle and illuminated the bleak surroundings. Suddenly, the atmosphere changed. Queen Glendalock, who had seemed defeated and frightened, dashed the chalice from Gridelda's hand. Bellatinks flew forward and caught it before the precious essence spilled. Josh raised his bow and aimed it at Michael. Except that it was not his brother he visualised. The arrow flew in a stream of golden energy and struck Shift directly in his chest. Instantly, he transformed into his gargoyle self. His eyes bulged with shock and outrage as he tried to pull the arrow from his heart. His body twisted and turned. His blood-curdling howls filled the chamber. But his cries were cut short when Queen Glendalock pointed her finger towards him and began to chant. As her spell-binding words reached him, his feet became rigid. His upper body writhed but slowly his scaly skin hardened. As the spell crept over him, each part of his body, limb by limb, turned to stone. Soon, only his head moved, his neck straining upwards, as if he was drowning and desperate for one last breath of air. Then the only movement came from his eyes. They swivelled towards Gridelda, begging her to free him. But she was desperately trying to catch Bellatinks, who still clasped the chalice. As Bellatinks rose towards the ceiling, Gridelda turned to Shift.

"Crush her then bring her remains to me," she screeched, then stopped abruptly when she realised what was happening. She pointed her cane at him and released its enchanted force. But she was too late. Her magic flashed feebly off his statuesque body and she was forced to watch in horror as his gleaming red eyes dimmed to grey stone.

Bellatinks, clasping the chalice, flew towards an open window. She had almost escaped when Gridelda spun round and caught sight of her fluttering wings. Realising that the chalice was slipping from her grasp, she lunged towards the window sill. She had sipped a few precious drops of the essence, not as much as she needed, but enough to defeat the pitiful fairy who believed she could escape by flitting between the branches of the dead trees.

Gridelda jumped to the ground and pointed her cane towards Bellatinks. The fairy moved swiftly. The chalice had to be saved and she was in mortal danger, unable to tap her fingers and release her own magic. She swerved to avoid Gridelda's flashing evil, knowing that one strike would bring her to the ground as quickly as a falling stone.

In the silence that followed Gridelda's departure, King Leafslear pressed his fingers to his temples and listened, his face crumpled with worry, as mind messages were relayed to him.

"Gridelda has rallied her ghouls for the final battle," he said. "Our warriors are weary and unprepared for the attack. We must return to our kingdoms immediately."

Queen Glendalock flew to Beth who had become visible as soon as Gridelda left the castle. "I must go with King Leafslear to rally my troops," she said.

"But what about Michael?" Josh demanded. "You were going to help us find him."

"Forester will remain with you—"

"But Bellatinks is in danger." The telltale blush mounted Forester's cheeks as he looked from the queen to the children. "She needs my protection."

"She needs your love, Forester, not your protection. She is a brave and skilful fairy, and a match for Gridelda."

"I know but . . . " Forester hesitated, torn between his heart and his head.

"You have to help us, Forester," Beth pleaded. "We have to find out what happened to Michael."

"When Michael has been found, you must return the shard to its rightful place," said the queen. "Go with speed, Forester, and serve me faithfully, as you always do."

The queen and king, with their bodyguards, turned into a whorl of light and disappeared. The chamber grew dim. The statue of Shift looked as hideous as the pictures Josh had seen of gargoyles on the high turrets of Notre-Dame cathedral. The black walls and ceiling created such a crushing atmosphere that he wanted to flee the chamber. But he stopped at the door, alerted by an amber glow that travelled across the floor and formed a spotlight at their feet. As he moved from the chamber with Forester and Beth, the spotlight remained with them. In the corridor they paused, unsure which way to turn. When they took the turn to the left, the spotlight swung right.

"It's a signal," Josh said. "It's Michael's ring. Remember what we were told. It would bring us to him if he was ever isolated from us."

Beth ran back and jumped into the amber circle. "Hurry, Josh, hurry," she shouted. Josh needed no encouragement. He sprinted along the corridor, Beth panting alongside him and Forester struggling to keep up. The tunnel slanted downwards, with foul-smelling passages leading off it in many other directions.

It grew darker but they did not use their twigs of light. The amber glow was all they needed to guide them. It never wavered as they descended lower and lower until Josh wondered if they were travelling to the centre of the earth. Trailing roots dangled from the ceiling, tangled in their hair, and caught in Forester's beard.

"Come out, or I'll fire." A crackling voice cried out and stopped them in their tracks. Beth immediately vanished. For the first time since their gifts had chosen them, Josh wished he too had the disappearing power of the necklace.

"Who's there?" he shouted and removed his bow, dreading the thought of using it again yet knowing he would not hesitate to do so. "We're heavily armed and dangerous."

There was a momentary pause before three figures drifted into view from one of the passageways. The amber glow immediately spread to illuminate them. Unlike the ghouls who were cloaked in dark shrivelled leaves, these figures were dressed in the brilliant russet and bronze shades of autumn. Their bodies were shaped like maple leaves and their skin was a pale, delicate green. Willow-green hair hung to their waists and they carried forked wooden spears.

"Don't come any further or I'll fire," said Josh but Forester stepped towards the figures, a broad smile on his face.

"My dear friends," he said. "I believed you had perished under Gridelda's reign."

"At times we believed that would be our fate." The tallest figure stepped forward in a rustle of leaves to embrace Forester. His wings were almost invisible and could easily be mistaken for leaves.

"Who are they?" Beth whispered, reappearing again.

"They are the guardians of the Shard of Decay," said Forester. "They belong to the legion of sylphs who are the true inhabitants of Duskcanister." Forester waved his hand towards the guardians. "Josh and Beth, may I introduce Subfusc, Ecru and Umber."

Josh wondered if it would be good manners to shake hands with a guardian sylph. Better not, he decided, noticing the brittle stems of their elongated fingers. The guardians dropped their spears to their sides and gazed curiously at the children.

"I see you have been gifted the golden arrow." Subfusc, the tallest sylph, eyed Josh's bow. "Have you used it wisely?"

"I hope so," Josh replied. "It has helped us recover the Shard of Decay."

The guardians rustled excitedly. Their voices sighed like a breeze through leaves.

"Do not mock us with false hope," sighed Ecru. "Until the precious shard was stolen, we had guarded its power for many aeons. To be born, to live and die, and to be reborn again, that was the cycle of nature until Gridelda seized control."

"She has seized my brother as well," cried Josh. "We're searching for him. The beam is taking us to him but we don't know where we're going."

"We fear he is in the Crypt of Duskcanister," said Forester. "I have heard of that loathsome place but no one knows its whereabouts."

"We will search together," sighed Umber. "We too search for the Crypt of Duskcanister." The amber beam danced excitedly at their feet and urged them forward. The sylphs fell into step beside them. Beth suddenly screamed as the ground turned into a resinous swamp. The sylphs quickly came together and formed a floating bed of leaves. They carried Beth to the other side of the swamp but Forester, his boots sticking to the gluey earth, spoke sternly.

> *"Resin! Listen to my verse*
> *And resist Gridelda's curse.*
> *Let us travel arm and arm*
> *Without hindrance or alarm."*

Unlike the resin in the woods, the swampy ground became firm again and so they continued on their way, around twisting and turning corners, the ground dipping then rising, then sharply twisting again. Suddenly, when Josh felt as if he could not take another step, the amber light lifted from the ground and shone on a door. It was padlocked but Forester did not hesitate. Josh held the shard while the little man worked the bamboo cane into the lock.

> *"Bamboo! You are now equipped*
> *To invade Gridelda's crypt."*

The guardians rose in the air and floated through the doorway into a small stone room. Three wooden biers lay side by side on the floor.

"Michael!" cried Beth, falling to her knees beside the middle bier.

"Stop!" shouted Forester. "Don't you remember what happened in the manor?" Beth halted just in time. She knelt outside the spell of immobility, and still holding the bow, Josh crouched beside her.

"We'll free you, Michael," he said. "Shift has been turned to stone and Gridelda will soon be destroyed." He turned away from Michael's gaze, afraid his brother would see his fear, and gasped when he recognised the elderly, silver-haired woman lying beside him. Great Aunt Graves. A lump rose in his throat when he looked at her faded cheeks, and the laugh lines that had always crinkled around her eyes. How could he have believed, even for an instant, that she had become that wicked harridan? But Gridelda had been clever and the children had believed what they saw, not what they remembered.

The crackle and rustle of the guardians grew louder. Josh turned to see what was causing their excitement. They had gathered around the smallest bier and were gazing tenderly upon a slender female sylph. She rested upon a bed of leaves. Like Michael and Great Aunt Graves, her eyes were open. Her gaze moved slowly towards Forester, who reached into his satchel and removed the Shard of Decay. As she recognised the flickering symbol of her rule, her eyes glistened with joy.

"Josh, take the shard and place it in her arms," Subfusc ordered.

"But I'll be frozen in Gridelda's spell," said Josh.

"The shard will protect you," said Ecru as the guardians swayed towards him. Tentatively, he stretched out his arm and laid the shard on top of her crossed arms. Immediately, the amber spotlight grew brighter. It radiated heat into the stone crypt, flowed in waves over all those who stood in its path. As if a gentle breath moved over the bier, Queen Patina's emerald tresses stirred. Her arms unclenched and grasped the shard. With the gentlest of sighs, she pressed it against her chest. Her pale-green skin deepened and her breathing became stronger. She sat up and smiled at the guardians who formed a dancing bed of oranges, yellows, reds and browns. They swept beneath her bier and swirled her triumphantly in the air. As they flowed gracefully through the amber glare, they cast dappled shadows over Michael. As if touched by magic, he was released from Gridelda's power. But Great Aunt Graves was still unable to move a muscle.

"She will remain spellbound until Gridelda is vanquished," said Patina. "The Shard of Decay must be returned immediately to its resting place."

Forester, who had been silent while the queen spoke, could no longer control his anxiety. "What about Bellatinks?" he demanded. "Gridelda will use her most powerful magic to destroy her."

Queen Patina stared into the crystal shard and smiled. "Bellatinks is a spirited and wily fairy. She is leading Gridelda on a merry chase. They are now beyond the Tree of Seasons and fleeing through the mortal world. Therefore, we can replace the shard in safety."

"What if Gridelda catches her?" Forester refused to be comforted. "I'll never forgive myself if anything happens . . . " He stopped, too embarrassed to continue, and sunk his chin into his beard.

"She will be safe." Patina placed her hand on his shoulder.

"Be reassured, Forester. She has every reason to hurry back to you." She tossed her emerald hair over her shoulders and tilted her chin. "Come, let us depart this wretched crypt."

"But we can't leave our great-aunt all alone," cried Beth. "What if the ghouls find her?"

Patina floated over the bier where their great-aunt rested and placed her hand on the old woman's forehead. Almost immediately, her mouth softened in a half-smile. Her eyelids flickered as she sighed, then sank into a deep, peaceful sleep. "She will be safe now, my magic will protect her whilst she sleeps." Patina said.

The spotlight flickered, a beacon demanding their attention. No time to waste. They hurried from the crypt and back to the tunnel. Perhaps it was the power of the shard that lent them speed but it seemed no length of time before they reached the chamber room. Patina wrinkled her nose at the smell of decay that still hung in the air. She exhaled, loudly. Her breath clouded, as if she was breathing into a frosty morning, and as the vapour drifted around the chamber the air was filled with the sweet scents of autumn. The amber spotlight spread over the dismal walls and bathed the chamber in russet tones. The guardians, led by Patina, and accompanied by Forester and the children, glided from the castle and crossed the courtyard towards the stagnant wastes of Duskcanister. Their gracefulness amazed Josh. He had become so used to the rushing onslaught of the ghouls and their reeking smell of decay that he had forgotten the beauty of autumn. Now he saw its splendour as Patina's breath transformed the dead trees into radiant colours. The guardians lightly drifted on the wind, and were joined by other sylphs who fluttered from their hiding places and joined the growing throng.

The children's feet crunched on crisp bronze leaves. Josh kicked them in the air, showering Michael and Beth. Soon, they were whooping and laughing, gathering up great armfuls of leaves and flinging them over each other. But when they noticed that the shard – still being held aloft by Patina – had deepened to a blood-red hue, they stopped their game and followed her. A battle still raged outside the Tree of Seasons and Patina was moving faster, as if the wind that carried her and her sylphs had grown stronger.

She came to a halt when they reached a grove of trees. The stump of a decaying tree trunk released a sickly smell.

"This ancient oak once protected the Shard of Decay within its roots." Patina spoke clearly above the rustling of her sylphs. "Gridelda cursed the tree with despair and disease then removed the shard to the mortal world, knowing we could not search for it outside our season."

A faint keening cry carried towards them. The sound was melancholic, as if voices wept and sighed somewhere deep within the stump. Josh, unable to resist his curiosity, leaned forward. The stump was hollow, like a bottomless well, he thought. He imagined the lost keening voices echoing mournfully within that yawning void.

"It's the lost joy Gridelda stole for the Chalice of Elentra," said Beth. Her face grew blank as she listened to the wailing. A tear rolled down her cheek and quivered like a watery firefly above the hollowed stump. She stepped closer to the edge, deaf to Josh's cry of alarm, as she leaned forward to catch her falling tear. He grabbed her pink jumper but the material slipped through his fingers. She made no effort to stop herself as she plunged head-first towards the yawning opening. Michael screamed as he too tried to catch her but he was too late. She made no sound as her head disappeared, then her body. Her trainers had mud and leaves embedded in the grooves. That was the crazy thing Josh noticed as he watched her legs vanish. His horror was too deep to think about anything else. A branch lashed his face, or so he thought as leaves whirred past him.

Although the guardians changed shape so often, Josh was still amazed by their dexterity as they wove themselves into a rope. They fastened themselves around Beth's ankles and whisked her up from the chasm.

"I wanted to free the children," she whispered as she collapsed on the grass. Her eyes closed, as if the light dappling the grove was too bright after the vortex she had entered. "They were calling for help."

"You heard the echoes of loss," said Patina. "A trick but true, nonetheless. The children who gave away their joy so willingly now cry to have it returned to them."

The sylphs, growing in numbers, flew across the sky like a gigantic flock of starlings, their burnished wings swirling and swerving before coming to rest at the feet of their queen. They recoiled from the stench that gushed from the stump but Queen Patina stood firmly between the roots. She spoke in a husky voice, addressing her words directly to the children.

"The interior of this stump has been polluted by leaves

and plants, by insects and animals whose life had reached its natural end. But if King Leafslear's seeding season is not followed by the growth of summer, and if, after the harvest, my season is not allowed to decay and make way for the fallow months of winter, there will be no new blooming, no renewal, no new seasons to help us understand how life and death are intertwined."

Patina turned to the guardians and held the shard towards them. "The Tree of Seasons would be honoured if you would protect this precious shard, as you have done since ancient times."

"It is our destiny to protect the Tree of Seasons," said Subfusc. "We willingly dedicate ourselves once more to this sacred duty and accept the Shard of Decay."

The guardians placed their arms on each other's shoulders and danced joyously in a circle, swirling so fast it was impossible to separate their slender forms.

Queen Patina touched the shard to her lips and uttered a husky incantation. "We release this shard to serve our harvest season." With a graceful flick of her wrist, she flung the shard towards the swirling guardians. "May it honour the cycle of birth, growth, decay and death. May the essence of our souls continue to exist in harmony, comforted by the wealth of memory, through the generations that come behind us."

Toe to heel, heel to toe, around and around the guardians danced until their nimble feet lifted above the ground. Holding the shard in their centre, they spun upwards in a blur of autumnal hues.

"With the shard protected once again by my faithful sylphs, joy will be restored to the mortal world of children," said Queen Patina.

The guardians hovered above the ancient stump. The wind, blowing stronger now, swished through their leafy dress until the eerie wailing faded.

A palette of colours beamed across Duskcanister. Golden grain and purple berries, russet fruits and hazelnuts, all those colours that had been lost swirled in the circle of energy released by the guardians.

Forester gazed down into the now silent tree stump and recited his magical verse.

> *"Root that carries knowledge deep*
> *Grant that nature does not weep.*
> *For what was lost must be regained*
> *Before this warring night has waned.*
> *Grant Bellatinks the might to fight*
> *And strike Gridelda's evil blight.*
> *Help her destroy those spells and charms*
> *And bring her safely to my arms."*

A slurping sound arose from the hollow stump. The children jumped backwards as a thick, mossy root wriggled to the surface and slithered past them.

Patina smiled as she watched it disappear from the grove. "May it travel a safe path to its destination," she said. "Thank you, Forester."

# 21

# the avenging root

While Forester was reciting his verse, Bellatinks was flying desperately towards Merryville Manor. Being in the air was her only advantage. Without Shift to carry her skywards, Gridelda was earthbound but her cane was as powerful as ever. With the chalice clasped securely in her arms, Bellatinks was unable to retaliate and had to use her wits to avoid the spells being cast in her direction. She'd almost been trapped in the resinous doorway at the entrance to Duskcanister. A moth in a spider's web would have struggled just as violently but, unlike the moth, Bellatinks had enough guile to free herself. She'd felt the weight of the resin on her wings as she escaped and it was taking all her energy to remain airborne.

Outside the Tree of Seasons, she'd entered the dark night. Under the tree's white light, the ghouls had screeched their blood-curdling war cries and the moon had glinted on the axes of the traitor goblins. With Gridelda's last command ringing in their ears, they'd flung themselves at their enemies, their lust for victory forcing the fairies and elves to retreat even closer to the entrances to Brightisclearen and New Blossomdale.

Bellatinks had faltered when she saw Queen Glendalock battling with a ferocious ghoul but the queen's mesmerising voice echoed through her thoughts. She must save the chalice above all else. So she'd flown onwards, hovering for an instant above the invisible boundary of the woods and the mortal world. But in that pause she'd seen something that added strength to her wings and hope to her heart. The grim, desperate sounds of a defeating army were changing.

Looking around she'd seen something so wonderful she'd almost crashed into the bough of a tree. The entrance of Icefroztica was flung open and King Darkfrost, astride his white stallion, and followed by columns of faithful goblins, had charged into the battle.

Gridelda's furious shriek left her in no doubt that she too had seen King Darkfrost's advance. Bolts of green light slashed through the leaves of the Tree of Seasons but Bellatinks had continued to fly onwards through the woods. Now, as she flew into the back garden of Merryville Manor, a dark shadow crossed the moon and a sudden rush of air almost blew her off course. Before she realised what was happening, a crow swooped across the sky and attacked her from the left. It nipped her arm then soared upwards with a triumphant caw. Unable to release the chalice and tap her magical fingertips, she could only fly onwards towards the protective branches of a horse chestnut tree. The tree was in full bloom. A length of rope hung from one branch but it was covered in cobwebs and bird droppings. She twirled around the chestnut candles, hoping to disguise herself between the pink sweet-smelling blossom. But another crow waited on a higher branch, its beak razor-sharp. Blood trickled from her arm and neck. Her wings began to beat more slowly. As the menacing crows prepared to attack again, she found herself losing height.

"*Featherixus, alopeaciam,*" she panted, amazed that her memory of magical spells could work under such danger-ous conditions. But as the black feathers fell from the crows, she realised she had chosen the wrong spell. Losing feathers was not quite the same as demanding that crows tumble from the sky. How did that spell work? Something about *plummetusis* . . . but it was no good. Her memory was blank and the crows were moving in again to attack. One nosedived towards the chalice, prepared to knock it from her grasp. The other, furious to see his feathers floating downwards, aimed for her legs and nipped viciously at her ankle. Desperately, she tried to continue flying between the branches but she was losing concentration. The crows' vicious cawing was replaced by quieter, satisfied screeches as they watched her falling. The flashes from Gridelda's cane revealed her surroundings; the earth – how fast it seemed to rise towards her. She could see the long summer grass and swaying daisies, the purple heads of clover sadly nodding.

I'll die first rather than hand the chalice over to Gridelda, she thought. But she knew that her death would make no difference. Gridelda would rule forever and it would be Bellatinks's fault. Frantically, she swerved from the path of a crow. She was almost within Gridelda's grasp but still she held on to the chalice. Her toes trailed over the grass. The crows had been joined by their entire flock. They flew in a dark stream from the trees and lunged downwards, ready for the final assault. They made such a commotion that Queen Glendalock's mesmerising voice was almost impossible to hear. Bellatinks forced her thoughts away from the approaching danger and listened only to her queen.

"Give me the chalice," screamed Gridelda, whipping the grass aside with her cane. She grasped Bellatinks's ankle. The skin was slick with the blood that dripped from Bellatinks's wounds and Gridelda was unable to hold on. The fairy rose unsteadily into the air again. Suddenly the crows scattered, cawing furiously. Looking upwards, Bellatinks saw Partlant and Bowrain flying towards her. They realised the danger immediately and lost no time whipping their arrows from their quivers. They fired at the crows who began to screech and scatter, allowing Bellatinks to reach Merryville Manor. The grim manor was in darkness, the window closed. Gathering her failing strength, Bellatinks made a last supreme effort to regain height. She flew upwards above the porch and collapsed on the eaves. She could hear Gridelda's footsteps crunching on the gravel. She was panting heavily, muttering as the powerful flashes from her spell cane became weaker. But there was still enough light for her to see Bellatinks peering over the eaves of the porch.

"How appropriate that you exhaust yourself at my mortal home," Gridelda crowed when she reached the porch. "When will your people realise that I now control your destiny? From now on, sunshine will forever cower behind the clouds of autumn." She pointed her cane towards Bellatinks, who, defenceless and exhausted, could see the crows re-forming and zooming in on Partlant and Bowrain.

"Hand over the chalice or you die where you stand." Gridelda pointed her cane towards the quivering fairy. "As you know, I do not make idle threats."

Bellatinks's head drooped. Her hands shook as she clasped the chalice to her chest one last time. She flapped her wings and flew unsteadily from the porch roof towards Gridelda.

"You have vanquished me," she cried and passed the chalice into Gridelda's keeping.

Gridelda's hands trembled as she placed her cane in its sheath and grabbed the chalice. She drank deeply, not stopping until she had drained it. A drop escaped, slid like a silver tear from the side of her mouth. Her tongue flicked and greedily licked the last drop of the essence of joy.

"Now, to deal with you," she screeched and swept her hand towards her cane. But her fingers were unable to whip it from its sheath. Shocked, her hand fell limply away and dangled uselessly by her side.

"The essence of joy," she gasped. "Where is its power?" She placed the chalice on the ground and used both her hands to try to release the cane. When it refused to budge, she staggered towards the front door.

"Shift . . . Shift," she shrieked then fell silent, knowing her gargoyle was lost to her forever.

The crows squawked furiously as they retreated from another hail of arrows.

"The joy you stole from those children has escaped." Bellatinks flew from the eaves and glided before Gridelda, making sure to remain out of reach of the queen's grasp. "I have received word from Queen Glendalock. The battle is over, Gridelda. You have lost everything."

"I do not lose," Gridelda snarled. "You are a fool if you think this cane is my only weapon." Her fury twisted her features so violently that Bellatinks flinched and looked away. That was when she saw the snake. At least, she assumed it was a snake writhing up the garden path. What else could wriggle so silently and at incredible speed? As it drew nearer, she realise it was a gnarled and mossy root, with loose tendrils clinging to it. Forester. She smiled to herself. She should have known the protector of the Tree of Seasons would not let her down.

Before Gridelda could turn, the root had wrapped itself around her in a sinuous movement and pinned her arms to her side. Within seconds, it had encircled her legs and before she could recover her wits, or utter a magical chant, she was trussed and immobile.

"Your power is over, Gridelda." Bellatinks's voice rang loudly through the garden. She swooped downwards and clasped the empty chalice in her arms. "On behalf of Queen Glendalock, I will tell you that you are wrong. Whenever clouds, no matter how dark or heavy, cover the sun, the light is always there, always present, always shining."

Gridelda began to wail as the root retreated, drawn back to the vortex from which it had arisen. It slithered through Grimsville Woods, moving at a steady pace between the trunks of the watchful trees. It paused for an instant when it reached the Tree of Seasons to draw strength from the healing light. The battle that had raged was over, the cries of victor and vanquished silenced.

Then the root crept through the entrance to Duskcanister. The way was clear now, no rotting gateway, no clammy resin. Without pausing, the root writhed through a tunnel lined with pyramids of harvest fruit, plump yellow pumpkins, sheaves of wheat and corn. Then it erupted into the courtyard where sylphs, camouflaged against the leaves of the trees now restored to their autumn glory, fluttered downwards to hear Gridelda's shrieking pleas. Bellatinks followed the root to a grove where the guardians waited. Leaves began to rustle joyously as soon as the root appeared. Bellatinks cried out with amazement when she saw the swirling guardians. Although they were entwined, she recognised Subfusc's spiky chestnut hair, Ecru's trailing willow strands and Umber's mop of burnished maple curls.

"I thought you were dead," she cried as they whirled around her. In their centre she could see the shard, throbbing to the rhythm of their dance.

"We survived," Ecru replied. "Patina has been restored to her throne and we are once again the protectors of the shard."

Gridelda screeched for mercy. What promises she made: wealth, power, eternal life. She would share her secrets, her knowledge, and the potent magical spells known only to her.

Forester ignored her entreaties and pointed sternly towards the hollow stump. The root wriggled closer to the edge.

*"With this root we banish slime,*
*Gridelda's gargoyle, ghouls and grime.*
*All those who aided her campaign*
*And fought to stop Patina's reign*
*Have NOT destroyed our season's time*
*And will be punished – by this rhyme –*
*With one – who tried for evil reasons –*
*To destroy the Tree of Seasons."*

Suddenly, a cyclone hit the grove. It whirled viciously through the trees, having swept the ghouls and traitor goblins into its centre. It claimed Gridelda's dismal furniture from Merryville Manor, the globs of mulch and streams of resin, the enchanted crows, and lastly, the stone statue of Shift. With a last dizzying whirl, it disappeared into the stump. Gridelda screamed, bribing, threatening, swearing vengeance on those who'd defeated her. But the root had had enough. With a final wriggle it too vanished into the vortex. Her screams surged upwards but grew fainter . . . .fainter . . . fainter.

"We did it." Beth shouted and danced on the spot, waving her arms in delight. Footsteps approached, crunching on a crisp carpet of leaves. Silence fell as three rulers entered the grove. Queen Glendalock smiled. King Leafslear winked. King Darkfrost bowed before the children.

"The Tree of Seasons chose wisely when it sought your assistance," he said.

"We knew we could rely on your courage," said Queen Glendalock. "Your tasks are now at an end."

Subfusc's voice rang out from within the whirling leaves. "The Tree of Seasons has sent a message in the wind and through the roots of the earth, asking us to enter the folds of its branches and give thanks."

It was time to give thanks. The Tree of Seasons released strong vines that curled around the children and lifted them high into its branches. They were joined by the four rulers, Bellatinks and Forester. Springy moss cushions resting on the boughs provided a comfortable seating area. The thickest bough on the tree formed a table. Light filtered down from the crown and threw a warm glow over the small gathering. Below them, the woods were hushed and peaceful.

As soon as they rested their hands on the table, Josh saw green sprigs trailing over his hands. Pale-green leafy shoots twined around his wrist, trailed to his elbow. Green leaves lay along the inside of his arms and when he looked at the others gathered around him, he saw that they too were being embraced by delicate, pale-green shoots. The stems looked so fragile but Josh felt their strength tingling his skin. The veins in the leaves pulsed against his own veins.

"Don't be afraid," Forester reassured the children. "The Tree of Seasons is communicating with you."

Bellatinks, also enfolded in the same gentle clasp, smiled when she realised her wings were adorned with tiny leaves.

"Welcome, Josh, to the Tree of Seasons." He looked around to see who was speaking then realised he was hearing the voice in his mind.

"The Tree of Seasons wishes to communicate with us and connect us to its energy," said Forester. The look of concentration returned to his face as the tree spoke again.

"We have been through a difficult time." The tree's voice was deep and murmuring. "Gridelda was a vile obstruction in the throat of two worlds – our enchanted kingdoms and your mortal world. Through her magic we could have choked and died. But we have rid our worlds of this obstruction and we are free to breathe fresh air into our lungs. But evil will thrive again unless we live in harmony and appreciate the value of each other's seasons."

A short silence followed. Queen Glendalock was the first to break it. "I admit, I have always been so engaged in creating a flourishing summer that I ignored the other seasons."

"I also have been interested only in budding a perfect spring," confessed King Leafslear.

"Winter has been my only preoccupation," admitted King Darkfrost. "I have always willed the other seasons to end so that I can nip the fingers and tingle the toes of mortal children."

"I will burnish my world and prepare it for winter," promised Queen Patina. "But I will not lose sight of what our seasons almost lost under the spell of decay."

"I am pleased to hear such unity," murmured the tree. "But mortals must also appreciate that they have to exist in harmony with their climate. If they do not cherish the natural earth they share, and take responsibility for its welfare, there are many others like Gridelda who wait for the right opportunity to destroy what humankind takes for granted."

When the Tree of Seasons finished speaking, sprites fluttered from the branches carrying trays of food and drink. They placed wooden beakers of juice on the boughs, along with platters of berries and freshly baked breads. A contented silence fell as everyone feasted and, when the dishes had been cleared away, three sprites returned to hover in front of the children. Each sprite held a tray covered by a leaf cloth.

"One final thing." The Tree of Seasons' deep voice sounded in their minds once again. "In nature, gifts are given and returned, recycled and re-shared. Your gifts were presented to you in a time of conflict and used to banish your fears. We are now entering a new period of peace so gifts borne from joy are necessary." The tree paused to give each child time to absorb what they must do.

"Josh, you will relinquish your magical bow," the tree continued. "It will be returned to the chamber of mysteries where it will lie in peace until conflict strikes again."

Without hesitation, but with a pang of sadness, Josh placed his bow next to the leafy cloth on the wooden tray. He plunged his hand in his pocket. Already he missed the reassuring touch of the bow.

Michael had already removed the ring from his finger and placed it on the tray. Beth touched her necklace and disappeared for the last time. The tree waited patiently for her to return – which she did within seconds.

"I had to do it one last time." She glanced apologetically at her brothers before placing the necklace on the tray.

Josh sighed with relief, glad he would no longer have to endure her sudden vanishings.

"Children, look under the cloths," ordered the Tree of Seasons.

Josh, Michael and Beth lifted the leafy covering and gasped with delight when they saw three exquisite miniature replicas of the Tree of Seasons.

"Each tree has been carved by the tree sprites from roots. They are powerful emblems and will help you to understand and absorb your worries and fears. All you need to do is hold the tree in your hands and concentrate on your problems. If you look closely, you will receive your answer."

A look of concentration appeared on Beth's face. Suddenly, a tiny ring hung from the branches of her tree gift.

"Hey, I've just given my truth ring back," Michael exclaimed.

She laughed, excitement sparking her eyes.

"It's not a truth ring, Michael. It's a gift from all of us to Forester." She lifted the ring from the branch and handed it to the guardian of the Tree of Seasons.

Everyone waited as the blushing Forester lovingly placed the ring on Bellatinks's finger. Queen Glendalock smiled and bowed towards them. Michael was the first to cheer. Tears rushed to his eyes.

"I kept thinking about them when I was in the crypt," he said in an apologetic aside to Josh and blinked the tears away with great determination. "I know it's cheesy and all that stuff . . . but still . . . " He clapped loudly and, as others joined in, the entrances to the enchanted kingdoms opened. Fairies, elves, goblins and sylphs emerged and gazed upwards. At a signal from their rulers, they joined hands and circled the Tree of Seasons. As soon as one circle was complete another formed, and formed again, spreading outwards beyond the tree, their faces iridescent as they danced beneath a sky of shooting stars.

Dawn was breaking when the dancing ended. The enchanted folk disappeared into their kingdoms and the children were alone, except for their faithful friend, Forester.

"Don't be sad," he consoled them when they reached the edge of the woods. "We are your family now. Come to the Tree of Seasons whenever you need us. This is not the ending, my friends. It is the beginning of new adventures."

The walked wearily through the woods, hoping their parents were still sleeping soundly. Merryville Manor was in darkness, except for the bedroom where their great-aunt always slept. They rushed up the driveway and stood outside the door. The gargoyle door knocker had vanished. They had seen it disappearing into the stump. In its place was a shining brass knocker.

"It looks like our tree," said Beth, touching her gift. "Do you think we should knock and see if she's all right?"

"Tomorrow," said Michael, his legs suddenly giving way. "I'm so tired I could lie down right now and sleep."

"No, you don't," said Josh as he and Beth supported him.

"I don't want any more adventures tonight."

"But we need to see if she's all right."

"Just breathe the air," said Josh as the light in their great-aunt's bedroom window was switched off.

They stood for a moment longer outside the dark manor and breathed deeply. Oh, the smells that wafted towards them from inside: beeswax polish, herbs, spices, potpourri, and, most importantly of all, the delicate lavender scent.

"She's back," sighed Michael and the three adventurers wended their weary way home.

# 22

# a change of mind

"*That* woman," said Mr Lotts at breakfast the following morning. "One minute she can't wait to have the woods chopped down. She torments me to get planning permission passed as soon as possible." He clasped his head in his hands. "Day and night she pesters me and when everything is finally ready to roll . . . what happens?" He stared at each of his children. "Tell me what happens?"

"She changes her mind?" said Josh, and tapped the top of his soft-boiled egg.

"Got it in one." Mr Lotts nodded and heaved a frustrated sigh. "She cancels the contractors. I won't tell you where she told them to put their chainsaws! Disgusting language for a lady of her advanced years. So, now we have a new plan. Conservation. All the trespassing notices are coming down and the hedgerow will have gateways to the woods."

"No motorway?" said Michael.

"Not as far as my aunt is concerned. I'd hate to be the official who tries to change her mind." Mr Lotts retreated behind his paper then peered over the top at his children. "Oh, I almost forgot. She wants to see you three scamps as soon as possible." He stared warningly at them. "No excuses or nasty comments. She actually sounded more like her old self again . . . Where are you going? . . . There's no rush . . . you haven't finished your breakfasts . . . " He sighed and returned to his newspaper as his children disappeared out the back door. "Children," he muttered. "Will I ever understand them?"

Inside Merryville Manor, the children were being embraced by their great-aunt. Beth was weeping guilty tears and apologising for all the nasty remarks she'd made. "Oh, Great Aunt Graves, I'm *really* sorry for calling you an evil witch. And I called you worse . . . much worse things—"

"The worst thing you called me was Great Aunt Graves," said the elderly woman. "Whatever happened to Lily-May?" She smiled and led them into her kitchen. "But that's a silly question. We all know the answer to it."

"Who will believe us?" asked Josh.

"They'll say we're crazy," agreed Michael.

"And I'll be blamed for telling whoppers again," said Beth.

"We know the truth," replied their great-aunt. "We do not need to share it with others who will not understand. The Tree of Seasons does not need the curiosity of humans to invade its space."

"But Dad says you're going to allow people into the woods."

"Merryville Woods will be protected and conserved. It's something I'd planned to do when I purchased it." Their great-aunt looked grim as she removed a tray of muffins from the oven. "I wanted people to study the trees and the wildlife. Of course, Gridelda had other ideas. But we don't need to talk about that now. When life turns upside down, it can always be righted again with a cup of tea. What do you say, children?"

"No, thank you," the children chorused. Despite all the changes they saw around them, the memory of cold, weak tea was still to the forefront of their minds.

They need not have worried. Their great-aunt poured mugs of steaming tea, just the way they liked it, especially when it was accompanied by freshly baked blueberry muffins.

"Won't people discover the Tree of Seasons if they explore the woods?" said Josh.

"Don't forget Forester," replied their great-aunt. "People will see what he wants them to see. And he, like me, believes that the woods should belong to everyone. He will protect the Tree of Seasons and only those who are allowed into its enchanted worlds will ever know of its existence."

When they had finished eating, they went outside to survey the wilderness that was once Lily-May's beautiful garden.

"No prizes this summer at the Merryville Festival," she said, ruefully.

"I'd like to help you," said Michael.

"Me too," said Beth.

"We've the whole summer holidays in front of us," said Josh.

"Thank you, children," replied their great-aunt. "I've also been offered help from a young lad who lives nearby. He's making a start by clearing the weeds and brambles." She waved at a boy who had emerged from the garden shed with a wheelbarrow. He wheeled it with difficulty, lowering it once and resting for a moment to recover his strength.

"He was discharged from hospital last night but he insisted on calling at my house first thing this morning and offering his help," said their great-aunt, then shouted across to him. "Johnny, come on over and meet the children."

The wheelbarrow wobbled as Johnny Welts picked it up and wheeled it towards them.

"What's he doing here?" gasped Josh.

"Why don't you ask him?" his great-aunt replied.

The children stood still as Johnny approached. He looked pale and puny, his face bruised from his last encounter with Josh. His gaze was steady as the two boys exchanged glances.

"You won that fight fair and square, Josh." He lowered the wheelbarrow and held out his hand. "Can we shake?"

"Why should we trust you?" said Michael.

"You have Gridelda's strength in you." Beth shuddered and drew away from him.

"My strength has gone," said Johnny. "But I don't care. I'm free from her tyranny at last."

"Your strength will have returned by the time you've finished my garden." Lily-May smiled at him. "And it will be your own strength, earned by the sweat of your brow."

"Will you shake my hand?" Johnny asked once again.

Without hesitation Josh accepted his gesture of friendship.

"Well, I'll leave you young people to get on with it. I have a wood to preserve." The elderly woman walked briskly back to her manor.

"We'll make her garden beautiful again," said Beth.

"Problem is, I know nothing about gardening," said Michael.

"Me neither," admitted Johnny.

"So, how will we manage?" asked Beth.

"Why not ask him?" said Josh as a flutter of butterflies entered the garden and swirled around a small, bearded man with a green cap tilted at a jaunty angle and a hemp satchel slung over his shoulders.